A SEAT AT
THE TABLE

Corinne Arrowood

Published by Corinne Arrowood
United States of America
www.corinnearrowood.com

ISBN: 979-8-9851087-4-3 (eBook)
ISBN: 979-8-9851087-5-0 (Trade Paperback)
ISBN: 979-8-9851087-6-7 (Hardcover)

Cover and Interior Design by Cyrusfiction Productions.

TABLE OF CONTENTS

INTRODUCTION

A Seat At The Table was originally *Gentleman's Dance* written in 2003 and published in 2006 by Authorhouse. The big push to write *Gentleman's Dance* came when I had a life-changing diagnosis, so I needed to start writing. Hannah, the main character, had been prodding me for years; thus, I wrote her story. However, I was too emotionally attached to the story to publish it, which defeated my ambition of becoming an author. The emotional attachment pushed me to write *Price To Pay,* a story I didn't think I'd get attached to—*haha*. I wrote and published it in 2003.

I wrote *Price To Pay* sharing my father's office. He was not only my dad but a tremendous support and my friend. When he became ill and the outcome was written on the wall, I wanted to have a copy of *Price To Pay* he could hold in his hand. Not knowing anything about the publishing industry, I jumped at the first opportunity to publish; I hired 1st Book.

In 2006, I decided to publish *Gentleman's Dance* and went back to my same contact, but the company had changed to Authorhouse. At that time, I still knew nothing about the publishing industry and considered my writing over and done.

I went back to the corporate world. One night in 2018, two characters (Rainie and Michael from the Censored Time trilogy) woke me wanting their story told. Thus, I seized the moment, retired, and opened up a career as an author, learning to surround myself with a coach, classes, professional editors, and designers, ensuring a professional product. After publishing the trilogy and a stand-alone book, *Friends Always*, I decided to resurrect *Gentleman's Dance*, giving it a new name, *A Seat at the Table*, and entrusted it to the professional editors and my designer.

It was like breaking the dam; new characters started lining up in my dreams, waiting for me to write their stories. The ride is just beginning and so far its been wild, fun, and crazy busy. I have one more finished manuscript, *Untouchable Love*, and a couple well on the way with many more to come.

Unravelling the Threads

The Family Tree

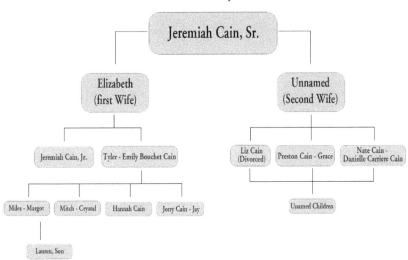

Cain & Sons Office Personnel (as they appear in the story)

Margaret – Tyler Cain's assistant
Sal & Deidre – Hannah's Design Team
Page Foster – Real Estate Investment
John Harris –Property Development
Millie – Preston's assistant

Investigative Team

Seth – New Orleans PD
Nick Messina – New Orleans PD
Ford McClain – Covington PD

Integral Domestic

Belle – Southern Manor, Covington, runs household
Porter – Jeremiah's right hand, Bogalusa
Ruby – Runs the house for Jeremiah, Bogalusa

Hannah's Love Interest…Nope, you'll have to read the book!

ALL IN A NIGHT'S FIRE

he screech of sirens penetrated the stillness of the night. Like runaway locomotives, fire engines barreled down the narrow streets of New Orleans. Flames ripped into the black sky and filled the block with thick, sooty smoke. Several homeless people on the street gathered and watched as the building gave itself to the wiles of the fire. Windows blew out, shattering in the street as hot embers floated from the sky. It was tragic.

The renovation of the quaint four-story building on Julia Street had recently gotten in gear after going through a smorgasbord of red tape. This historic site would have soon been the hottest boutique hotel in the New Orleans warehouse district. T.V. crews circled like vultures trying to catch any shot of the owners.

"Where the hell is Hannah? Has anyone spoken to her? Somebody get these damn cameras out of here!" Aggravated by the situation, the little man barked out commands to his entourage. They would jump to attention with each of his blasts.

Moments later, a 1973 classic English Racing Green MG squealed into the area, and a tall blonde dressed in faded jeans, a white tee-shirt, and plain black jacket stole from the car. She stood mesmerized by the flames. The madness was unfathomable. She could hear the firefighters as they called to each other. The intensity made her heart pound like the bass drum of a marching band. There was a mass of confusion; she seemed paralyzed by its awe. Gathering her wits, she looked around for familiar faces. A plague of camera crew battled their way closer.

She heard Preston's voice through the commotion, "Hannah!"

"Over here," she stood entranced by the fire.

"It's about time," he huffed his way over to her.

The cameras were on her, and reporters thrust mics in her face. "Miss Cain, Miss Cain—"

The barrage of questions started flying; it was too much to decipher, let alone answer.

"Is it true the city denied Cain &Sons the permit to tear this building down?" shouted one reporter.

Simultaneously another pushed, "Do they know if it was arson?"

Another piped in, "The word is your father is out of the country. Has he been notified about the fire?" The questions were coming fast like a firing squad as her muscles tensely knotted and her breath hitched.

She cleared her throat and held up a hand, forcing a quiet. "At this time, as you know, the building has been undergoing renovation. Sadly, this unfortunate tragedy will set us back, postponing the opening; however, Cain & Sons will get back on track as soon as possible. Presently, we have been unable to reach my father. To answer your question, he has not been informed of the setback at this time."

After several more minutes of hassling with the press, she caught up with the entourage. "Preston, has anyone reached Daddy yet? He should've landed in London by now." From the depths of her soul, her body shuddered as a gnawing sensation developed in the pit of her stomach. Fear and uncertainty had started to rake over her body.

Although consumed with seeming busy, Preston made time to answer her, "Margaret's been trying to get answers from the airlines; they're funny hush-hush about giving names and confirming passengers. It's a real pain, especially at a time—"

Margaret, her father's assistant, interrupted as she approached, "Mr. Cain, no luck so far. He didn't meet his driver, nor has he checked in yet. According to the airlines, the flight arrived more than three hours ago; he should have made it through customs and long since been at the hotel."

Hannah was exasperated, sighing loudly, "This is just great; he's gonna be pissed. I'm heading to the office. I can't do much else here." She turned on her heel and made her way to her car with determined steps.

By the time she wove through the crowd and arrived at the office, Deidre had the coffee dripping, and Sal had picked up some donuts.

He was arranging the napkins and placing the donuts on a tray in the kitchen when she entered, "Girl, what a mind blower, huh? But I gotta say, missy, you looked good for the camera." He sashayed out the room and turned at the door. "T.V.'s on in the conference room, if you're interested, hon." He buzzed from kitchen to conference room, all the while incessantly talking. "You took charge. The big guy will be proud."

Deidre entered, "Yeah, we could see Preston in the background with his little band of ass-kissers. Was he his charming self?" She poured the coffee into a silver coffee urn.

"He's a fool." Hannah rolled her eyes. Since abruptly being woken from a dead sleep, a fog took over her thoughts, making each remark a step out of beat. Hannah sipped her coffee as she gazed blankly at the screen. The back lines began to ring. She answered, "C&S."

She waited, "Hey, it's me."

Hannah intently listened while tapping her pen on a blank pad. The call was from Page Foster, the Director of Real Estate Investments, her father's right-hand man. He was trying to whisper into the phone, "They found a body."

She muted the T.V.. "What?" she could barely hear him.

"A body." This time he was a little louder. "It seems a vagrant must have moved in for the night." There was a lot of static, and he was beginning to break up, "This isn't good. I'm on my way to the office. Did you get your dad yet?"

"No, not yet. I'll see you when you get here." She plopped in a chair and buried her head in her hands, parting her hair with her fingers. "Somebody get Preston, please."

Deidre passed her the phone, "He's on."

"Preston, Page called me; you better get in here. Don't answer any questions; just get in here." He was rather put off but said he was on his way. It was always about him, the narcissistic bastard. She started walking to her office.

Moments later, Sal turned up the television and hollered down the hall, "Hannah, ya gotta see this." She was just in time to poke her head around the doorjamb. Big as day on the conference television was Preston, in all his glory, "People please, we don't know any more than you do at this point. I'm sure we, at C&S, know nothing about all this and certainly had nothing to do with it, and other than that, I'm not at liberty to say anything else."

Hannah went from zero to sixty in a New York second. "What is he going on about? He's made it sound like we're trying to hide something. Crap!" She stewed for the next fifteen minutes, pacing the hall until she heard him come in. She flew around the corner and bolted to the door. "What is your malfunction? Preston, didn't I tell you not to say a word. Now I gotta undo this feeding frenzy you've ignited. Damn!"

He had a look of shock which quickly turned to anger. "Hannah, get in my office right now." He stormed down the hallway, "Who the hell do you think you're talking to, one of your gofers? You will speak to me with more respect, young lady." *Give me a break*, she thought.

"Respect has nothing to do with this." She leaned against the doorframe to his office. "You have no idea what the press is gonna do with your statement, not to mention the man-hours it's gonna take to undo this mess; shit, I don't even know where to begin." She closed her eyes shook her head in disgust; her whole body felt shut down and defeated. He had pushed her past pissed, and before she said something she regretted, she quickly turned and walked away.

Preston yelled as she made her way down the hall. "Get your panties out of a knot and grow up. Do you think for one second the press wasn't already thinking we had something to do with all this? Pleeze. I wanted to set the record straight."

"Pompous ass." He wasn't her favorite person in the world to start with, and his arrogance served to anger her even more, twisting her gut.

"Han-nah!" It was Page. She turned into his office. He was red in the face and obviously concerned. "What kind of damage control is this dead body mishap gonna take? We have to do something. The Old Man is not gonna like this one." From his expression, she could see the wheels spinning in his brain.

Hannah stood in front of his desk with pad and pen in hand, busily making notes. "Did you hear Preston's glory moment?" she asked.

Page looked up, somewhat dumbfounded, "How bad?"

"Pretty bad, but hey, it's my department; you ain't got nothing to worry about, friend." Her tone was laced with her anger from Preston.

"Yeah, right." She knew whether it was his job or not; he always worried and felt responsible, especially when Tyler was out of town. It had been a long day. The press camped at their front door, and there wasn't one moment of peace whatsoever. Little did she realize it was going to go from bad to worse. Sal and Deidre were utterly spent; she sent them home around four. As she let them out, the fire investigator and one of his cronies entered.

"Miss Cain, can we have a moment of your time?" The two men had wearied expressions, with frowning foreheads, knitted eyebrows, and tightly pursed lips. They had purpose in their gait.

"Sure, why not?" she sarcastically retorted. "I'm exhausted, guys, shoot. Whatcha got?" She put her hands on her hips with her famous Supergirl stance.

"Miss Cain, there's clear evidence, even though it's preliminary, the fire was no accident. Are you aware we found a body?" the fire investigator inquired. He wiped his brow.

She sadly nodded and ran her hand through her hair, wishing this nightmare would end.

"We also found something else," and they handed her a ring.

She looked up quite puzzled, "Where did you get this?" Her thoughts ricocheted through her mind like the silver ball in a pinball machine.

"Do you recognize the ring, Miss Cain?" The investigator spoke again.

"Yes, where did you get this?" This time she was a lot louder and demanding moving into their space, "I asked you—"

"In the debris from the fire, ma'am."

She was confused. "What would my father's ring be doing in the building? That was his wedding band; he never took it off. Certainly, you don't think my father had anything to do with the fire?"

'No, ma'am, we don't," they answered almost simultaneously.

"Then what are you saying?" and her voice trailed off. "Oh my God, there's no way." She punched in some numbers on the PA system, "Page, now." She was shaking uncontrollably and felt as though she might vomit any second, but she had to hold it together. This was all such a horrible nightmare.

A NEW KIND OF REAL

he next few days seemed like a blur. There were people in and out of her house and office. It all seemed to run together. This morning seemed even more like hell. It was unbearably hot, and the humidity was 100%. Streaks of condensation formed on the windows, but when she looked out, the sky had an almost wintry gray look to it and not the smothering heat of reality. Perhaps it was just the fog over her mind. She watched as the cars below lined up in what seemed to be a never-ending parade.

She stood before his full mirror. In the reflection, she caught a glimpse of that once impish face, now much wiser. She possessed a beauty that turned heads, and she was growing more beautiful with time. The once rebellious young woman had grown with each and every battle, and the scars were defined in her determination, but then again, she knew where this characteristic had come from, and she had acquired it quite honestly.

"Excuse me, Hannah honey, but it's time to go." A soft voice came from behind her.

She turned to face the one person who had always been there; in fact, she sometimes thought Belle had come with the house. Although tiny in stature with a creamy cast to her coffee-colored skin, she had an innate almost mystical strength about her; no one dared defy. Her word was the one and only word, and they complied. Belle had taken charge of the house, the help, and the children, long ago, even while her mother had still been alive. She had run the place well, but more importantly, she knew the eccentricities of its family and would take them to her grave. Her loyalty and love, beyond reproach, came straight from her soul.

"I'm coming, Belle." Hannah took a closer look in the mirror, sizing up any would-be circles or bags, and turned away. "Tell the others I'll be down in a minute if you will." Her voice echoed through the room as she looked out his window, but it didn't sound familiar. *How strange*, she thought. She remembered waiting in that very spot, waiting for them to come home from a night out. Her nose would be pressed to the window in anticipation. Two tiny patches of fog would appear with each breath.

She glanced around the room, almost as though taking inventory. The raised four-poster bed, topped with an imported lace spread, hosted a multitude of matching pillows of all shapes and sizes. Their wedding picture encased in a sparkling silver frame remained, as always, on his side of the bed.

How many frightening stormy nights had she stolen into their room. She would struggle to climb to the top of the bed, where she knew the storm could not reach her. Her dad's mighty hand would sometimes reach down to meet her, scooping her effortlessly and setting her down where she could crawl between them under the safety of the heavy covers. The room and everything in it had always seemed larger than life.

Hannah walked over to her father's bureau, where a stack of envelopes awaited, just as he had said. She remembered his instructions and could almost hear his voice. Hannah would not stray from his directives; she'd follow them step by step. She smiled; this would be a first. Carefully tucking the letters into her purse, she stopped by the mirror to adjust her dress and brace herself for the morning's event. It was a struggle, but she inhaled a deep breath as she tried to take control of her trembling hands.

Everyone was there, present and accounted. The atmosphere was somber and grave with a sea of idle chat and sorrowful confirmations, precisely what one would expect from her socially predictable family. As she descended the stairs, all heads turned with the same faux sympathetic nods and acknowledgments she had seen and heard only the night before. She wished they would vanish and allow her to grieve.

There seemed to be people everywhere, and with Hannah's descent, they clustered in their appropriate groups, a few of them checking their watches in disapproval of her tardiness. She was void of feeling and didn't care who approved or disapproved. Her face was deadpan, devoid of any emotion. The twinkle in her eyes was gone, the light in her soul extinguished, and her heart ached at its very core.

She would ride in the car with her brothers, Miles, Mitch, and Jerry. The others would travel with their families in the limousine procession. Much to outsiders' dismay and raised eyebrows, Tyler would have insisted the help ride in one of the cars. They were to be part of it all. They were as close, if not closer, than family and certainly more loyal.

As she reached the bottom of the grand staircase, her Aunt Lizzie fluttered over in her naturally insincere way. Taking Hannah's hand, she patted it and spoke as though gasping, "Hannah dear, we were all getting so worried about you. Are you okay, Suga'? It's going to be a hard day for all of us, but we'll get through it." After giving her hand a slight squeeze, she let it go as she slipped away to re-join her little group. Hannah remained silent but gave a slight half-hearted nod.

Miles had already begun ushering everyone outside to the cars. Hannah stopped on the porch, went over to the side, and gazed at the beautiful rose garden in the side yard. What a tranquil setting. Intricate wrought-iron benches amidst fragrant rose bushes of every imaginable color set the perfect scene. She envisioned her father on bended knee proposing to her doll-like mother. She'd heard the story many times.

Belle cradled her waist, "It's time, darlin'. Things goin' to be fine; jest you wait. Belle's gonna make things fine. Ya mama and daddy sure made a handsome pair, yes ma'am, sure did."

Once again, Belle had amazed her. Hannah had always felt Belle could read her thoughts. It was through Belle's vivid storytelling Hannah knew so much about her mother, her parent's courtship, and the early years after her mother's death.

As they walked down the brick path, Mitch came up from behind with a quick nudge to their ribs, "C'mon ladies, let's get this charade over with." Although not very eloquent and the proverbial black sheep, Mitch had made his own way through life, and Hannah respected him for it.

Jerry was distant, almost withdrawn, a total contradiction to his usual outgoing personality. Charming and strikingly handsome, all the unmarried ladies in New Orleans found him irresistible.

The drivers awaited with doors open as this somewhat questionable clan approached. Miles stood by Travis, their father's driver and the first car in line. He gave the signal for the rest to hurry along.

Once inside, away from all the relative's ears, the four of them could finally speak uncensored.

Hannah spoke first. "I don't know about y'all, but I'm scattered and still in disbelief. I'm waiting for the phone to ring and for him to be pissed because he was detained in customs or the arrangements for a driver were poorly executed. Ya know? It's weird. Like some horrible nightmare I can't wake up from."

Mitch touched her hand. "These kinda things ain't never easy, but we'll stick together and get through it. Think like the old man. 'Be a Cain, stand proud.'"

"Give me a bucket," Jerry looked at him with disgust, "Sorry, Mitch. I wanted to throw up when Dad said it and outta your mouth. Shit!"

Hannah cast her eyes on Jerry. "I was wondering if Belle had cut your tongue out. I think those are the first words you've uttered today," she patted his knee.

Miles sat ever-so-composed. No expression. Just blank. After listening to the banter, he finally spoke. "Hannah, Margot said she called you offering the guest room. She said you wanted to stay home, is that right? Think about it, even if only for a few days. It's gonna feel weird in the house at first. Right now, there's a houseful, but it'll be only you after today. Think about it, please."

To keep peace in the car, she nodded. "We'll see." She had no intention of staying anywhere but home. She'd have to eventually anyway; no time like the present to begin getting used to the quiet.

The time from Covington to the city had flown by quickly; it seemed only minutes had gone by as the limo pulled up to the stately white columns of the funeral home. Miles and Mitch got out, and as Hannah leaned forward to exit, Jerry grabbed her hand tightly, "Han, ya gotta stand by me. I'm gonna need someone to lean on through this." The tears welled up in his eyes; she squeezed back.

"I'm here," she winked back at him, "Remember, this is the show; we'll have our time later." She could feel her insides binding as though donning a protective armor cocooning her heart as an extra fortification. The thought of her relatives caused the taste of bile to purge into her mouth.

The four of them walked together into the funeral home. Something to do with the old cliché, united we stand. Although they had been there the night before for the wake, it all seemed distant and blurred, as though an eternity had passed. It played through her mind like a reel of film.

The funeral home had the eloquence of days gone by with wide planked floors, magnificent high ceilings adorned with artful plaster medallions commanding voices to a hushed whisper.

The register looked like something out of the who's who— Congressmen, Mayors, and even the good Governor and his wife made their appearance. Representatives from each of the old moneyed families were donned in their tastefully conservative funeral togs. Quiet conversation passed with comments on the heat, the humidity, and of course, the shock of Tyler Cain's death. The receiving line seemed to go on forever. The crosses and rosaries were out for the show as the procession passed one by one with their sympathetic faces and empty condolences.

Hannah watched as some old biddy cornered Miles. He had the physician's demeanor attracting older ladies and their barrage of maladies.

"Miles, you who, Miles. I'm so sorry dawlin' about your father's passing. Hon, I don't think I've seen you since your wedding. My, how time flies." She smiled with one of those too practiced Southern smiles. Hannah looked over her shoulder at him with a mocked expression; he returned the look. It was the first bit of lightheartedness she'd felt in days.

Hannah noticed more than once some young debutante offering her condolences to Jerry. Some of them would go so far as to whisper in his ear. Hannah laughed to herself. She knew he could handle them, and they ate up his attention. He was the picture of his father, just a smaller version. Standing at 5'9," his mass of sandy blonde hair set off piercing green eyes, the kind of eyes that mesmerized.

She was proud of her baby brother. Jerry was doing quite well for himself. Working part-time in an art gallery on Royal Street, he attended Tulane working on his Doctorate. He hoped to get an offer to teach in a university Fine Arts Department, but that had not materialized. The Museum had already made several offers, but perhaps there'd be a change with Tyler's death. Everything seemed to be in the hell-hole of limbo.

It was an eerie silence that served to emphasize any noise. The rustling of people taking their seats had ceased. Finally, the moment had come. The tension was in the air; onlookers would never be able to determine if it was the occasion or just the Cains' way unto themselves and most stoic. What the family did know was their every move was being scrutinized. For the most part, they were good at putting on a show and going through the motions of life, but no one ever truly knew what they were thinking; they'd all been doing it a long time.

"I can't believe this. God, I'm gonna miss him," Hannah whispered to Jerry.

He held her hand, "We'll all miss him in our own way." She had faith in her brothers, even Mitch; as wild as he was, he would never do anything to hurt her. He might have been a bit rough around the edges, but he was still a Cain, through and through.

A blanket of exquisite red roses draped over the casket at the front of the aisle. She felt like reaching out and touching the coffin, protecting it, never letting anyone take it away. She needed to be near him, just one more time, "Oh, Daddy." A single tear rolled down her face. He would've forgiven that one, but she quickly wiped it away.

The priest stood at the pulpit and described their father as though he had been a close friend since birth. To the best of her knowledge, her father had only brief encounters with the church. He had established his own relationship with God. Above and beyond anything else, he was a good man. He provided for his family with everything they could ever want, and he loved them all equally and dearly. Their mother had been the love of his life, and he took that untarnished love to the afterlife. She thought, *yes, Belle, they were quite a pair.*

Her dad had been born in a blink of a town just south of Jackson, Mississippi. His parents, Jeremiah and Elizabeth Tyler Cain, had in their brief marriage two sons, Jeremiah Jr., and Tyler. Soon after Tyler's first birthday, his mother took ill with the fever that plagued the South and died. His father remarried a much younger woman, later bearing him a daughter and two more sons, but most importantly, she provided the motherly rearing needed for his first two sons.

Hannah seemed to fade in and out with each testimony. Hearing bits and pieces, it all seemed to run together in a rambling monotonous drone. Pin drop silence in the church abruptly brought her back into reality, heightening her senses and capturing her full attention as she watched her Uncle Jeremiah walk to the podium.

Jeremiah was two years older than her father but lacked the sophisticated polish. He stayed to himself and was a man of few words. Some thought he was insane, but Hannah knew differently; he was plain old shrewd. *They'd never see him coming,* as her dad had said many times. He had those same intense eyes like her dad, and if one looked close enough, there was a strong resemblance minus the country-cut hair and rugged, sometimes shaven face.

As a child, she would ride with her father to see the "Old Coot." She played by the river with some of the local kids while the two of them would watch the grass grow or argue the plight of Louisiana politics. Jeremiah would say it was the reason he stayed just across the Mississippi state line. He had never married, but rumor had it there were a few children in the neighboring town bearing a striking resemblance to him. At age 70, he stood with the same strength and determination she had seen in her father and, more recently, looking back at herself from the mirror.

He cleared his throat, then paused and took measure of those in attendance. His voice was strong, like that of a much younger man. He shook his head as he looked out into the crowd. "Today's a day I never thought I'd see. It wasn't supposed to be this way. Out of the two of us, I thought it would be me. To those who don't know me, that's just as well. And those of you who do," and he smiled, "you know who I am, and believe me, I know who you are, all of you, and I'm watching.

"What happened to my brother shouldn't happen to no man. My brother and I were real close. Not your meeting every day close, but in the spirit close. Cut from the same cloth, if you will." His voice dropped low almost to a whisper, "There's talk, speculating, who done this horrible deed? I know who it was folks, and they're sitting in this room. Could be next to you," and he pointed, "or you." Hannah could hear the unsettled creaking of the seats from the people behind her. The atmosphere of the room became uneasy and the air thick. His voice began to swell, "Tyler leaves behind a legacy, a real fine family." He dropped to a dramatic whisper again, "These old ears of mine have heard rumblings; things shouldn't be whispered, let alone said. You fine folks talk about my brother." His voice boomed again, "A pinnacle of a man." He raised his fist in the air and slammed it down on the wooden stand before him. "The strength, wisdom, and power, yes power of an army of men, and this may all be true, but," he became even more intense. "Make no mistake, dear ones, should any harm befall any one of his heirs, should they accidentally fall into ill fate, or doom cast shadows on their otherwise sunlit path, he or she will answer these acts of disloyalty with a wrath unlike any felt before." His voice crested, "there will be no rewards for you beyond them Pearly Gates."

Hannah had to do everything she could to refrain from laughing. As she looked around, she saw faces of utter shock, mouths agape, and looks of horror and confusion. Her eyes locked in on her Uncle Preston and Aunt Grace, who sat beside her Aunt Lizzie, her two snobbish daughters, and their families. She watched as they made obvious but whispered derogatory remarks and seemed overly angered by his witness. Preston's eyes fixed on hers, and for a slight instance, she saw something strange in his face. Was it fright? Within half a second, he re-grouped and had the same sickening look he'd been wearing since the fire. As she scanned the pews, she was taken aback by the sight of her Uncle Nate. Tears ran like rivers from his eyes as though his heart had been shattered like glass. Jeremiah returned to his seat and put his arm around Nate's shoulder. Maybe there was more to Nate than she knew.

The priest regained the composure of the service and commented on the different ways people handle death, and no one should judge too harshly. She had hoped this ten-minute dissertation had not been for the benefit of her Uncle Jeremiah; if so, it was all in vain; he wouldn't give a rat's ass. The ceremony ended, pallbearers carried the casket out, and the congregation departed for the cemetery.

As they drove down the winding path of the cemetery, Hannah couldn't shake the horrible sick feeling in her stomach. It had been a long time since she had been back to the family resting place. She remembered going with her dad when she was a little girl. He would walk her through the city of tombs, pointing out a great uncle or great-great-aunt or cousin twice removed, and so on. At the back of the cemetery, the sun always shone the brightest, as though warming her mother's tiny, frail body. She would hide behind the headstones while her father would walk over and talk to her mother as if she were standing right there. Those times didn't bother her but certainly were no preparation for this day, as she was about to lay her father to rest.

Hannah felt violated as she watched people flood into the private family area. *They have no business being here*, she thought. She wanted to ask some of them why they bothered coming when all it appeared to be was the wealthy and prominent social gathering. She could hear some of them complaining about the heat. *Then just leave*, she thought. For some strange reason, she hated them all, even the ones she knew in her heart that she liked. Today was different.

The service went as expected; the hot sun had burned through the overcast clouds, and steam rose in a suffocating thickness. The crowd dispersed, and Miles, Mitch, and Jerry waited patiently for Hannah to return to the car. Something kept her there. She stood by his grave, looking blankly with despondency in every breath. She admired the collection of wreaths and sprays, then focused on the graves again. Her parents were soon to be side by side, and for the first time, it hit her. Through tearful eyes, she whispered to herself, "I guess I'm no one's little girl anymore."

Miles came up behind her, "Han, come on. He's not there, he's with us, and through us, he'll live on. You know what he would say, 'Hannah Lee, pull yourself up by your bootstraps, girl. There's work to be done; get on with it.' That's what he'd say."

She clung to him, sobbing, "I feel so hollow, so afraid. Oh, my God, Miles, I don't know if I can do this. He's always been there."

She cried in his arms like a lost child, and her pain reached to the pit of her soul, "C'mon, Hannah, let's get home."

The car ride back to the house was silent; each one of them engrossed in their own private memories. Had her father truly been proud of her, and did he ever completely forgive her for moving to New York? Did he understand she had to? She was sure he did. Memories of that horrible fight still haunted her. No one would have ever taken her seriously in New Orleans, it was still very much a man's world, and she'd never get a seat at the boardroom table. She would have been Tyler's daughter, Miles' sister; no accomplishment would've been just hers. She had to go and make her mark. That awful night played back like a bad dream.

It was May, and the family had gathered to celebrate Jerry's birthday. They had a private room at Arnaud's, in retrospect, thank heavens! All was going well; everyone was there. Her dad, Miles and Margot, Mitch and Crystal, Jerry and his friend Elise and she and her plus one came to the celebration. It was a night full of announcements. Miles announced he and Margot were expecting their second child; Mitch had made it to his sixtieth day of sobriety, so why not make her announcement?

She felt the bubbles of excitement and apprehension gurgle their way up the back of her throat. "I, too, have a bit of exciting news. The advertising agency of Tisdale, Elliott, and Martin has offered me a position. These opportunities don't come very often." She remembered the feeling of pride in her accomplishment as her posture got a little taller, and her chest puffed out with her words.

Everyone at the table touched glasses, and then the hum of congratulations and conversation returned.

"Hannah, this is exciting," Jerry piped in with enthusiasm. "Tisdale, Elliott, and Martin are powerful people even by New York standards. I didn't realize they were opening an office here. When did this come about?" He was thrilled for her, and it rang true in his dimpled smile and a quick squeeze of her shoulder.

"They haven't opened an office here, Jer," she proudly explained. "I'm moving to New York; I can't wait. I leave next week to find an apartment. Tisdale, himself, is taking me around and says he knows some great studios. It's been like a whirlwind."

Margot spoke up, "Hannah, hon, did I hear you right? Did I understand you were moving to New York? What a bold move. Southern girl in the Big Apple, better hold on; it's gonna be quite a culture shock." She had a warm smile and caring eyes.

Tyler interjected, "My girl's not moving to New York; she said they made her an offer. Big compliment, I admit, but she's not moving to New York." He was reticent in his statement. Not even the beginning of a smile on his face and his voice spelled out, not up for discussion.

Offended, Hannah shot back, telling him she had thought it out, weighed the pros and cons, and planned on taking their offer. Tisdale was taking her to look for studios, as she said, and it was pretty much a done deal.

Once again, silence. Everyone was rustling in their seats, trying to ignore the obvious crash of wills. "We'll talk about it tomorrow; enough of this speculation for now. Now, where was I, Miles?"

Hannah blurted out, "Not this time, you don't. I will not be poo-pooed. 'Of course not, Hannah, don't be so silly, Hannah, you're acting like a child, Hannah.' Sorry, Dad, I don't want to find a good man to marry and have a house full of kids. I don't fill the role of the little woman very well, like it or not. I'm going to New York, and I'm taking the offer, so how about a congrats or job well done instead of telling me how ridiculous I am. This whole thing just pisses me off. You piss me off." She got up, told her date it was time to leave, and bolted out of Arnaud's.

As the car turned onto the estate, her mind spun back to the present. Her dad had been right; Southern Manor was a slice of heaven. The gate slowly crept open, revealing magnificent grounds, still very much left in the hands of Mother Nature. Hannah and her brothers had roamed every inch of the property, living wild fantasy adventures; the place was perfect for it. They explored it all, except for their mother's rose garden; it was off-limits.

The driver pulled to the front of the house ahead of the other cars parked alongside the circle driveway. Although Travis had only been their dad's driver for a few years, he had won favor.

As she entered the house, tempting aromas from the kitchen drew her to the back of the house, straight past the royal feast in the dining room. She tasted the etouffee, then grabbed a bowl of ambrosia, kicked off her shoes, headed for the back porch and the comfort of the swing, the perfect escape.

Inside, Belle was directing temporary staff to get the food out, Reginald, the bartender, to pour easy, and Margot's nanny to keep the young'uns upstairs and out of the way.

Jerry watched as the calamity became merely organized chaos. For such a little woman, Belle ruled with command.

"Belle, it looks like you've gotten everything taken care of, as usual, and it all looks scrumptious," Jerry reached for the Stoli and poured himself a good strong drink. He had such polish and poise to him; it was alluring to many.

"Git, you. You an' ya sister always comin' up in my kitchen, now go on out an' join ya company." She reached in her pocket and pulled out a crumpled piece of paper, "Jerry, bae, before I forget, there was a call for you from some Ted fella, said you knew the number and call when you got a chance. I told him you wouldn't have any chance to call today, so not to wait 'round, but I'd pass the word on, so consider it passed. Just between you and me, I didn't like the sound of his voice; he talked like he thought he was something or somebody, but what does an old lady like me know?"

She was asking, but Jerry knew it was one of those questions one would stay away from answering; there wasn't an answer acceptable. Besides, he couldn't think of a time when Belle was wrong. If she said someone was no good, sooner or later, one would discover why and indeed, they were no good. His dad had always said to listen to Belle. She, like some others, could hear untold tales in the wind.

As a child, he remembered, there was always the old folks from the country, someone's aunt or cousin. Things were distinctively different growing up on the outskirts of Covington than anywhere else in the world. Time seemed to stand still. No worries, life was simple.

Had he stayed at Southern Manor, life would've probably never changed, but graduation from the esteemed St. Paul's beckoned him on to bigger and better things. Big cities with impressive universities and, Lord knows, he had the grades to get in anywhere. He recalled sitting in his room filling out applications to prestigious east coast and west coast universities, the likes of NYU and Berkeley, and of course Northwestern. His dad had believed Southern people should attend Southern universities and keep their money in the South, close to home. When questioned about Harvard or Princeton, his dad, while reluctant, agreed to those as a possibility, but the west coast was out of the question. He remembered one discussion particularly well in his senior year when college decisions were finalizing. Seated behind his mahogany desk in the study, his dad summoned Jerry from his room to discuss schools and what the rest of his young life had in store for him. Jerry found it curious but humored his dad as he tried to absorb this Neanderthal way of thinking.

"Jeremiah," he said, "Rumor has it you've been talking about going to art school," there was the proverbial pregnant pause. "Son, that's a good hobby to have and can rest your mind from proper business, but the family could use a good lawyer. I'm tired of paying all those sons a bitches. It'd be better to keep it in the family, you know what I mean," and he winked. "Before you go making any hasty decisions, sleep on it; we can talk again. Accounting could work well; you have options. Son, the Lord gave you the intelligence and learning capability beyond measure. Use the blessing and put your brain to work. You can always paint or draw in the evenings on the veranda. It would be nice; every man needs a hobby, keeps him out of trouble and off the streets at night."

Talking to himself, his dad proclaimed, "Jeremiah, my son the lawyer, sounds good, nice ring to it. I'm glad we had this talk. See you at dinner." And that was it; Jerry was surprised his father hadn't gone into the one-day wife and two children. That would be another day and certainly a battle far past anyone's wildest dreams.

Jerry was always submissive and went with the flow, not out of fear but laziness. It was easier that way, and besides, he'd do what he wanted anyway; there were no points to prove. He knew who he was and felt good about it, most of the time. Only time would tell whether his father would bankroll his college adventure to Northwestern and Chicago. At least he'd be majoring in business and maybe go to the art institute also in Chicago. There was something about going to school in Chicago, no particular reason. Jerry already knew he was up for a scholarship if his dad wouldn't pay. He knew he would've had his mama's blessings had she still been around.

Before she died, she had become ever-so frail. With the loss of her last pregnancy, Jerry had heard his mother never regained her physical strength and would take to the bed quite easily. Jerry had beautiful memories of sitting with her in the rose garden. It was her treasured spot and off-limits unless invited, but sitting with her amidst the beautiful blossoms was like a walk in Heaven.

One time, the driver had taken them to the city, New Orleans, that is, to the big museum in City Park, and then to an art supply store where she bought him sketch pads, pencils, paints, anything and everything a young budding artist could possibly want or need.

They had an understanding from the beginning, and he felt comfortable talking to her about anything. Oddly enough, even though he was only seven when she passed, she shared precious secrets with him; it was that kind of relationship.

His mother's skin was fair, so much so, in the mild heat of September and October, as the days were becoming shorter and the sun was dimming, she'd still use her parasol or, as she called it, a sunbrella. Her steps were quiet, as if she glided across the floor, making her totally undetectable and often able to catch the boys or Hannah in some rule-breaking act. The worst punishment of all was her stare, the look of disappointment or hurt to the heart. That was enough; it was more than anyone could bear, but it was the end of it; it would never go any further. He remembered some of his friends' mothers threatening them with the likes of their dads, screaming and wailing. She never did anything of the sort and never raised her voice. Perhaps that's what drove them crazy and riddled them with guilt. In a traditional Southern manner, she regarded business as Tyler's territory and the children's shenanigans a matter for her and the help. He hated to think of what might have happened if his dad had any inkling of his mama's disappointments. He chose to dismiss the thought instantly.

His parents were deeply in love; it radiated from his dad's eyes, and it seemed the old guy particularly delighted in her story of the day's events. Her eyes would sparkle with life, like a child seeing something for the very first time. She was innocent but wise at the same time. Her emotions were pure. Between the two of them, there was the feeling of storybook romance. They were a remarkable couple; Tyler, strapping and handsome, towered over her. She was delicately beautiful with a classic look that would quietly and unobtrusively turn heads. Make no mistake, Emily Bouchet Cain was a lady, and everyone treated her with the utmost respect. She never demanded it; it was understood.

While she kept her opinions to herself, she was knowledgeable and well-read, something his father greatly admired. Her sisters had married well, lived in the Garden District, and visited a few times a year. Jerry still felt the void, that dull aching hollowness of loss. Even though it had been twenty years since her death, he could remember the smell of her faint gardenia perfume. It was feathery light.

The bite of reality came with a vengeance when Belle returned to the room. "Boy, you still in my kitchen? Don't be pickin' out the fridge. Get that scrawny butt of yours out in the parlor. Folks have been asking about you and Hannah. Where is that girl?"

He navigated through the dining room, main hall, and into the parlor, where he found Miles trapped by one of Covington's leading wedding planners. Her deceased husband had left her with more money than sense. No one could guess why she worked other than weddings, and their planning involved just as much gossip as the local beauty parlor.

"Miles, I understand you and Margot bought the big white house on Jahncke. You know, aside from my wedding planning, I've been dabbling in interior decorating. I'll have to give Margot a call." He spied Jerry as he entered the room.

"Nice speaking with you. Do give Margot a call. Jer, Jer, hey been looking for you kid." Once out of earshot, "Thank God you showed up when you did. That woman drives me nuts. I know she's lonely, but she finds any reason to come to my office. I'd like to tell her to get another doctor."

Jerry watched her, "She's not bad looking, Miles. Might be good to keep in the hip pocket, never know when things will change between you and Margot." Miles returned a smile dripping in sarcasm. "I was only kidding, bro."

They began to walk into the dining room. Jerry continued, "It does me good to come over here every now and then. I keep forgetting how wonderful it is over here. Death always seems to bring out our own mortality, don't you find? Here today, gone tomorrow. Like when I saw your daughter, Lauren, she looks like a miniature Margot. I don't know your kids—sad, really. I'm gonna make a point of coming over more; it'll do me good." They made their way around the food, both filling up a sizeable plate.

Miles took on a serious and concerned look, his brows heavy over his eyes. "You need to come over more. Since Hannah came back from New York, she's been a little distant, kinda closed. She and Margot talk a lot, but even Margot says Hannah's got something going on some kinda dark cast. Maybe she'll open up to you. Y'all were always close."

A loud commotion came from the front parlor. It sounded like Mitch's voice, followed by the crash of glass against the wall and a woman's scream.

As they made it around the corner into the dining room, they found Travis standing between Mitch and Preston.

With arms grabbing toward his uncle, Mitch continued on his rampage. "Get outta here, you slimy cold bastard. Get out and take your money-hungry family with you." He continued to reach for Preston.

Preston was red in the face and ranting, "You're crazy! Absolutely insane!" Not taking his eyes off Mitch, Preston continued to rant and rave.

"You want crazy, I'll give you crazy," he grabbed Preston's shirt.

Travis was all over Mitch, trying to hold him back.

"You don't go talking shit about my father in his own damn house. You got a lotta balls," he swiped in Preston's direction again.

Preston fueled the fire in a loud demeaning tone, "You're nothing but a loser. A foul-mouthed gutter drunk. Nothing more than an embarrassment."

Most of the guests had flown the coup with the first outburst. The few remaining seemed to try and get out of the way but watched as though it were some kind of sideshow.

Jerry jumped in. Always the peacemaker, he coaxed, "C'mon guys, it's been a long day, and emotions are running high. Let's settle down and return to your respective corners." He turned to Mitch's live-in, "Crystal, hon; you want to go into the dining room with Mitch?"

He instructed Miles, "Take Uncle Preston so he can freshen up his drink."

He put his arm around Travis and led him into the kitchen. He briefly turned to the room full of guests standing with their mouths agape. "The entertainment's over everyone. There's plenty of food, so help yourselves."

Travis was sputtering, "Man, it all came down so fast, first, um, first. Oh, man."

Trying to calm the situation down, "Slow down, Travis. Ya did good. Now, slowly what happened?"

Travis was trying to gain his composure, but it was apparent his adrenalin was rushing. His hands were trembling, "It wasn't Mitch's fault. Man, I don't blame him. Preston was talking about your dad, the Will, stuff like that," he ran his hand through his hair in exasperation, trying to put his thoughts together. "Hey, Mitch asked him, nice like, at first, to stop talking business, but you know Preston, he wouldn't let it go. Preston was wrong, man, really wrong. I'd have done the same thing."

"Thanks. You did a great job. Go get yourself a real drink, and I understand we make a mean turtle soup around here," Jerry thanked him again and told him to go relax. It had been a long day.

He made his way to Crystal and Mitch. He could hear Crystal trying to soothe Mitch. She may have been trailer trash at one time, but she certainly made the climb out and could control Mitch better than anyone else. She loved him, the bad and the good, "Baby, is there anything I can get you? Don't let Preston get to you; you know he's egging you on, the old prick." Mitch wasn't very responsive; he was still seething. "Aw, Mitch, let it go, baby. He thinks he's something because of the Cain name. You are your father's son, not Preston."

Jerry smiled at her as he entered the room. Her hair was almost as big as her breasts, and they both made a statement. Actually, he thought, she was a good-looking woman despite the big blonde hair that gave her a passé look. She wore the country-western style to a tee. Every top she owned was skin tight and cut to the navel. Her curves were in all the right places, and she worked out hard to keep them. Overall, she had been a good influence on Mitch; she was tough enough to keep him in line.

"Hey, Toots," Jerry called to her, "You got your guy settled down?"

He put his arm around Mitch, "Before you start, Mitch, Travis told me the whole thing, and I don't blame you one bit. Preston's an asshole; everyone knows that. I'm just glad Hannah hadn't been here; she would've made a bigger stink. Let it go; it's over."

Mitch couldn't turn it off and on as easily as some people. It would take a while for him to calm down, "It's easy for you to say, Jerry, you're not the one to catch the shit all the time. He's got a lot of balls comin' in here and talkin' about how he's the big chief now and how things are gonna change, he can kiss my ass."

"Better watch what you ask for," Jerry gave him a wink.

Mitch stopped him, "Sick, Jer, you are one sick mother—"

Crystal glared at him, shaking her head, and scolded, "Mitch, not here."

The crowd, for the most part, had dispersed. Miles and Preston were into one of their serious manly talks. Miles could play Preston's game and win it every time. Jerry finally made it into the kitchen, grabbing bites off the trays as he passed. Belle stood in the back doorway gazing out with folded arms. She smiled back at him as they both could hear the distinct rhythmic creak of the porch swing. Quietly he came up behind Belle. They watched in silence. Curled up on the swing, with her eyes closed, hair down and barefooted, Hannah seemed at peace.

He whispered, "It's been a long day, Belle. Been thinking maybe I'd like to stay around for a few days, just until things settle a little. Clear my head."

A MUCH NEEDED RIDE

The morning seemed to drag and he wasn't use to the slow pace of Covington, so he headed to her bedroom.

"Get your lazy butt out of bed!" Jerry plopped on the bed, almost bouncing Hannah onto the floor.

"Good God, Jerry, give me a break," she tugged at the covers. "What time is it anyway?"

"C'mon, sleepyhead, it's ten, and I'm going crazy sitting around here, gotta get out, go somewhere, anywhere. Get up!" He pulled the covers completely off her.

"For cryin' out. You're still the same brat you were when we were kids. I guess some things don't change, do they? I know there's no point in arguing; get outta here and let me get myself together."

Without further ado, he made his way down to the kitchen. Belle had her back to him. He came up behind her, gave her a hug, and whispered, "Belle, Belle, my sweet caramel Belle."

"Boy, shut yo' sassy mouth. Someone musta slapped you upside the head or something cuz you sure is crazy!" Repeating to herself in a giggle, "Sweet caramel Belle, where you come up with your nonsense?"

Although still a bit sleepy, Hannah looked like a breath of freshness in a white cotton dress and sandals. She twisted her hair up in a messy haphazard fashion yet managed to keep a chic appearance. She grabbed a cup of coffee, and the two of them headed out the door.

Covington was a neat little town, well-planned and unspoiled. It still had an old country charm. With the radio tuned to the oldies station, memories of younger years were brought to mind leading them along memory lane. They capped it off with a stop by St. Paul's School. Even though Hannah was 29, Jerry couldn't help but notice the few young boys at the school turn their heads as she walked by. Her white cotton frock flowed with each step giving her an almost angelic look. Although average in height, her long thin legs, and lean body gave the illusion of someone taller than five feet six. She resembled her father but had the delicate features of her mother. The combination made for a stunning picture, but her most remarkable attribute was her authenticity. She didn't put on airs or play games.

After a leisurely visit, they headed through town, down Boston Street. Old brick buildings lined the streets festooned with flower boxes brimming with vibrant blooms. Jerry was taken aback by the array of artisan and specialty shops along Lee Lane. Slight twinges of hunger coaxed an early lunch at one of the quaint cafes along the lane.

It had been a long time since they had pal'd around together, yet he was comfortable with her as though they saw each other every day. It was then he realized how much he missed her. In true Southern tradition, they shared a relaxed lunch free from the urgency and stress of time or schedules. It was peaceful, a break they both desperately needed.

Lazy from lunch, they returned to the car tootling around town beneath the unforgiving heat of the June midday sun. They continued on Boston and kept going heading toward the country. Out of the city limits, glorious trees to either side created a canopy over the roadway, a most welcomed refuge from the sun.

"This day has been nice. I'm glad I decided to stay instead of going back to the city." He put his head back, letting the wind toss through his hair. "They'll get by without me for a few days. So, Hannah tell me," he turned the radio down, "Besides helping Dad with P.R., what have you been doing? I'm sure you must be bored sick. Going from the fast pace and high profile of New York to here, let's face it, Covington isn't a-buzz with excitement, nor is New Orleans on the cutting edge of any industry, let alone P.R." He adjusted himself sideways in the seat so that he could face her. "Like, what do you do for fun? You ought to move to the city; at least there is some nightlife." At twenty-seven, he still possessed a boy-like charm.

"Actually, I love the quiet and slower pace. Believe it or not, C&S does provide me with challenges, and I don't just mean the family politics, although I must say, it can get interesting from time to time and will probably enter a whole new dimension now." She focused straight ahead as the road began to wind and cars picked up speed.

Jerry smiled. They rode in silence for the next ten minutes. His mind was like a blender without a lid, thoughts flying all over. "Who's the latest beau? Any guys hanging on the hook?" Jerry asked quizzically.

Preoccupied with her own thoughts, her voice trailed off with a soft, "no, not really." She seemed sad, almost vacant. Although she didn't want to get into it, her thoughts took her back to the heartbreak in New York. She pushed the images from her mind as quickly as possible. It hurt too bad.

Jerry watched her intently. "You okay?" No response. "Sis, is there something I can do?" Still no answer. "Ya want me to drive?" He furrowed his brow as he watched her. Things were way off.

"No, Jer, that's okay. Other than the obvious, nothing else is wrong, but thanks for asking." Changing the subject, she asked, "Up for an adventure?" She looked over at him with a devilish smile.

"You're scaring me; what kind of adventure? I'm the wild child, not you!" he looked over at her. In some ways, she still had a naughty little girl smile, and she flashed it on command, only now it seemed somewhat hollow. She would have a hard time without the old man, and everyone knew it.

"Let's go to the Pearl, see what the Old Coot is up to," she took him off guard.

"You're outrageous." Throwing on a Jamaican accent, he played, "Sick, you know, sick in de head, but what de hell. I hear it runs in de family, mon." She playfully slapped his arm. He continued, "Boy, Uncle Jeremiah was out there yesterday. I think too much solitary living is finally taking a toll; he's lost it. He musta been drinking too much of the homemade hooch, and it's rotted his brain."

Hannah laughed, "Nah, he's just out there naturally, but don't let him fool you. He's clever like a fox."

Jerry interrupted, "You know what really scares me? Have you ever noticed how much Mitch is like Uncle Jeremiah? Sometimes it's downright uncanny. I mean, that stuff Uncle pulled yesterday is something I can see Mitch doing; give him another thirty years." She gave a slight giggle; she wasn't sure how funny Mitch would find it, or maybe he would. Memories of the day before crept into her mind.

"Yesterday, in the car, I looked at you, Miles, and Mitch. Y'all are so different but special. It's strange how we grew up together in the same house and turned out completely different. Take Miles; he's gotten stone serious. Remember when he was in college? He was wild. I wonder if he's changed because he thinks he has to or if it's real. He seems uptight." She sat up straight in the seat to check out her make-up in the rearview mirror. All of a sudden, her face lit up.

"You know what the four of us should do? We should get together once a month, no wives or partners. Wouldn't that be great?" When she hadn't heard a response, she looked over at him, "I think we all need it, Jer. I know I do. I need y'all."

He knew if he didn't answer the way she wanted, she would go on and on; he decided it might be better just to agree, "Sounds good, Hannah. With this happening to Dad, who knows?"

The stench of the paper mill was a strong indication Bogalusa was nearing, and it would only be another hour or so until they reached The Old Coot. Hannah remembered the many trips with her dad to her uncle's house over her lifetime. It didn't seem right going there without him. The more she thought about it, the more awkward she began to feel.

"Maybe we shouldn't do this, Jer." Insecurity rolled through her like a wave. Her second-guessing had to stop; it was out of control. All because she refused to read the signs while in New York. Raised with three brothers, she knew the male psyche. How she hadn't seen it created and fueled her insecurity.

"Do what? Go to Uncle J's?" she nodded at him. "Hell, Hannah, we're just about there. After we get there, if you don't think it's right, give me a signal, and we'll bolt. Okay?"

She thought about it for a moment or two, "okay."

When one crossed the Mississippi state line, it was almost like time travel, not that Louisiana was anywhere near up with the times, but backwoods Mississippi was more like a hundred years behind.

The winding road leading to his house was just to the right after crossing the bridge. It led deep into the backwoods. Several small wooden homes along the dirt road, once used as slave quarters restored with rooms added on, created a charming cottage appearance. Children played in the yard while adults visited on the porches. The neighbors waved, knowing full-well it must be family. The locals drove pick-up trucks proudly bearing full shotgun racks hitched to the rear windows.

Jeremiah came out on the porch to welcome his visitors, "What the hell? If it's not the city folks, what do I owe this honor?" he came down the steps to greet them. "Don't tell me you were just in the neighborhood. C'mon in, you two." He put his arms around their shoulders and walked inside. He called out as they entered, "Porter, guess who's here? Guess who made the journey from the city?"

Porter looked the same; he never changed, still looked strong as an ox. He had a head full of white fleece, and his skin had the appearance of dark worn leather with deep crevices from years of working hard side-by-side with their uncle. Porter had one of those toothy smiles that would light up his whole face. He was a large man standing as tall as Jeremiah. Age may have worn his face, but his back was still straight and tall.

"Miss Hannah and Mista Jerry, y'all look mighty good on this hot afternoon. How about some lemonade? Just made a big pitcha."

Hannah loved old Porter's lemonade; it was by far the best there was. She reckoned it must've been the sweat, at least that's what her daddy had said.

They sat in the parlor and exchanged niceties about the day, the drive, the changes in Bogalusa, and, of course, the heat. They briefly talked about the funeral service. Jeremiah was the first to cut the small talk, "Got a question for you, Missy. Have you heard from your Uncle Preston today?"

"No, sir," she replied. "Why, is everything okay?" She paused for a second, "Not to overstep my boundary and at the risk of sounding rude, what's the deal with Preston? One couldn't help but notice the tension. Jerry told me there was some altercation between Mitch and Preston."

Jeremiah listened and interjected the occasional, "hmm," "uh-huh," and "ya don't say?"

She went on, "I know my father always thought Preston to be a bit pompous and verbose, but I also know he thought he was harmless, just a pain in the—"

Her uncle cut in, "ass? I know that's what Ty thought, he and I talked about that, but I'm not so sure 'bout that. I think his poison streak goes right down to his heart. There's something out of sync with him. Always has been."

Footsteps creaked from down the hall, heading toward the parlor. Unlike Porter's more solid strides, the steps were quiet, then Nate entered the room.

Hannah was surprised. "Uncle Nate, I didn't know you were here. I guess I'm a lucky girl, two birds with one stone," as she got up and hugged him. Jerry also got up and embraced his uncle.

Nate had always been a little different, quiet and to himself. He followed in the shadow of his older brother Preston. They were only a year apart in age, and Preston had always come off as brighter and the leader of the two. Between his sister's nagging and Preston's verbosity, Nate had grown up to be a man of few words. Preston talked to him like he was a dog and came across as if he was superior. In actuality, he was far less handsome than Nate and much shorter. Terms like conniving and swindling came to mind when thoughts of Preston came about. Nate was more like his half-brothers, Tyler and Jeremiah. He favored them in appearance and mannerisms but was more shy and unsure. He came across all brawn and no brain, but hardly was the case, more like still waters run deep.

He was married to a striking woman, Danielle Carriere Cain. She had fiery red hair and sported a contagious laugh. She was strong in a steel magnolia kind of way and took great care of him. Nate provided a heart full of love for her, the name, money, and prestige all in one package. They enjoyed a great relationship.

Childless after ten years, they adopted three Romanian children, all girls. A year later, God blessed them with a daughter with his wife's fiery red hair and stereotypical feisty disposition to match. Nate was a manly man and had his hands clumsily full with ribbons, lace, and frills. It was a house of women.

He'd occasionally flee to Mississippi for a good dose of the rugged outdoors and guy conversation. He rarely visited Southern Manor; thus, Hannah knew little about him. She had always figured he was like Preston since they were so close in age, lived a few blocks from each other, and traveled in the same social circles. She might've been wrong about Nate; time would tell.

Nate had a sorrowful look. His lips had a downward turn, and his eyes had a bleary-from-too many tears look. She knew that feeling well. "I know I didn't get to talk with y'all at the service; I did want to convey how sorry I am, I really am. Your dad was the best, one of the good guys, and will be missed terribly. If you kids need anything, just holler," he seemed painfully sincere, and there was something else in his voice. The tears welled in his eyes, and he excused himself from the room.

The doorbell chimed; Porter called out that he was getting it as he moved to the front door. Hannah heard the door creak open, followed by a friendly unfamiliar voice accompanied by almost bouncy steps. The voice was Southern with the distinct Mississippi drawl; Hannah was intrigued. Jeremiah and Jerry were talking, but she was somewhere else trying to place the voice in the hall or hoping to catch a glimpse of the face that went with it. A door shut, and the voice was gone. *Curious,* she thought.

"Uncle J., seems like y'all have company, Jer and I don't wanna be in the way we'll be going. Thanks for the visit and the wonderful Porter lemonade." She started to stand.

"Whoa there, y'all just got here. Besides, missy, y'all are my company," he instructed them to stay seated.

Hannah sat on the edge of her chair, ready to stand at any moment. "You had a caller at the front door, and we don't want to impose; after all, we did come unannounced." She was hoping he'd tell her who the mystery guest was. She started to stand again.

Her uncle patted her arm, encouraging her back into the chair. "Girly, sit yourself down; that's just the preacher here to see Nate. Suppose he'll be joinin' us for supper. I think y'all will like him, the younger crowd, from what I hear, think he's, what's the term, oh, yeah, rockin'.'" He leaned back in his chair. It was uncanny how much he looked like her dad. He had the same sparkly green eyes, full of thought and silent opinion. One might call him cagey, but he was just ever-observant.

Jerry excused himself for a couple of minutes. Hannah moved into Jerry's seat, a little closer to her uncle, "Do you mind if I ask you a question about yesterday?" She leaned in with a not quite shushed whisper.

"Not at all, darlin', I figured you'd be wonderin' what on earth I was talking about," Hannah was listening and waiting.

She guessed it was her turn, "Yes, sir. It's hard to believe Dad's gone. I'm trying to wrap my head around it; it feels like a bad dream, ya know?" She crossed her legs.

He nodded that he understood, "Yep, darlin', I know." He leaned forward with both hands on his knees and looked her straight in the eyes.

She had to ask, "What was that stuff about? You know who did it, and they were there? With all respect," she whispered, " it sounds a bit—"

He interrupted, "Crazy?" His eyes lit up.

She wasn't sure what to say but shrugged and said, "Kinda."

After a studdered chuckle, almost a cough, from deep in his belly, he answered. "Hell sounds crazy cuz it is crazy, but it's true. Just wait. It'll all clean up in due time."

She sat there in disbelief, "Who?" tilting her head slightly to the side.

He sighed, closing his eyes, barely shaking his head, "Can't tell you that, just yet, darlin'."

Jerry returned, and the three of them took a walk down to the river. Spook and Shine, Jeremiah's labs bounded ahead. One thing for sure, they loved to fetch and were relentless with never-ending energy.

Upon their return to the house, Nate was sitting on the porch with someone, maybe the preacher man, but from a distance, she thought he sure didn't look preacher-like. In fact, he had the look of a college student with scruffy khaki shorts, a faded plaid shirt, and a baseball cap. The man was sitting in a chair, so she couldn't tell how tall he was or what the whole package looked like, but she was intrigued, a feeling she hadn't felt since New York. Maybe this was a warning rather than intrigue, and what the hell was she thinking? He was a preacher, a man of the cloth.

"Hey there, Mr. Cain, you're looking mighty fine today," the preacher called out from the porch. As he got up to his feet, she could see the Lord had blessed this little lamb. She estimated he was 6' and a buck eighty.

"If it ain't my favorite preacher man," Jeremiah extended his hand as the preacher walked toward them. "Reverend Joshua B. Delery, I'd like to introduce you to my nephew Jerry Cain and his lovely sister, my niece, Miss Hannah."

The preacher put his hand on Jerry's shoulder, "I'm truly sorry for your loss. Your father was a good man, and I enjoyed our talks; he was a knowledgeable guy and spoke of y'all a lot. He was extremely proud of all of you."

Jerry was first to respond. "Yeah, I have to agree; he was one in a million," they all headed for the porch.

Hannah watched as the men postured themselves. The butterflies in her stomach started to land more between her legs, raising her temperature and turning on a sensation she hadn't felt in a while. She could feel a glow developing on her skin, and her cheeks began to pink.

They settled in for what she suspected would be some good old boy conversation. She'd just mosey into the house, freshen up, and get control of the heatwave.

She examined herself in the mirror. She felt hot and sweaty but was managing to conceal it. Running cold water on her wrists, she then patted her face with a cool, damp washcloth, wondering what the preacher thought of her. She tried to dismiss the thought as quickly as it came. But *wow*, she thought, *he had some presence and that smile, a man of the cloth or not, he has a winning kinda smile, the kind to light a woman's heart or was it libido?"*

"Enough," she said to herself aloud, "get a grip."

She knew the problem; it had been a long time since she'd been with a man, too long. Here was a new face and a rather attractive one at that. She rationalized the whole brief fantasy and retreated to the kitchen. Ruby was at the stove, and Porter sat at the kitchen table, sipping on lemonade. The conversation came to an immediate halt as Hannah entered the room.

"Okay, what were y'all talking about?" Hannah fussed, "Don't y'all hush on my account; I had to get away from all that testosterone. Besides, if it's juicy, you know I want to hear."

Ruby piped in, "Child, there ain't nothing juicy in these parts; we're too old and decrepit. We talkin' about ya Uncle Nate. He's been spendin' an awful lotta time here. Miss Danielle's been callin'; she's worried too."

"How long has he been here?" Hannah asked.

"Lemme see, had to have been right after Carnival. He's been back and forth but spends most of his time here. He don't go into the city, except to go to his house. He ain't himself. Old Porter and I were just sayin' we hope Preacher Delery might help him find his way."

She sat at the table with them. "Jer and I were talking about how unreal things seem on our way up here. I feel like I'm spinning around and around, and the rest of the world is either stopped or in slow motion. Life has taken some odd turns. How long has Uncle Nate been talking to the preacher?" Just as Ruby was about to answer, Hannah continued, "In fact, Reverend Delery said he met my dad. When was that?" She cocked her head in curiosity, almost like an intrigued puppy.

"Honey, your dad has always been close with your Uncle Jeremiah, and since the two of thems been getting older, they been spendin' more time together. They called themselves playin' cards, but I'd be surprised if more than three hands were dealt. The three of them, Nate, your father, and Mr. Jeremiah, would spend hours chewing the fat and throwing back some beer."

Hannah leaned forward on the table, twisting up a paper napkin nervously. "That's interesting; I didn't know Dad was close with Nate. I always figured Nate, Preston, and Lizzie to be thick as thieves and Dad and Uncle J to be the odd pair. Learn something new every day." As she made her last comment, she noticed Porter and Ruby exchange glances, "What gives? I saw that look; something's going on."

"Ain't nothing goin' on, now make yourself useful and go set the table." Ruby took her crumpled paper napkin, handed her fresh ones, and pointed to the silver.

She'd buy the BS for the time being, but she knew eventually she'd get to the bottom of it all; there was something they were not saying, at least not to her. She gathered the silver and set the table.

Coming back in for the glasses, she asked Ruby how long the preacher had been coming around. "What's his story? Does the good reverend play Poker too?" Mocking a southern belle attitude, "I declare what else does the good reverend do?"

"Girl, you got a tongue like a razor; you best lower your voice before you go embarrassing yourself. Take these glasses and call them to supper." Ruby handed her the glasses and turned to the stove.

As they came into the house, the preacher removed his cap, revealing a head full of soft wavy brown hair framing an almost angelic face. His eyes were a warm brown that emanated goodness, but that smile not only lit up his face but turned on a devilish sparkle in his eyes. *What a combination*, she thought. If she didn't know better, she'd bet he came out of an Abercrombie ad. He had a carefree, casual, but gorgeous look about him; he'd easily be described as eye candy. As they ate, she could feel his eyes watching, no, observing her. It made her nervous.

The men continued their conversation from the porch, following, of course, a heartfelt grace offered by the preacher.

She couldn't help herself, "Reverend Delery,"

"Joshua," he interrupted.

Ignoring his interjection, she continued with a snotty, almost sarcastic air, "Now just what is it you do in Bogalusa? You better be careful, you know folks have called it Sin City. It just might drive a good preacher man like you around the bend," she paused a moment. "The Lord must deem you special, Reverend. He certainly sent you on a tough mission; things can get pretty ugly from what I hear in Bogie." She didn't mean to come across quite so snide. It was not her nature to be rude. Maybe, she'd be quiet before she said something worse.

Everyone looked at her in surprise, probably in total embarrassment, but the preacher, without skipping a beat, said, maybe it was the tough that kept him going, but then again, it could be his penance. Whatever the case, God had sent him on many a rugged road, and he guessed he had a lot of repenting to do, or maybe the Big Boss was pleased.

"Joshua, please forgive my sister," Jerry quickly interjected, "She's generally not so rude. With the recent turn of events, we're all a little off-center." Jerry was always so damn polite and composed, but he was right; an apology was in order.

She looked down and, indeed, was embarrassed. "I am sorry, my mama always told me, even a fish wouldn't get in trouble if it kept its mouth shut. Please forgive my rudeness." She humbled herself well.

In his sweet Southern accent and with an ear-to-ear smile, he retorted, "Darlin' you couldn't be rude even if you tried, no harm, no foul, but if you'd like to see what's goin' on here, you're welcome anytime," he took a sip of his drink, "in fact, Sister Hannah, do you have any penance you need to serve?"

"Touché!" her Uncle J. chimed in from the end of the table and raised his glass for a toast.

Everyone had a good laugh which broke the ice. The rest of dinner was enjoyable and relaxing. It started to get dark, so Hannah and Jerry began their journey back to Covington.

The first few minutes of the car ride, they both commiserated on how full they felt, then a deafening silence invaded the air.

Finally, she spoke. "I don't know what came over me at the table. I was such an ass. For some reason, I felt this intense hostility," Hannah confessed.

Sarcastically Jerry retorted, "You don't say? I don't know what your deal is, but you need to come to terms, dearie. Even considering all that has happened, you seem overly uptight."

She got a distant foggy feel and murmured, "Don't mean to be."

"Why the game of cat and mouse, talking to you about you is next to impossible," he seemed frustrated. "Take a look, remember me, your brother? We were always confidantes and pal of pals. If you talk, maybe I can help, who knows? What is it? Love problems, like problems?" he pulled at the steering wheel. "Pull over, Hannah; I can't stand it; you gotta talk. It's killing me to see you like this."

She kept on driving, "Don't touch my steering wheel again; you're such an old woman. I'm okay, just going through some lonely times and pissed the old man is gone." She started to ramble, almost as though she were talking to herself; only Jerry was sitting right there, ears wide open. "Even though we fought like cats and dogs, he was my rock. We had a friendship; I felt like I was just getting to know him as a person, and bang, he's gone. Then, to hear Ruby and Porter talking," she turned and looked at him. "Did you know Dad had been going to Uncle J's visiting with Nate and the preacher?"

"Good for him." Jerry smiled and nodded. He was happy for his dad.

She shot a look of daggers at him, "Good? How do you know it was good? Also, why didn't I know about it? Jesus, we drove into town together a lot, and Lord knows he could talk about everything else. Why not this?"

She sat silent for a few seconds; Jerry thought she finished, but just as he was getting ready to say something, she started up again. "It takes a surprise visit to the Pearl, a by-chance meeting of some preacher and walking in on a hush-hush conversation between the help to discover Dad had some secret life."

He'd had enough, "What are you going on about? So Dad went to play cards with his brothers and chew the fat. Hannah, they weren't getting any younger, and it was about damn time they started acting like family. You're acting as he betrayed you; that's sick. I certainly hope your life has more than the day-to-day life of an old man who just happened to be your father. If it isn't, then it needs to be." His face flushed, and he was aggravated but concerned.

She was offended, "That's not what I'm saying; you're twisting it all around."

"Am I? Just for grins, when's the last time you went out on a date? Better yet, what was the last thing you did for fun?" He was animated as he spoke, punctuating with his hands.

She was getting pissed and felt her stomach churn, accompanied by tense muscles in her neck. "Ya know, it's easy for you to say, Jer. You don't work 24/7. Everyone thinks my job is some cushy thing." The tears started flowing down her cheeks, "There's a shitload of demands on me. I know what the people in the office think of me." Her gestures became wild, "Daddy's little girl, some brainless twit who inherited her job, makes stacks of money only to leach off the old man even more by living with him. News flash, it's not easy; in fact, it's damn hard. No, I don't have a life; thanks for reminding me. Date? Hmm, let's see, my last date was with an investment broker, obviously trying to get next to Dad. The whole dinner, we talked about business and what a great guy Dad was," she was bordering on hysterical, "not even a damn good night kiss."

"Hannah, you need to pull over." He tried to calm her down by speaking calmly.

She kept going. She was getting angrier by the second. Jerry was a bit taken aback but glad she was venting; she obviously needed to vent. She looked over at him, "You know, sometimes I see how the bag boys at the grocery look at me, and I think 'yep, I could get one of them to do me.' Let's just say, Jer; it's been a long time. I had my chance at love and ran, there you have it, the exciting life of one Hannah Lee Cain. Every day brings forth another wonderful adventure," she remarked sarcastically.

"All I can say, Sis, you need to take off a month or so; no one will question it. Get your head together, go to the beach. I'll go with you if you want." He was quiet for a while, and as they came closer to the few city lights of Covington, he playfully grabbed her hand. "Ran from love? Do tell. Who knows, he may still be waiting, call him."

She smiled. There was so much her family didn't know. They all still thought of her as a little girl, but she'd been a woman for a long time and had made her mark on the world. Whether the people in the office acknowledged it or not didn't matter, she knew, and so did the people that counted. Maybe it was time to return to New York again or give it a go on the West Coast. She'd made enough contacts and impressed enough people in the know, getting another position was a no-brainer. No, she thought, she'd have to play out the rest of the saga at C&S, at least for then.

"Not tonight, but one day I'll tell you the whole sordid tale. It's fair to say, he's not waiting, and even if he were, I sure as hell don't want him."

They pulled up to the house. As she got out of the car, she batted her eyes and smiled, "Still pals, even though I was the wicked witch from the west?"

"Witch, don't you mean bitch? Only you, my dear, can get away with it. You do it so well."

The next few days would prove to be uneventful. She did a lot of hammock hugging, strolls on the grounds, and heart-to-heart chats with Jerry. She even broke down and told him about Davis, Peter Tisdale's younger brother, the love she ran away from, how they had moved in together, how he had proposed to her, and how the M-word was becoming more and more a reality. She said the date had been discussed, but she decided to leave New York. When Jerry questioned why, she was evasive and told him she had a gut feeling it wasn't right, so left. It still hurt too bad and best left unspoken. It had been a long few days, and she retired to her room for the night.

She was in a deep sleep, and somewhere in her dream, she heard the voice of Belle as she gently tried to wake her. "Hannah, oh Hannah, you gotta get up; there's an important call from the city. Hannah, wake up, it's Deidre. She said you gotta get on the phone. I told her you were sleepin', but she said she needed you now."

Rubbing the sleepy blur from her eyes, she turned over and picked up the phone. She turned to Belle, "Thanks. Can you be a love and get me a cup of coffee?"

"Hey, Deidre, what's up?" Her voice still had a sleepy grog to it.

"Sorry to wake you, but I thought you might like to know when I got to the office this morning, there were some detectives and a slew of police officers going through the office. I don't know what they're looking for, but it's intense. I thought you might like to know. I know John called Preston. They're going through Preston's office, John's, and your dad's right now."

"Thanks for calling and let them in my office; tell them they are welcome to go through anything they want. Cooperate, and I'll get there as fast as I possibly can. Let them know I'm on my way." She rolled out of bed and was showered, dressed, and done in twenty minutes.

The ride across the Causeway seemed to go on forever. She couldn't figure out what the police would be doing at C&S. They always played things strictly by the book. It was her dad's rule, no hanky-panky. She rummaged through her purse; she knew somewhere she might have her Uncle Jeremiah's phone number. Even though he only came to the city once in a blue moon, he was still Chairman of the Board and needed to be advised of the situation if he hadn't already been called. In her search, she came across the envelopes from her father. She'd forgotten all about them. She thought *one more day won't hurt; right now, Uncle J's number. Screw it!*

She dialed the office, and Deidre picked up, "Hey, it's Hannah. I need Jeremiah's number in Mississippi. Thanks, you're a peach."

She quickly dialed the number. The phone rang about ten times, and Porter picked up, "Good morning, Cain residence."

"Porter, Hannah here. I need to speak to my uncle right away. Is he around?"

" No dawlin' he and Mr. Nate left for the city about an hour ago. If I hear from him, you want him to call you?"

"Thank you, no, I'll see him at the office." She pushed the speed to an even eighty. At times like these, she wished she lived in the city rather than so damn far away.

The office was in utter chaos; Deidre, Hannah's assistant, and Sal, the Art Director, arrived at the office about ten minutes before the police. A barrage of uniformed officers flooded the building. There were police cars everywhere. No one was allowed to enter the individual offices. Hence, Deidre called Hannah.

Moments later, two detectives arrived on the scene, requesting to see Preston and John Harris, the Director of Land Development. Since neither had gotten into the office yet, they took a seat to wait. Deidre had a way with people, especially men, and it was evident Detective Seth Parsons had quickly given her the once over. She was an attractive African American woman. Deidre wore her hair in long braids tied loosely back. Her skin glowed, and her eyes had a mysterious quality men loved, and she knew how to flash them.

"Would either of you gentlemen like a cup of coffee? I had just started the drip when y'all came in; it won't take but a few. I suspect Mr. Harris will be in within the next fifteen minutes, but until then, how do you like your coffee, light or dark?" she gave a sexy smile as she headed toward the kitchen.

"Thanks, I like it sweet and dark, " Seth remarked with a broad smile and coy sound to his voice. He watched as Deidre walked down the hall. He looked at his partner, "m,m,m, that is one fine woman." Nick shook his head.

Seth was the proverbial brick wall, about six feet five, tipping the scale around 250. There wasn't an ounce of fat on his bones; he was sheer muscle and a good-looking man. Seth played football for Southern, a predominantly black university, and would have been drafted into the pros if not for a thrown knee his junior year. He never recovered thoroughly enough from the injury to go pro. Anyway, they wouldn't have wanted him; he was damaged goods. Seth was a well and outspoken man. He had a happy-go-lucky demeanor, whereas Nick was a bit more high-strung and far less eloquent.

Nick had a rough appearance like he'd grown up on the streets and could've gone either way, cop or criminal. His quietness was almost unsettling, but nothing got by him. His dark hair, olive skin, and dark eyes suggested Italian heritage. At first glance, he was nothing much to write home about, simply average.

Deidre, with a sassy smile and strut, returned with the coffee. By the time Mr. Harris arrived at the office, one would've thought Seth and Deidre were long-lost friends, but then again, in New Orleans, that was the way of everyone.

Harris came barreling through the door, "What in the hell is going on around here? I had trouble getting in the damn parking lot. It looks like—

Deidre quickly interrupted, "Mr. Harris, these men are from the police department and have been waiting for you and Mr. Cain for the past few minutes. I told them you'd be in shortly, and here you are," she smiled big and gave him a nod.

She tried to soothe the situation before he said something embarrassing. He tended to be opinionated and annoyed everyone around him, "Thank you, Deidre." He turned to the detectives, "If you gentlemen will follow me, we can speak in my office. I have a busy day ahead of me."

"Mr. Harris, your office is off-limits," Nick instructed. "We'll find somewhere else to speak." Harris saw two police officers going through his things as they passed his office. He had a look of being appalled, which both Seth and Nick ignored. Seth looked in; Mr. Harris had a well-appointed office with an array of impressionistic jazz paintings and sketches on his wall. His credenza hosted an array of what appeared to be family-type pictures, even one with a dog. Like the other offices at C&S, his was classic and elegant, wreaking success and old money. He had his putter and practice game in the corner.

They came to a break room, "This'll do." Seth started the ball rolling as he pulled out a chair for the man and sat down himself. "The NOPD received an anonymous letter suggesting things here at C&S have been less than forthright, and given the recent murder of Mr. Cain, um, do you have any idea what I might be talking about?" Nick was leaning on the doorjamb blocking the break room into the hall.

It was apparent Harris was uncomfortable, "I have no idea what you're talking about."

"No idea? Let me see if any of this rings a bell; then you can fill in the blanks."

Harris' hands were a bit shaky, telltale of intense nerves, " I assure you everything here at C&S is strictly above board, and you and anyone else are more than welcome to see for themselves, I'm afraid, officer—

"Detective," Seth interrupted.

Corrected and irritated, Harris continued, "Detectives, someone has led you on some wild goose chase, for reasons I know not."

To this, Nick responded, "Ya know, we thought this might be bogus. Like a disgruntled employee, but then, we figured, what the heck, let's look into it. Low and behold, we talked to some people, and things didn't add up. By this, I'm referring to dealings with the Julia Street property. It seems like I remember C&S, only a coupla months ago, wanting to take down the little building and hop in bed with one of those, whaddya callit, oh yeah, boutique hotels. From what I understand, the city turned y'all down. I'd be pissed too; I mean, if I owned a building, I'd figure I can do whatever I want with it, ya know? But, you're an educated man; you can see how this might not look too good for your company." He shrugged his shoulders and stared at Harris.

"I suppose if one were to be unfamiliar with the ins and outs of property investment and insurance ramifications, one might deem things could look peculiar." While nervous, Harris had a haughty air, which totally pissed off Nick. "But for those working day in and day out with valuable assets such as the Julia Street building, they would inevitably see the loss and tragedy. What you are implying, Detective Messina is ludicrous. Yes, the city turned us down for demolition, but they were more than supportive and thrilled at the prospect of renovation to suit the same need. Just think, a new four-star property, blocks from the Convention Center." While irritated, Harris remained calm and to the point.

Seth continued, holding a pleasant, non-threatening look upon his face. "There are several allegations. We just want to look into them, you know, check it out. What is your position, Mr. Harris?" the questioning had begun, like it or not, and Harris would have to answer like everyone else.

As the interview went on, Seth could see his partner's patience running thin, "Nick, why don't you find out when we can expect Mr. Cain. I think his secretary called him at home and said he'd be here soon." He knew he better get him out of there before he blew or insulted someone.

It was about that time Hannah got there. Before going into her office, she stopped to look at the message pad at the receptionist's desk.

Nick turned the corner, "Hey doll, you know when Mr. Cain is due in?"

A bit startled, she said, "Excuse me, which Mr. Cain are you looking for and who might you be?" Her matter-of-fact attitude took him by surprise, and he quickly realized this was not Preston Cain's secretary. She had a strong presence, something he admired.

He decided to try again, "I'm looking for a Mr. Preston Cain, and I somehow think we got off on the wrong foot." He reached out to shake her hand, "Nick Messina, NOPD Detective."

His face was a little embarrassed looking, which she gathered some mirth from; she smiled, "Hannah Cain, C&S Marketing and Public Relations." She paused a second, picked up her briefcase and purse, "Now, how can I be of help to you, Detective?"

She was sincere, he could tell, and he appreciated it, "My partner is talking to Mr. Harris, and we need to get a hold of Mr. Cain as well."

With that, a voice boomed into the office. It was Uncle Jeremiah. Hannah thought to herself that if she had made this Nick Messina nervous, how was the poor bastard gonna deal with Jeremiah? This would be interesting.

He bellowed, "You got him, sonny." There was a look of surprise on the detective's face. Even with city clothes on, Jeremiah looked a little on the wild side. His gray hair was long by city standards, shaggy over the ears, and the back passed his collar. He had a rugged Marlboro man kind of style. His skin was a weathered tan, and his teeth stained from years of 'chew.'

Hannah broke in, "Uncle J, this is Detective Messina with New Orleans Police Department. He was asking about Preston." She turned to the detective, "Detective Messina, you'll soon find there are Cains from one end of this place to the other," she smiled at him, poor guy.

Nate came in behind, and the detective was introduced to him, as well. Nick told them to wait in the conference room; they would call them in one at a time. Jeremiah seemed happy to oblige, whereas Nate was jumpy.

The conference room had the same classic style as the rest of the office. There was one wall filled with bookcases floor to ceiling and a mammoth table with twenty-plus leather chairs centered in the room. A small table at the opposite end hosted a silver coffee service and two telephones. Nick thought this was impressive, very impressive. Even more so was Hannah Cain. Within minutes the room started filling with people as the police escorted them to await their interview with the detectives. Nick watched as they filed in, making notes on a pad.

Hannah leaned over to him and whispered, "That's Page Foster; he's Director of Real Estate, and the man behind him is Charlie, he's in charge at the lumber yard. Believe me; you'll know when Preston gets here." Everyone was taking seats; Jeremiah came in and took one of the seats at the head of the table. There was an obvious vacancy next to him. The staff chatted idly and looked each other over. Nick could see the wheels turning. He wondered how many were involved and who knew what. They all seemed a bit put out. Everyone's attention was drawn to the door when Seth walked in with Harris, who now seemed beyond frazzled.

Seth inquired of Nick, "Preston Cain? Any word?"

Nick shook his head no. The two detectives started to exit the room.

The sound of voices trailed from down the hall. The male sounded exasperated, "Oh, for heaven's sake, Millie." Instantly changing to butter sweetness as he approached the detectives.

"Good morning, gentlemen." Nick thought this had to be Preston.

"Glad you could join us," Nick sarcastically commented, "and now, follow me." Nick took the lead and started for the break room.

"Gentlemen, perhaps we would be more comfortable in my office." Preston was Mr. Smug Pompous Ass.

"Nah, this'll be fine," Nick pulled up a chair, "Here, take a seat."

Seth sat across from him, and Nick resumed his position at the doorway, standing at Preston's back.

They grilled him for two hours. Preston's good humor wore thin quickly, and he, at one point, became enraged. Seth defused the situation where Nick seemed to make a point of inflaming him.

Nick pulled a chair up close to Preston and got in his face, "Preston, you're really pissing me off. I just wanna know how the hell did you get your position? According to your answers, you don't know shit. Either you think I'm fucking stupid, or you're lying through your teeth. Now, which is it?"

Preston pleaded and looked to Seth for help. "I have told you all I know," Nick disgustedly pushed his chair as he got up.

Seth laced his hands together and stretched, knuckles popping. "Okay, Mr. Cain, let's go back to the denial from City Hall about Julia Street. You are trying to tell me you knew nothing about the request. Am I supposed to believe John Harris did this all on his own?" Preston sat straight in his chair, posturing attitude. Only his head swiveled as he held a look of contempt with a set jaw, flushed cheeks, and almost robotic movement.

"I'm sure he didn't, but without being able to go to my office, I can't get the file to look at it. If I could get to my office, maybe I could answer some of these questions." Preston was flustered and put out at the insult of being detained and interrogated by the detectives.

They went round and round. Seth had a lot more patience than Nick. Even under these circumstances, Preston came across as a pompous ass and way too snotty for Nick's liking. He appeared to be one of those people that took themselves way too seriously and thought he was too important for the rest of the regular Joes.

A CHANGE IN THE TUNE

t had been a long day, and everyone was happy to go home. Hannah had never remembered seeing Preston as red in the face. She had no idea what went on with the detectives, but she hoped he hadn't been his typical asshole self. Uncle Jeremiah seemed rather indifferent and not bothered by the whole business. He sat around drinking coffee, shooting the breeze with some of the uniforms, and snacking on a sundry of food he had catered for the office.

Everyone was waiting to find out something, some juicy bit of scandal. Each employee secretly had their suspicions or fantasy about which one of the big wigs had gotten caught with their hand in the cookie jar. Nothing like this had ever happened at C&S before. It wouldn't have with Tyler Cain at the helm.

Hannah spent time catching up on family phone calls. She had only had brief conversations with Mitch and Miles since the funeral. They had each said they were doing fine, but she hadn't gotten the chance to talk to Margot or Crystal, so this was the perfect time to call them. After speaking with them, Hannah felt more grounded. She and everyone else at C&S were glad when the day ended, and they were free to leave.

"Miss Hannah Cain, where you headin', girl?" she turned to find Detective Messina following her.

She smiled, a bit off-guard, but remained composed, "Hey there, Detective, I'm heading home," she paused a moment, "I'm sorry, I thought we were free to leave." She held a determined look on her face.

He quickly caught up with her. "You are, you are. I just thought maybe we could talk a bit, away from the office. There were a few things you said today that piqued my curiosity. I was thinkin'—"

She thought it had been a long day, and it might be nice to unwind a little before hitting the bridge. Cutting him off, she answered, "You'd like to find somewhere to chat? There's a new place down the street; we can go there unless you have any objection. I've wanted to try it out. Talking to you will give me the perfect excuse." She was pleasant but not overly friendly.

"I'm game," he smiled.

The restaurant was empty, only two tables were occupied, which made her wonder how long the place would stay in business, but it suited her fine. She didn't want to fight crowds. No crowd, no chaos, a perfect setting for an extra dirty martini and French bread.

"We're here; what did you want to talk about?" she waited. "I know my family must've frustrated you, they're an unusual bunch at the best of times, and I think it's safe to say," she smirked, "this isn't the best of times, to say the very least."

He chuckled but then took on a more somber, straight from the heart expression, "First, I wanted to tell you how sorry I am for your loss." He looked straight into her eyes. "Some of your family members are a little out da box, but you wouldn't believe some of the stuff we see, but let's start this right. It's Nick. I didn't necessarily say the curiosity had everything to do with business." She caught a twinkle in his eyes.

Fortunately, the waitress came at the perfect time. Hannah ordered her martini, and Nick got a draft with a dozen oysters. She felt a little uncomfortable but knew she had brought the whole thing on. There was no one to blame but herself. The entire day she had played eye games. She had figuratively knocked, and he had opened the door. Had she not made a point to run into him all day, whether it was in the copy or lunchroom, he probably wouldn't have been as bold to ask her for a drink.

Getting totally off the subject, Hannah began the conversation, "Have y'all been able to find out anything yet? I figured something must be going on with Land Development since y'all honed in on Preston and John first. However, I have nothing to do with that aspect of the business and know very little. Anything I could tell you would strictly be on a personal level, like family, personality, and things I've overheard from time to time, but nothing business."

Nick explained how sometimes it took getting to know the personality and family stuff to get the whole picture making it possible to put the pieces to the puzzle in place. "Are you close with your uncles?" He relaxed at the table with a look that screamed curiosity.

"What do you mean by close? We do weddings, funerals, and the occasional holiday, but not the every Sunday family gathering kind of thing, if that's what you mean." He watched her intently; she had a naturally sexy way emanating with her every move. She felt uncomfortable; she didn't know what else there was to say, anything else would be sheer babble, yet she babbled despite herself. "As kids, we used to do Thanksgiving, Christmas, Mardi Gras, and Easter together, but that was years ago." She paused, and he waited to respond if she had something else to add. Watching her made his heart smile, a feeling he had once before but thought was gone forever. Continue she did, "It's kinda like a story of two families, but it's one. There's my dad and Uncle J, and then Lizzie, Preston, and Nate. I mean, if you think about it, it all makes sense because my dad and Jeremiah were from the same woman, and the other three from Grandpa's second marriage. They're older and different. I guess you could say they're not as socially conscious as the younger three. Uncle J. and Dad never had anything to prove; sometimes, I feel Preston has something to prove, and Nate, I always thought he was a bit thick. I know I sound horrible, but you asked." One side of her mouth upturned in a half-smile.

He was holding onto her every word. Finally, the server brought the drinks. Hannah raised her glass, "To life as we once knew it."

"Here, here," they touched glasses.

He looked over his notes, "I had a different read on the family dynamics. I got the feeling Nate and Jeremiah were close." He stared her in the eyes, not in a distrustful way, but it made her uneasy like he was weighing her honesty, and how dare he?

Hannah sat quietly, sizing him up for a few moments but then completed her thought. "Funny you should say that, because it wasn't until recently I learned they spoke at all. I always thought Nate to be more like Preston, but evidently, he's been going to Uncle J's a lot from what the help over there told me. But, as I said, I don't know them well." She brushed a wispy lock of hair from her face, "In fact, I'm just learning how much I don't know. Amazingly, you can see people day in and out but not know them. Scary," she hesitated, "or maybe I'm just self-absorbed and miss out," she took a long sip of her drink, trying to catch the olive with her tongue.

"This is the third time you've said, 'more like Preston,' just how is Preston?" His face took on a frown with eyelids hooded and brows drawn together but more in an answer-seeking way, not a look of displeasure.

Clearing her throat, she gave a slight chuckle, "Other than a pretentious self-serving asshole, you mean?" She plucked the olive out with her fingers and smiled with instant gratification. "There's truly not one answer. Preston's got some ego thing going. He, his wife, and his daughters have always been big into appearances. Not saying my family can't, at times, but it's different. They seem fake or superficial. I don't know." Her mind seemed to drift off as she concluded the thought, "I guess I've never been close to that side of the family, that's all."

He had taken a few notes. As Hannah spoke, she studied him, too, as well. She watched as he made his notes. He was into arrows, circles, and underlines. The more she looked at him, the more she felt an attraction like love denied or something along the lines of look but don't touch. He wasn't overly handsome, and one couldn't call him cute, but he had something. He was one of those men that just had the moves, the package wasn't great, but the way it moved more than made up for it. He was sexy in a bad boy kind of way, something she found intriguing. She could hear his voice, but she wasn't paying attention; she was more into her rambling thoughts. He snapped his fingers in front of her nose.

She jumped, "Sorry, my mind was drifting. What were you saying?" she was embarrassed.

"I'd like to talk with the domestics; when would be a good time to jump the pond?" He shrugged his shoulders with a pivot to his head in a sarcastic manner. His hands had been steepled until he showed an exaggerated curiosity.

Feeling called out, she fired back. "Anytime. They're always there during the day except for Sunday, of course, unless it's some special occasion. Call the house." She tried to be more attentive.

His expression changed, "I don't see a wedding band. Is that a professional move, or are you unattached?" He blind-sided her.

"What?" she couldn't fathom the question. She scrunched her eyebrows as her shoulders dropped.

"I asked are you married, hitched, involved, ya know, spoken for?" he was unnervingly intense in his frankness.

Hesitantly she answered, "no."

"Ever been?" He smiled.

Once again, she answered but rather slowly, "Uh, no, what does this have to do with anything?"

Matter-of-factly he answered, "If you were married or attached, I couldn't very well ask you out, now could I? It just ain't my style." He was so self-assured and cocky.

With this, Hannah decided maybe it was time to get on the road. With all the eye games, bumping into him, and a friendly flirtatious drink, she wasn't planning on taking things down this road. Copying his phrase from earlier, she said, "Looks like I gotta call it a night, I still gotta jump the pond. Gotta get on my way."

"No ma'am, not with that very dirty martini in your gut and nothing to soak it up, you didn't eat any bread. Can't let you do that." Nick held himself smugly.

"What do you mean, can't let me do that? I'm not drunk. Look, I'll drive extra cautious, mister policeman." Hannah was throwing the sarcasm right back at him.

"Sorry, I can't do that. I'd offer to drive you home, but then that leaves the problem of your car. If you stayed in the city tonight, you could get it in the morning. Maybe stay in, eat pizza, catch a good movie." His look was unwavering.

He had her blown away; she couldn't believe the conversation. All of it was sounding way out there, "Just what are you saying? Are you suggesting I stay the night with you?" *How audacious!* She thought.

"I wasn't, but now that you mention it, sounds good. You're certainly welcome." She looked like she was going to come unglued, so he quickly added to the thought, "I was actually suggesting I take you to your brother Jerry's or Mitch's or the Corporate condo." Then, jokingly he teased her, "but mi casa es tu casa."

Firstly, she was embarrassed to have assumed the way she did, and secondly, she was blown away at his outspokenness. She knew Jerry wasn't home. He was back in Covington, and she didn't want to deal with his roommate Jay. She loved him, but he could be a bit much, and she wasn't up for it right then. She hated the corporate apartment; it was so corporate.

"Are you really not gonna let me drive home?" She questioned in a pleading voice.

He nodded, "yep." He closed his eyes as he nodded in confirmation.

"For crying out loud, it was one martini, don't be an asshole; I don't need it tonight."

Sternly he countered, "And I don't need you on my conscience tonight."

Aggravated, she told him to walk her to the company's place; it was only a few blocks away. She hated to stay there all night by herself. Staying the night in the city made her nervous, especially in the warehouse district. The more she thought about it, the more uncomfortable she was becoming. She didn't want to be alone, "If I have to stay at the condo, you know what that means? You'll have to stay there too for a while. Eat some pizza, let it soak up the beer you just threw down your throat." She waited a moment, no response. "I hope I still have some spare clothes there." She remarked as they walked; she wondered what she was getting herself into. She had to admit it; something had been brewing all day.

She dug around in her purse and eventually found her keychain, which had the key to the condo. It had been months since she'd been there. In fact, it was the night of the ball. Now thinking back on it, the night had been crazy. Everyone was beyond drunk, more like plastered.

The walk was only ten minutes or so. The condo was in one of the renovated warehouses, a product of the catastrophic World's Fair, something she'd heard about but not even born to witness. They stopped along the way and bought a bottle of wine, some beer, microwave popcorn, and a couple of bags of chips. He seemed offended when she pulled out her wallet.

She glanced in his direction, "Get over it."

He shrugged, "I didn't say nothin'."

"Good, don't." She abruptly turned toward the cashier and away from him.

The condo had a different style than the office. It was a mixture of antique and modern, a trendy, artsy feel in step with the district. The ceilings soared, and while the floors were of old heart pine, the design of the contemporary angles created an interesting but austere look. The living area and kitchen flowed with a loft bedroom overlooking the living room. A set of French doors led to the master bedroom on the main level.

"Okay, Detective, there's the phone," she pointed, "You order the pizza; I'm gonna check to see if I still have clothes here." While not suited, stockinged, and heeled, she still needed to shed the stress of the day, and changing clothes always served as the perfect symbolic gesture. She returned in a pair of hot pink bike shorts and an oversized tee balanced on her shoulders, threatening to plunge off at any moment.

He had already popped the top to a cold one and was putting things away in the kitchen. Hannah reached for a glass, and when she turned back around to get the wine, he was there, face to face. He grabbed her by the waist and roughly pulled her into him. He looked into her eyes momentarily, then pinned her to the cabinets with a deep hard kiss. The moment escalated while in the throes of passion, and without further thought, she unbuttoned his shirt and began to undo his pants. He scooped her up and carried her into the bedroom. It was one of those almost ugly sexathons. Hard, groping, and aggressive. There were no tender words or intimate touches, no sweet little pecks of a kiss; it was almost savage. Both of their bodies gleamed with sweat, their hair drenched to the scalp. Sometime later, they came up for air, and that was the first time Hannah thought about what had just happened.

She got up to run the shower. Nick watched her as she crossed the room. He couldn't believe this feminine creature had stirred his life so quickly. She was an exciting person, astute businesswoman, spoiled little rich girl, innocent in many ways, and innately passionate and practiced in others. *A piece of the pie*, he thought. Her body was slender and graceful; nothing overly spectacular. Everything was average but richly and perfectly assembled.

He heard the shower turn on, gave her a few moments of privacy, and then entered the bathroom.

"Room for two?" he inquired. It was the first time a word was spoken since the kiss in the kitchen.

"Sure," she found herself uncomfortably quiet. What did one say after such an adventure? Whatever she had to say would sound trite; she lathered up and smiled.

"Thank you, Hannah; it's been a long time since I've been with anyone." He gently dotted her nose with soap bubbles and delicately kissed her lips. He touched her face and looked deep into her eyes.

For the first time she saw it, the pain, a hurt that stung so bad he'd covered it up with layers and layers of tough guy.

She whispered, "I usually don't do this sorta thing."

He touched her lips; he didn't want any apologies, no excuses, it would ruin the whole thing, and he hoped she had no regret, "I know, I wouldn't be here if I thought you did."

He turned her around and sponged her back. Hugging her tightly, he said, "Thank you, I hope you enjoyed."

There was an obnoxious chiming; they both zoomed into reality simultaneously.

"The pizza!" It was a mad dash.

"I'll get it," she grabbed a towel and ran.

When he came out of the bedroom, the tempting aroma of pizza had filled the air. Hannah was still in her towel. He had on most of his clothes, "I'll take over from here; you get something on."

"What's wrong? You don't like to eat pizza in the buff," and dropped her towel.

"Girl, you some kinda crazy," he proceeded to undress. She watched him as though he was part of some show. He looked a hell of a lot better without the clothes. His body wasn't overly muscled but big enough and well-defined. He left his briefs on.

"Cheater," she laughed, grabbed his shirt, and threw it on.

The rest of the evening, they laughed, ate pizza, drank wine and beer, and indulged in more great sex. The intimacy was a bit slower and gentle, a perfectly choreographed number. They fell asleep in each other's arms.

In the distance, she heard her phone buzz and buzz, vibrating across the dresser as it buzzed. It occurred to her through her haze; the buzzing wouldn't stop until she answered it.

"Hello?" who would be calling so early? But then again, she had no idea what time it was.

The voice on the other side was sassy and chipper, "Where were you last night, hmm?"

"Jer, I'm sorry, I told Belle I was staying in the city, and I'd call you when I got a chance. I guess I didn't get a chance. Sorry."

There was a brief pause, "Well, I'm waiting. Where were you last night that you couldn't come home?"

"It's a long story," she mumbled.

"How long," and he howled; he loved those dirty penis innuendos. "Jay called me this morning and gave me an ultimatum, either I come home, or he's coming here. Whaddaya think? Should I dare? God, Covington would never be the same. There's enough scandal right now; I'll leave it for another time. Join us for lunch? I'll have Jay cook up something, and the three of us can chat it up. I want all the details, and I mean all."

"You're sick. Anyone ever tell you that? I'll be at your place around one, okay?" She rubbed her eyes, trying to read the tiny numbers at the top of her phone, "What time is it anyway?"

"Nine thirty, sleeping beauty, one it is, ta," he hung up.

She got up, looking around; she figured Nick had left at some point in time. She dressed in her clothes from the day before, figuring she'd stop at one of the boutiques around the corner for an outfit. There was a single rose and a note on the table as she walked out.

Beautiful lady,
Have a great day. Call me.

She headed out the door, stopped at the first boutique, and outfitted herself for the day. It wasn't quite office attire, but a sundress and sandals would have to fit the bill. She continued to the office after dropping a quick six hundred dollars. On the way to the office, she pondered if the police were still there in hopes of seeing Nick again. They were.

Margaret greeted her as she arrived, "Good morning, darlin', no one knew if you were coming in today. The phone's been ringing off the hook for you."

"I'm here now, I think." She grabbed some coffee and headed back to her office.

Deidre came in, "Ooh, girl, I love that dress. You look like a burst of summer." She put Hannah's hat on and checked herself out in the mirror. "As I'm sure you know, the cops are still here. Those two detectives are with Jeremiah, and I think Nate just went in, too." Still checking herself in the mirror, "Girl to girl, what do you think of Seth, think he's hot? I dunno." As though having a debate with herself. "I can't see myself with a cop, it's not me, but he's sooo buff."

Hannah found it curious, "What do you mean you can't see yourself with a cop? Why not?" She rocked her chair back with her head at a tilt.

"Cuz they don't make no kinda money, honey. I have a lot of wants, ya know. I'm looking more for a doctor, lawyer, accountant, even a real estate agent, but cop, shiiit!"

"I see what you're saying, but as long as he's nice and a good person, what does it matter what he does?" Hannah rocked forward and leaned on her desk, her head propped in her hands. "I think he's a hotty. He's built and certainly seemed into you yesterday. What can it hurt? Has he asked you out?" Her mind drifted; she wondered how discreet Nick was going to be; only time would tell.

Deidre turned with a smile. "Not yet, but I think if I let him know he can, he will. Maybe. I'll think about it," she handed her a stack of messages.

"Who knows, Deidre? He could be Mister Right." Hannah winked at her with a slight giggle.

Lunchtime came quickly, she had returned all of her calls hadn't seen Nick yet, but it was time to go to Jerry's. It seemed Nick had been with Jeremiah and Nate for quite some time. She didn't know if she was more curious about the problems with the company and what she'd heard from the grapevine or what his reaction to her would be now, now they'd crossed a boundary. She speculated the whole way to Jerry's.

As usual, Jay had outdone himself. He had fresh-cut flowers floating in a crystal bowl and a crisp white linen tablecloth complete with matching napkins and sterling napkin rings. The soft sound of string instruments provided the perfect background.

"Your garden is gorgeous; y'all did a good job." It always impressed her to see their place. She couldn't imagine Jerry being domestic.

"Honey, there is no y'all in garden work; that's all Jay. Make sure you mention the flowers on the table; they're from the backyard. He's out there cutting some fresh mint as we speak."

A shrill cackling came from the backyard as the screen door screeched open. "Do I hear the sound of my favorite sister-in-law?" He rounded the corner from the kitchen with arms spread wide, "Don't we look like a breath of freshness. Let me guess another Mimi's excursion?" He turned her around, "Look at you, sandals and hat to match, why you could be on the front cover of Southern Living, just a little Southern belle."

Flattering Jay, she declared in a perfect drawl and a bat of her eyes, "It would only be perfect if I were standing in front of your beautiful flower gawden." She spun around, letting her dress twirl in a soft bell.

Jay puffed his chest with pride. "Ya think so? They did bloom well this year, and I was afraid they were gone after those few cold nights early spring. I'll have to give you some cuttings to take home."

She stood next to him and put her arm around his waist. "I'm not good with flowers; you'll have to come across the lake and show me."

"Meee, come to Covington, what a hoot." He touched his fingers to his chest. "My sweet little closet queen would put his foot down. What would the neighbors say? Maybe it's time for him to come clean and strut his stuff down Boston Street." He cackled again.

The two of them went on and on, pouring it on, to the total frustration of Jerry, "Give me a break, y'all. Jay, isn't it time for lunch? Hannah does have to get back to the office sometime today; besides, I think she has a story to tell, full of wonderful graphic details."

They sat at the table as Jay scurried around filling ice tea glasses and serving their plates. Once he sat down, she told them about Nick, the police stuff at the office, how he stopped her as she was leaving, the martini tale ending up in the condo, the pizza, the kitchen episode, and great sex.

"What does he look like?" Jerry asked, leaning into the conversation.

She patted her lips. "Nick's okay looking, kinda y'atty. He grew up by City Park, and he's Italian – dark hair, eyes, olive skin. I guess he's about thirty. Kinda rough, but a nice guy and a lot of fun. Great smile."

"And?" Jerry asked.

"And what?" she looked bewildered.

He stared back at her, "you know." He wiggled his eyebrows.

"Oh, God, Jerry, you are sick, worse than an old woman. Let's put it this way, he's gifted but better than that, he knows how to share the gift," Hannah could feel herself blush.

Jay scolded Jerry, "Look what you've done now, Hannah honey, don't pay him any attention; he's a pervert. Jerry, enough, you've embarrassed her. He's always complaining we don't see you enough, but I tell him it's his own fault; he doesn't know how to treat guests. You ought to hear him with Elise. It's no wonder that poor girl hasn't had success with a man. Every time she thinks she's found Mr. Right, she brings him to meet Jerry, and poof, she never hears from him again."

The two of them made a good couple. Jay was good to Jerry. He was somewhere in his late forties or early fifties and had been a nurse for several years before going into anesthesia. Jay was extremely intelligent and well-read. He put up with Jerry's antics and pranks, almost in a motherly way, scolding him when necessary. He had been a good friend to her brother, and she liked him a lot. They had been an item for four-plus years. She thought it was time Jerry brought him to Southern

Manor; he'd love it. She bid them goodbye and headed for the office. She hoped Nick would still be there.

Just the telling of the last evening's escapades to Jerry and Jay revved her engine, raising her heart rate and temperature.

Nick's car was still parked outside, *good*, she thought. She made it into her office, picked up her messages on the way in, and had begun to settle when he stuck his head in, "Uh, Miss Cain, are you just bothering to come to the office at three o'clock, or have we been out on a long lunch?" He threw a devilish grin her way.

"Detective Messina, are you asking for the record, or do you have some ulterior motive?" She threw it right back.

He entered her office and plopped in one of her chairs. He gave her a broad smile, and she could feel her face blush like some lustful teenager.

"Last night, you said you might want to talk to Belle or Porter. How about Friday and you can stay in Covington for the weekend? Promise you'll have a good time," she gave him a flirty smile batting her eyes ever-so-coyly.

"Sounds great, but this is a big weekend; it's my daughter's tenth birthday, and we're having a family party for her on Saturday. After all, she is now in double digits."

The look on her face must've been one of shock, "Wow, why didn't you tell me you were married? I would've never, whoa," she put her head down in thought.

He became animated in urgency with both hands pressing the air as though trying to stop an invisible train. "You got it wrong, Hannah, wait, wait, I was married. My wife died two years ago, as I said to you," he leaned forward and whispered, "It had been a long time since I had been with a woman. My daughter and I live with my mother given my hours an' all. Look, I'd like to be with you, any other offers in your little bag of tricks or does havin' a kid mean it's caputs. Cuz if that's how ya feel, it's okay, you being all footloose and fancy-free."

Thinking, she responded, "No, it doesn't matter; I think it's great you have a daughter. What's her name?"

"Michelle, and she's a real charmer. She's got me wrapped around her little finger."

She wanted to know more. It seemed the more she learned, the better the package got, "How long had you been married?" She was absorbing his every word and hanging on to his every emotion. His answers would be the tell of his character.

"Ten years, I married my high school girl. We'd grown up a few blocks from each other. Our families had been close—the perfect life. Yeah, Sylvia was my girl, " he smiled weakly, transparent with the pain. "We'd been at a crawfish boil. My mama was babysittin', we were havin' a good time, like kids, ya know. I got called out and had to leave. I kissed her goodbye, told her I'd see her at home, and it was the last time I saw her. She had only a beer or two. While making the bend round Bayou St. John, she lost control and ended up head-on with a pickup. Our small Toyota crushed like an accordion." He sucked in a deep breath, trying for a stoic look, but failing miserably. His heart had broken that night, and it was apparent.

"I'm sorry, Nick," and after a brief moment, she added, "and I'd be pissed if you missed your daughter's party; after all, you only turn double digits once in your life, right?" he smiled at her comment and understood that she read the situation perfectly.

He invited her to the party, but she thought it premature; however, she'd like to meet her, and maybe he could bring her to Covington on Sunday. Michelle could ride horses, and maybe Lauren, her nine-year-old niece, could come over. They could swim and play. He agreed and said he would mention it to her, but it sounded fun, and Michelle was always up for new things. The big question was, when could he see her alone again?

"Hm, we never got to see the movie. Don't you need to interview me?" Hannah rang Deidre, "Detective Messina wants a few minutes of my time; please hold my calls."

She got up and locked her office door. She stood poised against the door frame, slowly unbuttoned her dress, exposing a glimpse of her breasts, then a peek at her sensuous navel. She seductively walked up to him, then straddled his lap, pressing her breasts in his face. He obliged with soft kisses and a tickling tongue. They managed to unzip his pants, and he slowly slid into place. They were quiet yet pensive, both desperately trying to maintain the secret while wanting to sing the song of exquisite ecstasy. Mission accomplished.

"How was that for being alone, soon enough?" she raised her eyebrows, "Now tell me, Detective, how long will you be hanging around here doing your investigation?"

As they managed to get themselves back together, he gave her a wink, "I think I'll be in and out of here for the next few weeks, at least," he chuckled.

She repeated, "at least," nodding her head in agreement.

He did need to get back to work, and she had a stack of messages. One was from Uncle Jeremiah asking her to call him in his office when she got back, so she did, "Cain, here."

"Uncle—"

He interrupted, "Hannah, that you? Can I hitch a ride back to Covington with you? Seems Nate is goin' home, and we came over in his car today. I'm in a bit of a pickle."

"Of course, I'd love it," she looked forward to the company, and he was quite a character.

A ROUND WITH UNCLE J.

eremiah was an interesting bird; he talked non-stop the whole way across the bridge to Covington. He spoke of being a boy and how the bridge had only been one lane. His papa kept a place in town and stayed there all week until Friday, and at 5:00 sharp, his driver would take him home for the weekend.

"Course, that was after he moved the family from Mississippi to Covington. We, your dad, and I were a lot older and just about ready to go off to college." Looking out over the water, he rambled on, "I never did take much to Louisiana, something about the people, ya just couldn't trust. According to your Grampa, I had a little too much fun in college. In fact, Ty and I graduated together. He finished in three years, and I finished in five." His wiry gray eyebrows knitted together. "Your dad was a more serious kind of fellow than I ever was, then and now," his voice trailed off. The stillness was deafening after his last remark.

He broke the silence, "Hannah, I know you're a big city girl, I mean, you've worked in the biggest hell-hole of all, New York City, but darlin' you gotta watch your back. You might see people smiling to your face, but those are the worst of the lot; they'll stab you in the back quicker than," he snapped his fingers.

She patted his hand, "I'm watching, don't worry yourself with me; I'm always watching. By the way, can you tell me what in the hell is going on in the office? I always thought we did things above board; at least, that's what my dad always led me to believe. Now there's this mysterious letter and scandal. It's all so peculiar, don't you find?" She briefly glanced his way.

"There have always been some peculiar things going on, but it was always on a personal level, and your dad and I looked the other way. No concern of ours, who's keepin' company with who, if you catch my drift?" She certainly caught his drift, but she couldn't see for the life of her any of the people fooling around, especially with each other.

Like a little girl telling a secret, she giggled and asked who was foolin' with who.

"C'mon, city girl, don't tell me you don't know about Millie and Harris? That's old news, hell, it's been going on for years, but the latest surprise was when the cleaning lady walked in on, what's her name, she's the new girl in Page Foster's department, common name, like Susan or Ann. Oh hell, anyway, the cleaning woman walked in when she wuz under Preston's desk. We all got a good hee-haw outta that, cuz to tell you the truth, it wouldn't have surprised me if it had been the fairy on your staff, Sal. I always thought Preston might butter his bread on the other side. Anyway, the cleaning lady is a Jehovah's Witness or something and took personal affront to the indiscretion and quit," he started to laugh. She thought, *Oh my gosh, did he just say fairy and butter his bread on the other side. How embarrassing!*

He had a good old belly laugh. At one point, Hannah was concerned he would choke to death, but he calmed down and would only periodically chuckle. "Uncle, you can't say things like that. Sal is gay, not a fairy. It's not okay to say those things; I hope you know."

They had about fifteen minutes to go, the light was red, and they were sitting listening to the radio. He turned down the radio, "Hannah, I'm gonna share something with you, only a couple people know, ya gotta keep it tight under your cap. Can't tell your brothers, not even Jerry. You especially can't tell your beau. Also, girlie, I don't give a flying flip who likes or doesn't like what I say. I'm old enough to talk the way I damn well, please. If it offends you, get the f- uh, heck over it."

Hannah looked over with surprise, not only with a close f-bomb slip but beau?

"Little missy, everyone knows about you and the detective, don't look surprised; you think the walls don't have ears? Your business, no comment one way or the other coming from me, where was I?" He thought for a minute. "Remember under the cap, tight under the cap," proudly he announced, "I sent the letter to the police. It's too long a story to get into right now, but you come on up to the Pearl, and I'll fill you in."

She looked baffled, "Why would you send a letter to get the company in trouble? I don't get it. You can't leave me hanging," she turned the car abruptly before getting to the gates of Southern Manor, throwing Jeremiah against the door.

"Now hold on there, darlin', hold on. Darlin', it's a long story. Turn this dang car around. For starters, remember the ball, where Nate's daughters were on the court?" She shook her head. He smoothed the air with his hand and held it still for a minute. "Story is, Preston was skunk drunk shootin' his mouth off about business and some dealings with a rather undesirable businessman. Your Uncle Nate overheard and tried to talk to Preston, who started his quick talk bullying treatment. Nate played the part of the dummy but told Tyler, and the three of us talked. It took some time, but we finally found out what Preston was up to, and your dad invited him to the house. According to Belle, there was a heated argument, and it was the last night anyone saw your dad alive."

Hannah looked puzzled, "Let me see if I got this right; Preston was in cahoots with someone y'all didn't approve of—"

Jeremiah interrupted, "Yes, actually, we didn't know he was in cahoots. We didn't know about anything. He was doing this all behind our back cuz he knew we'd never go for any business dealings with that sorta fella."

She thought for a minute, "Because y'all put the kibosh on the deal, you think Preston murdered my dad? I don't see it." She slowly shook her head from side to side, squinting her eyes, but with a strong sense of nausea building in her belly, like after eating just-off shellfish. Vomit rolled up the back of her throat.

"Hannah, it's only one theory, darlin' besides, it's not what I said. Hell, Preston doesn't have the guts or the strength to have done it, but I think he had something to do with the planning. Somehow, he's involved. I don't know exactly how yet. FYI, Preston has had numerous transactions, which we haven't known about until too late. Julia Street is just one. Come up to the Pearl, and I'll get into it further."

She pulled the car into the drive, and they got out. "This blows me away," she shook her head.

He grimaced, "and that's not the half of it. Travis can drive me the rest of the way, or I'll get Porter to fetch me."

It was a lot to digest. Jeremiah was out there; could this be some outlandish act of a man driven to paranoia from being in Mississippi too long? The country people tended to be a little around the bend; maybe Jeremiah joined the ranks. She'd have to think about this new information.

The weekend was upon her, and all went perfectly. Nick and his daughter Michelle came for a visit to Covington. Lauren, Miles' nine-year-old, and Michelle got along famously, and it ended up they stayed the night. The girls stayed in one guest room; Nick stayed in another, and Hannah remained in her suite. After the girls were fast asleep, Nick crept into her suite for a quiet rendezvous and then returned to his room. The following day he headed into the city bright and early. Hannah promised to bring Michelle in when she went to work.

Belle had fixed the girls a big breakfast and had served them like grown ladies out on the veranda. Hannah sipped her coffee in the kitchen and watched as Belle polished, ever so carefully, the silver service out of the dining room. Her dad always expected the silver to be polished and the crystal chandelier to glisten; those were two of his quirks. Hannah found it amusing how Belle always talked to her like a nursemaid to a little girl, never woman to woman or even person to person. She wondered if Belle realized she had grown up and was no longer a little girl.

"How are you holding up, Belle? You okay?" she asked, looking out the window at the girls on the veranda. She could feel her stomach twisting in angst.

Diligently polishing the silver, Belle casually remarked, "I'm just fine, honey. I've seen a lot of people come and go in my lifetime. Ya miss 'em, but before ya know it, ya turn around, and there they are, and they say, 'shore is good to see you.' Like no time had passed at all. We all got our turn, and I guess it was your daddy's turn. If ya think about it, he missed ya mama hard; now they're up there together, watching over you four."

She thought about asking Belle questions about the night when Preston visited her dad. She didn't want to contribute to the rumor mill; she wanted to hear from Belle herself.

Hannah turned and faced Belle. "I miss my dad so much. It's strange going into town without him. I only wish I had been home the last night; maybe things would have been different." In her mind, her comment sounded innocent and reasonable.

"Suga', things happen the way they're meant to be. Don't know why, but not mine nor yours to know why." Belle stared her directly in the eye. It felt like the old gal could read her soul.

"At least you were with him that night. What was he like? Did he seem different, like something was wrong?" she thought this might be a good lead-in.

"Girl, you knew your daddy well enough to know he'd never let anyone know what was on his mind. If he were worried about something, no one ever knew." Belle wasn't giving in, not even the slightest, and continued to polish the silver.

"Something doesn't feel right, I can't put my finger on it, but something isn't right. Were you in the house that night?" she pushed again and took a sip of her coffee.

"Yep, I was in the house 'til ten or so."

"Ten? Why on earth would you be in the house so late? I wish I had been home that night. Then I'd know if he did anything unusual or was acting funny like something was wrong, maybe things would have been different, maybe—"

Belle snapped at her, "Enough of such nonsense, child. You gonna maybe yourself to death. Maybe this and maybe that, enough." She went so far as to stomp her foot, punctuating her command.

"Why were you here so late?" Hannah dug in; she wasn't dropping it.

"Cuz ya daddy had company, and I was washin' up," she got up to bring the now shiny tea service back into the dining room and came back with the candelabra.

"Had company? Who?" Hannah waited, no answer, again she asked, "who?" Clasping tight to her coffee.

"Girl, you some kinda owl, who, who? Your uncle, that's who."

"Which uncle?" She thought, *just push a little farther.*

"Hannah, darlin', what is it you want to know? All these questions are running up my last nerve. I know Mr. Preston was here, and they had a difference of opinion. Honey, your daddy had it all under control. Things quieted down. Don't you need to get into town? Lawdy, look at the time."

"Belle, I need to know what you think about the whole thing," she pleaded.

Belle put the candelabra down and sat. She had a strange look on her face as she pondered her answer. "They're some things, child, you just don't wanna know. Like a man neva wants to hear his woman is playing games behind his back, he don't wanna hear it, cuz he already knows, he just don't wanna face it. Sometimes a mama don't wanna know if her child is lyin', all the whilst she knows, but don't wanna hear it. What I think ain't of no consequence; it's what you think, Missy, that's what counts in your heart. I can tell ya what I know, but you gotta look into your heart. You can see the answer to your question; you just don't wanna see it. Tell Belle, whatcha thinkin', baby. What's troublin' your heart?"

Hannah began to sob. These were the first real tears she'd shed since the graveyard, sad tears. Every other time she would start to cry, she'd shake it off. There was no shakin' off these tears. Belle cradled her as she cried, "It's okay, darlin'. As I told you when we put him to rest, I was gonna make everything alright."

"Belle, I think he did it. Oh, my God," and she burst into uncontrollable sobs.

"Baby, calm yourself down; you goin' to bring on an attack, calm down. There some folks in this world ain't happy with nothin', cuz they don't like themselves. I don't know for sure, but when I close my eyes and picture the night, I can see the two of them. Your daddy was sitting behind his desk, and Mr. Preston was pacin' back and forth in front the desk. I went to see if they wanted their cordials, and I could hear Mr. Preston raisin' his voice, then he dropped it low like. When I went into the room, they were both quiet. Your daddy looked like I never seen him look, real angry, like no forgivin' kinda mad. Hannah, you know your daddy wasn't that kinda man. I think Mr. Preston brought it out in him. He told me, 'Belle, my brother was just about to leave, we won't need any after-dinner cordials, but thank you just the same. Turn yourself in for the night.' I had a few more things to settle in the kitchen. Your daddy excused himself from the room, and Mr. Preston left," she shrugged her shoulders, "You know the rest." She sat in Belle's arms for the better part of an hour. Belle stroked her hair and face with a touch so full of love it made her heart feel full. She felt more at peace than she had in a while.

She rounded the girls up; it was long past time to head into the city. Michelle was a chatterbox; Hannah got the inside scoop on Nick's family, including her father had only been on one date since her mother's death, and it was with some cop's sister, named Maria. The date was a total bomb, according to Michelle. She said she thought Lauren was cool even though she was younger; Michelle said she acted older like she was ten. Hannah got a kick out of the foolishness. As only kids could, she asked Hannah if she loved her dad. Ticklish situation. Hannah told her she thought her dad was a great guy; they had a good time together and left it at that. She turned up the radio. Good luck followed her; a popular song was on the radio and changed the subject to music groups and pre-teen heartthrobs.

They arrived at Nick's mother's house, and she walked Michelle to the door. Nick's mom was right there, giving Hannah a three-time look up and down, called to her sister, Nick's aunt. She yelled back; the girl Nicky was seeing from the country was at the front door. Hannah explained she had to get to work, but the aunt made it to the door before Hannah could escape. She was trapped, and it looked like there was no way out of coffee and fresh pound cake. Antoinette, Nick's mom, brought out scrapbooks and photo albums. Finally breaking away, both sisters hugged and kissed her like a long-lost friend or even family member, registering a ten on the unbelievably uncomfortable scale.

On the way to the office, she reflected on the visit and decided things could have been much worse, and it actually felt good; she felt like she could connect to Nick's past. He was a good guy, whether meant for her or not.

Hannah arrived at the office, and things were still in a state of commotion, so she decided to take the rest of the day off. She saw Nick down the hall as he vanished into the conference room.

She leaned her head into the doorway and, in a deep New Orleans dialect, called in, "Hey, Nicky, Antoinette said ya betta not be late fa suppa, or it'll be T.V. dinna fa you."

He laughed but looked a tad uncomfortable.

Hannah continued, "Captain of the Nord baseball team, you were precious in your cute uniform, a real little stud."

Embarrassed, he pulled his hand down his face. "I'm beyond sorry, don't tell me, the scrapbook too?"

She nodded with a grin, "You bet."

"Aw, jeez, that woman, ya gotta love her." He shrugged his shoulders like it is what it is.

A few people in the conference room basically ignored the conversation as they were involved in their own stuff. Hannah walked up to Nick and whispered, loud enough for others to hear, "You were great last night, babe," and laid a kiss on him, smack dab on the lips. Everyone noticed, and she headed out the door.

He followed behind her, blushing like a bride and mumbling to her, "What has gotten into you? Hey, haven't you heard of discretion?" He touched her shoulder lightly.

"Lighten up; everyone knows anyway. Now it's out in the open for real. I'm heading to Mississippi, going to see the Old Coot. I'll be home tonight if you still want to call me." She batted her eyes and gave him a flirty smile.

The ride to the Pearl was quicker than usual. She called Jeremiah when she hit a half-hour out, confirming it was okay to drop in. He sounded thrilled; his enthusiasm rubbed off on her. Other than the country slang and twang, he sounded like her dad. It was almost unnerving.

Hannah couldn't help but notice; nothing ever changed at the Pearl. The same people were always hanging around on the porches doing the same things on the way to Jeremiah's, whereas, in her life, things seemed to always be in a state of chaos and change.

Jeremiah's pickup, geared to the nines with hunting lights and gun rack, some gray Chevy, and an old obnoxious banged-up bright blue pickup were parked out front. She thought she recognized it but couldn't place it and dismissed the thought as quickly as it came.

"Good afternoon, pretty lady, and how is Miss Hannah Cain on this fine day?" His bouncing steps and beaming smile gave an air of welcome.

Yep, she thought, he's just as good-looking as remembered.

She played it back, "Reverend Delery, you're looking mighty fine yourself; how the heck are you?" She put her hand out to shake his. Instead, he put his arm around her shoulder.

"They forewarned me that you're a spitfire, and it seems those rumors are accurate, but I wouldn't expect any different from kin of Jeremiah." He was a sincere kind of friendly.

"Don't be messing with my family," she laughed. They walked into the house, Jeremiah was at the stove cooking up some shrimp and okra gumbo, and Ruby was on the back porch raising hell that he was dirtying her kitchen.

"What are you doing at the stove? Uncle J., Ruby's right you've made one helluva mess," she walked to the pot and breathed, absorbing the savory aroma. "Looks like a parking lot outside; you having a party?" Grabbing the ladle, she tasted the gumbo. "Wow, this has a kick, but it's good."

"Nah, just me and the preacher," he called out to the porch, "Ruby, ya wanna finish the gumbo? I'm gonna visit with my niece." He ushered Hannah toward the back porch.

The preacher followed.

Jeremiah inquired, "How's the investigation going? Things still a mess at the office?"

"I guess the investigation's coming along okay, but business is still on hold, and the news channels continue to be hot on the track for a story," she hesitated for a moment. "I know you told me not to say anything to anyone, and I tried, but I did talk to Belle about our conversation." Her eyes cast down, trying to avoid eye contact and perhaps a look of disappointment.

He opened the door wide and ushered her onto the porch. "Darlin', you can talk freely in front of the preacher. He knows the whole stinkin' mess right from the start. He's trying to help out old Nate. Poor man is carrying the guilt, thinks he could've stopped things." The three of them sat on the porch rehashing the sordid murder and the chain of events that led to the ghastly end. Hannah asked question after question. She remembered the night of the ball, but nothing about the night of the ball stood out. She wondered how all the hostility could've been going down between the brothers, and she hadn't taken notice, but more puzzling was why her dad hadn't confided in her from the beginning.

"Where does it go from here?" she wanted to know, "You sent the letter, and the NOPD are looking into it. Let's say they prove things haven't been above board. How will that affect business for C&S? I mean, are you and Nate gonna get hung out because of Preston's screw-ups?"

Jeremiah grinned and patted her hand, "Little missy, you're getting all wound up. Nothing's gonna happen to C&S. All the monkey business has been with certain projects in Land Development, specifically involving John and Preston. John has no backbone and is going to roll over on Preston easily. He's said as much to keep his name out of things. John implied he knows Preston had something to do with or knows something about the murder and supposedly has proof, which he will be more than willing to give to the police for a free ticket out," he leaned back in his chair and folded his arms across his chest.

He continued, "Shit, Preston knows I sent the letter; he also knows I know about the night at Southern Manor, he may be a fool, but he's far from stupid. Preston's too full of himself to do the right thing; no, the police will have to drag his butt out of the office kicking and screaming. Suga', you can bet your bottom dollar I'll be there to see the whole thing. As I told you, I don't think he did the deed, he may not have even ordered it, but somewhere along the line, he had his grubby mitts in it, yep. It's got his stink all over the damn thing."

She felt a little reassured, but the whole ordeal was weird, to say the least. They were talking about her father's death, no murder, as though it were some story they read in the paper or saw on T.V., and her uncle, may or may not, have murdered him. Was she the only one to find this bizarre, outrageous, unfathomable? Even if she had been in the big world only a short time, certainly this type of thing was not commonplace. They drank another cup of coffee, and Hannah began to bid her farewell.

The preacher grabbed her arm, "Don't go so fast; I've heard story after story about you. Besides, I've gotta go to the shelter for a few minutes. Take the ride, maybe get some ice cream; I'd like to visit with you for a spell."

The preacher took her off-guard. How do you tell a preacher no? She wasn't up for Bible-thumping; church wasn't her thing, but what should she say? She didn't want to be rude. She didn't know if she'd ever spoken to a preacher, one-on-one. Come to think of it, she'd never been in a conversation with a man of the cloth, other than her insanely rude comments the first time they met.

Bubbles developed in her gut, like a case of the jitters before an exam. "Sure, I guess, but I do have to get home fairly early tonight." Her shoulders drew upward as she eeked out a cautious smile.

"All I'm talking about is an hour, maybe two at most," he gave one of those too sexy for a preacher kind of smiles.

"Alright, let's go." Feeling bamboozled, she followed apprehensively.

Talking with him was a lot easier than she thought it would be. He was a music lover and had a great playlist. She found out they had a great deal in common. She found herself forgetting he was a man of the cloth, and it was a good thing.

The shelter was in an old, run-down building in town and looked like it needed major renovation. Hannah was surprised to see so many teenagers just hanging around shooting the breeze and watching their cohorts play in a rather heated basketball game.

They called a time-out when the preacher and Hannah walked up.

"Wha'sup oh righteous one?" called one of the boys.

To her surprise, he responded, "wha'sup, my man, An-ton-y," giving each other a fist bump. The boys eyed her with question marks in their eyes, "and this, Hannah, is the basketball court slash gymnasium slash summer camp area, and these fine boys are the next NBA superstars," he made a broad sweeping gesture. The boys responded with some b-ball hot doggin'.

He led her to the office area. Greeting them was a round black woman who was extremely upset, "Am I glad to see you, Revr'n J., Latisha's in your office, it's even worse this time. You gonna have to do something about this poor little thing," she quickly exited to the next room, closely followed by the preacher.

Hannah heard them talking to someone, but the answers were quiet and muffled. She stood in the outer room alone. Through the window, she could see a little into the room. There was a young black girl with a split lip and a swollen eye. Someone had done a number on her. The round black woman was putting a sheet around her, instructing they would be taking her to the hospital. When the girl stood up, Hannah noticed the blood trickling down her legs; it was apparent she had been brutally attacked.

The reverend was on the phone; he was speaking loudly, "Claude, Bettina is taking her to the hospital right now. You better send someone to her daddy's house pronto, get them there before I get there. He's taken it too far. I want him locked up for good this time."

He was fuming; he hung up the phone with a vengeance. His eyes were full of tears as he looked up, "She's only a baby, Lord, a defenseless child. Help me, Lord. Because right now, my compassion is pretty much spent, and all I feel like doing is, dammit," he slammed his fists on the desk.

Hannah wasn't sure what to do. She went into the room, put her hand on his back, and stood silent. It was like he realized for the first time that she was standing there. "Looks like I'm gonna have to take a rain check on the ice cream. Sorry, I was looking forward to it. Let's get going; I gotta drop you quick and meet the police."

She told him to go on; she'd call Jeremiah to get her. He took her up on it and left. Without him there, the place was spooky. She called her uncle, and he said someone would be on their way and for her to stay inside the office. *No kiddin*, she thought. She cozied herself at the desk and looked around the room.

There was an assembly of crayon drawings taped to the wall, all with words of great adoration to Rev. J. He was their hero, their knight in shining armor. He was neither black nor white; he had transcended color and risen above; he was an entity unto himself.

The picture of the girl was playing over and over in her head. She felt her stomach turn leading the way to nausea. She nearly jumped out of her skin when a knock on the door broke the silence of her thought.

A tall, powerfully built black boy stood in the doorway.

"Miss Hannah, sorry, I didn't mean to startle you". He was well-spoken and very polite, and he knew her. He must've seen her puzzlement, "I guess you don't remember me. I'm Lawrence, Belle's grandson." He had a sweet smile and gentle ways about him.

"I'm sorry, Lawrence, God you've grown up." Still, a bit unnerved, her hands had a slight tremble.

"Yes, ma'am, I'll be seventeen next month," he led the way. It was the bright blue truck she'd seen earlier.

Finally at ease, she walked alongside him, looking over with a grin on her face. Her body relaxed, shoulders dropped with her body in a graceful flowing gait. "I knew I'd seen this pickup before. You must come to get Belle on Sunday mornings."

He nodded politely. "Yes, ma'am, me or one of my brothers. We share the truck between the three of us." Unsolicited, he told her about his brothers, how one was in the Marines and how the other had gotten in trouble and had done some time in Texas, but he was home now and doing fine. He also talked about his mama and how she worked in a beauty parlor in town since his daddy walked out on her. He said his daddy was struck with some kind of stomach sickness, and everyone knew it was cause his grandmother was making him pay for all his ugliness, even though he was her own son. His grandma didn't go for ugly ways and knew how to deal with them. Hannah asked him what he meant. He described all kinds of things Belle had made happen and that she was connected to the other world. Lawrence said Belle would call upon her people living in heaven to help her in times of trouble or make the wrongs right in her family, and sure enough, it worked every time. No one messed with Belle or her family, usually, if they were smart. He said both Belle and his great auntie Rose, Belle's sister, had the gift. She half-heard the boy's chatting; her own demons were running havoc in her mind.

It was about then that they pulled up to Jeremiah's. Hannah went in, told her uncle about the craziness, gave him a quick kiss, and headed home.

On her way home, she passed by the hospital. Her heart broke for the girl. She pictured how he must've held her down and when she fought back against him, he probably belted her in the face until she was almost unconscious, and then he punished her with each thrust into her tiny body. The picture in her mind was nauseating; she leaned out of the car, retching her gut and sobbing. Her demons had caused many a fretful night, and she didn't always deal well with being alone with someone, anyone.

She finally got control. Maybe she could help the girl; after all, she knew the pain, that dirty pain. If anyone understood, she knew she could. The poor child, she thought, for her, it hadn't been any man; it had been the one who was supposed to be her protector, the one keeping her from all harm. What would make a man do something like that to his own child? She couldn't fathom it. She knew it might be awkward, but something deep inside was drawing her. Perhaps this would be part of her healing. She was nervous, but compelled to listen to her inner pulling, tough as it was gonna be.

She headed toward the emergency room and saw Bettina talking to a police officer. They acknowledged each other with a nod.

Hannah called from the other side of the curtain, "Latisha?"

There was a timid reply. Hannah entered. The child lay there looking at her through glazed guilty eyes. Hannah sat on a stool by her and tried to comfort her. The two of them looking at each other, the pangs raced through her gut. Hannah solemnly nodded as the tears welled in her eyes, "I know," was all she said and held the young girl's hand. They shared a bond.

After a time of heartfelt silence as their demons danced in the windows of their memories, a quiet conversation gently ensued. "Latisha, it's nothing you did, sweetie," Hannah stroked her hand.

The girl looked at her with tears streaming down her cheeks. Still, Hannah blamed herself and carried the guilt like a two-ton anchor permanently suffocating. She didn't want this precious child to feel the guilt; it wasn't hers to bear.

"I know you feel numb right now, and you probably are trying to get it out of your mind; I know that's what I did, but, little one, don't make the same mistakes I made because the hurt only gets worse, not better. Let me help you. Together maybe we can both get rid of our bad thoughts. The sooner you can talk about it, the sooner he'll be punished for hurting you. Then, you'll be able to put it behind you and start again." A big lump developed in her throat. Hannah had a hard time finishing her last sentence; she almost felt like she couldn't breathe. The girl squeezed her hand, releasing Hannah's welled-up tears. They cried right along with each other, and the door opened to her pain and horrible secret. They sat there silent, looking into each other's eyes. Bonding. Knowing. So deep were they into the zone, Hannah didn't hear the preacher enter. He put his hand on her shoulder. There was a distinctive gentle tenderness about him. He saw the tears in her eyes and knew.

He said to the young girl in a comforting, healing voice, "I see you're in good hands, Latisha. I guess you've met my friend, Hannah. She musta snuck in here while I was talking to your mama. She's waiting outside, do you want to see her? It's up to you." His mere persona exuded positivity and calmed the turbulent waters.

"Yeah, I guess," she whispered.

The reverend left to get her mother. They could hear her coming from down the hall, and she was hysterical. Hannah hoped she would calm down before seeing her child, but she didn't; it escalated.

Hannah gave Latisha her card with her home number written on it, "You call me anytime you want to. That's my cell," the girl looked at the card. "Can I visit you again later this week?"

The girl nodded yes, and Hannah excused herself and started to her car.

The preacher came after her, "I'm almost finished with the police. You still up for something? I could use the company."

Ditto, she thought, "yeah, I'll wait here."

About forty minutes later, he appeared out of the door. The time alone gave her a chance to re-group and get her thoughts together.

"That was really special coming to see Latisha. She seemed to respond to you. On a selfish note, I'm glad you stopped. Sometimes the anger builds in me to the point I feel like I'm gonna explode. There are some real sick puppies around here, and sometimes I feel like what they need is a good beating, I know it doesn't sound very Christian of me, but it's how I feel. Part of me would like to take my anger out on Tyrone's face; the other part says I need to pray for him."

"Pray for him, my ass," his facial expression changed, "Sorry if I offend you, Reverend."

"Please, Hannah, call me Joshua." His head tipped to the side.

"Sorry if I offended you, but anyone raping anyone, especially his own daughter, deserves to be slowly tortured, castrated, and then executed. Maybe it might discourage any other would-be offenders." He listened carefully and didn't seem too offended by her occasional slip. She figured he must've heard it and a lot more from his clientele at the shelter.

"It's got to get to you being with that element all the time. I know you say the boys are basically good kids, just haven't had the benefits of a stable home life, but I saw some of them, and they're not as innocent as you may believe." Here eyes squared with a determined glare.

He held a patient, kind demeanor. "Darlin', I never said they were innocent; I said they were deprived, neglected, abused but not innocent, not by a long shot. All I'm trying to do is offer them a safe place and the hope and peace of Jesus Christ. I try to help them closer to God. Some of these kids had never even heard of Jesus Christ and certainly not of His Good Works. For them, there was no hope. Some of them are finding it now, and hopefully, they will pass it on to their kids. Most of the boys playing ball today have two or three kids. We need to get the message to their kids," he ran his hand through his hair. "It gets depressing, and sometimes I feel like I'm losing the battle, then one of them will come by and ask me to baptize their child or ask me something from the Bible, and I know it's working, slowly but surely, and I pray in thanksgiving. Our God is good, Hannah. So very good." He truly believed what he preached. She could see he wanted to make a difference and was willing to do what it took to make it happen. "You want Chinese take-out?" he asked.

"I'm game; where to?" she had no clue where she was going.

He directed her to the take-out, and they went to his house. He had a cute bungalow decorated with a Native American flair. They had a light conversation over fried rice and won ton soup.

He became very pensive, "You want to tell me about it?"

"About what?" she asked.

"How long ago did it happen?" He swirled the soup in the container.

"What?" she wasn't going there with him, and her body began to stiffen like a wooden board.

He became quiet again.

She played with her food and looked around the room, "Spend a lot of time in the West? I like the look, it's—"

He interrupted, "Just know when you want to talk about it or are ready to work through it, I'll listen. Anything you tell me will be confidential; no one else has to know." He turned her face toward his, "Promise me you'll share your burden; I know the way to lighten the load. Jesus always lightens the load."

She looked up, her eyes full of tears, "promise." She weighed in her mind about telling him, but it hurt too bad. It would have to hold for another time.

They talked briefly about the plight of Native Americans, then the original Odd Couple came on the television, and they silently watched until dozing off.

The next morning when they woke, she was lying curled up with her head in his lap. For her, the first moments were uncomfortable; she felt conspicuous and wished she could disappear.

He sensed the awkwardness and smiled, "Darlin, you're not the first to fall asleep on this sofa. It's a curse, you sit on it for more than an hour, and the next thing you know, it's mornin'." She wanted to hug him. There was something so rich about him she knew words would never come close to addressing. Her attraction to him was on a plane she'd never been close to before, and she wasn't sure how to deal. He smiled as though knowing her thoughts and gently pecked her on the tip of her nose.

He got up and made some coffee, "Want some?"

It sounded good and was already smelling delicious. Hannah watched him as he poured the coffee. His back was to her. He quickly turned and caught her looking at him; she blushed and began to fidget, "best coffee in all of Bogalusa," he said, "so I'm told." He handed her the cup and flashed his winning smile.

She needed to clear the air. She could feel her face reddening by the minute, "ya know, where I come from, preachers don't look like you. So cut me a little slack, I mean with the way you look and all."

He looked perplexed behind his smile. Finally, he whispered, "Hannah, I'm not a priest."

"Of course, you're not, and before I embarrass myself any more, I think I need to drink my coffee and get back to Covington, but thanks for the night and the company. Would it be okay to come up later in the week and visit Latisha?"

He nodded and agreed it might be good for not only Latisha but for Hannah as well. They made plans for later in the week. He told her to drive carefully, and he would see her soon.

Hannah had an overwhelmed feeling the whole way home, almost like a schoolgirl crush. The preacher had swept her off her feet. He was unique and completely unavailable. Then, she started thinking about the curves life throws. Until her relationship with Davis in New York, she had never been seriously involved with anyone. She had her stable of lawyers, doctors, architects, and judges as escorts for fundraisers or parties. Still, no one ever stacked up enough to rate as significant, and here in a blink, she meets two people who could easily rate as significant in her life. It was all perplexing.

Well, she thought, *this is what I do for fun, Jerry.* She knew he'd have a stroke when she told him about the preacher, and maybe she'd leave it a secret.

When she pulled into the driveway, she saw several cars, including Nick's. She heard his voice when she entered. His classic New Orleans dialect brought a smile to her face. He was walking with Mitch, Crystal, and Travis.

"Good morning, y'all," she called out.

Mitch walked to greet her, "Hey, li'l sis, where ya been?"

"Long story, you wouldn't believe me if I told you," she made the rounds with kisses on the cheeks.

In a professional manner, Nick explained, "To catch you up to speed, Hannah; we've been going over the incident with Preston after your father's funeral. We've almost wrapped it up if you want to hang around." His eyes had a questioning look but, at the same time, hopeful.

"I'm gonna go shower and change. That'll give you time to finish up." Nick watched her exit the room. She was a sight for sore eyes.

Mitch continued talking with Nick, "He pissed me off. He's one cocky little man, and his whole family has a snobbish way. I shoulda just popped him. But, like I told ya, Travis was standing right there, Preston egged me on." Mitch's hands balled and flexed involuntarily, coinciding with words coming from his mouth.

Standing with his hands on his hips, Travis confirmed, "That's the truth, Detective. I even told Jerry, you can ask him; he'll tell you I told him. If it woulda been me, I'd have done the same thing, maybe even more."

"Thanks, Travis, I've made a note of it," Nick continued, "Mitch, from all accounts, everyone has the same story. Can you remember what he said and who he was talking to?"

The conversation continued, and the consensus was Preston had been talking to John Harris and Billy Bankston, a long-time developer who occasionally worked in conjunction with C&S. Preston had been talking trash about the Will and the business. Crystal excused herself, and the guys continued to talk.

Hannah was in the shower when she heard Crystal, "Hannahhh, where you at, girl?"

"Almost done, be right out, hold on a sec." Quickly wrapping a towel around herself, she held another towel in her hand.

Crystal was something. She was the perfect Cupie Doll. She had on a tight red western shirt, accented by pearl tone snaps, sprayed on jeans with a flashy buckle and red cowboy boots. Her hair, as always, was perfect and probably wouldn't move in gale-force winds.

Hannah came out of the bathroom toweling her hair.

"What's the word, girlfriend? I hear Detective Nick is your main squeeze. Well?" she plopped on the bed, ready to hear Hannah's story.

Hannah told her they'd been on a few dates and were getting closer but not to start ringing the wedding bells. She could right any of those rumors before they started. They chatted while she got dressed, and then they joined the boys in the library.

Nick got up thanked everyone for their time and help. He and Hannah strolled off for a walk outside. "I tried to get ya last night," he faced her and put his arms around her waist. He looked deep into her eyes, "Should I be worried, like is there someone else?" he paused for a moment, "if it's none of my business, just tell me."

"Okay, none of your business." She said with a half-smirk.

He looked shocked as his eyes widened and his mouth dropped open in an almost caricatured manner.

"Just kiddin' I stayed in Bogalusa last night. She told him the whole story minus the falling asleep at the preachers. She felt awkward telling him about it; besides, she didn't want him to worry and would do no one any good. If it happened again, she'd tell him.

About an hour passed, Nick said he had to get back to the city. They briefly talked about the case and how things were going. She said she'd been thinking about things she may have overlooked or dismissed over time, but there may have been some things with significance when looking back. Crossing her mind was that maybe Joshua could tell the police about his conversations with her dad, and his testimony may help. She hurried Nick along, and they made a date for the weekend. He'd come over after work and bring Michelle, and she'd arrange for Lauren to come to the house.

As soon as he left, she called the preacher. Sitting at the kitchen island, she reached in the fruit basket for a handful of cherries, popping one in her mouth. She grabbed a notepad and pen as she waited for him to answer.

"Joshua, hi, this is Hannah. Hannah Cain."

"Miss me already, Miss Hannah Cain?" and then seriously, "I'm glad you called; I haven't been able to get you off my mind," she felt uncomfortable.

Just the mention of the night before twisted her gut as it brought back memories of her horrific experience, a wound she thought she'd closed and sealed forever only to find it had been festering beneath the surface and had grown worse with time.

He broke the silence, "Hello, anyone there?"

She apologized and asked if he could speak with the detectives regarding her dad's murder? Since he had gotten close with her dad, she felt sure he could possibly shed some light on the subject. Although he said he wasn't sure how much help he could be, he told her he was more than happy to talk to them and agreed to meet the police later in the week. Joshua said it would give them a chance to have lunch afterward. Hannah agreed but felt turmoil developing in her stomach. Apprehesiveness was clouding her thoughts. What was all this confusion? Was it about her dad and the murder, or deeper, more carnal feelings?

"Joshua," she hemmed and hawed, "There are some things I should have told you."

"Okay, like what?" he sounded curious.

"For starters, I have this friend, this guy I've been seeing." She doodled on the pad out of nervousness.

He interrupted, "W-w-wait before you go any further; I hope I didn't give the wrong signals. Hannah, you're one terrific girl, and I hope we can get to know each other better. Maybe even one day you'll view me as a friend in Christ or maybe a spiritual helper, but I'm not looking for a relationship, at least not now."

She felt like an idiot. Open mouth, insert foot, "Now aren't I the embarrassed one?"

"I didn't mean to embarrass you, Hannah. I have a feeling I know what's going on, and it's perfectly normal" She suddenly felt extremely uncomfortable and began fidgeting in the chair. "Many times when someone goes through the emotional ride you've been on, their emotions get all confused and start crisscrossing. Know what I mean? You hear of it all the time. People in a crisis pair up, but they realize they have nothing in common after the crisis is over. Kinda the same principle. Darlin', there's a lot of stuff you're going through right now; it's no wonder. Plus, being I was kinda close to your papa throws us closer. It's a real common thing." Pregnant pause.

"Maybe you're right," she was silent for a moment and commenced making starry doodles. "The detective I want you to talk to, he's the guy I'm dating. I'm not sure what his and my relationship is; I think he thinks, no, I know he thinks it's for keeps. Also, the point you brought up about crisis relationships, I definitely think it might apply."

Joshua stammered. Obviously, she had shaken him a little, "I see what you're saying; everything will be fine. Hannah, you worry too much. Okay? Is there someone else you'd rather me talk to?"

"Nah, the more I think about the whole thing, ya know, it doesn't matter. I don't know Seth too well, and I think I'd rather you talk to Nick or maybe both of them. It's up to you, preacher man." She was completely befuddled by this time. She felt she'd been around long enough to know when a man was interested in her, and it felt like Joshua had been interested, but maybe she was way off base, and he was right; her emotions were all confused. In fact, she wasn't sure of anything.

He broke in, "instead of waiting until Thursday, why don't you come back to Bogalusa today? You and Latisha might get some good work done."

Thinking it wasn't a bad idea, Hannah went to Bogalusa for the day. She spent most of the time with Latisha and barely saw Joshua. Hannah's numerous hours of researching rape and its psychological effect proved helpful. She and Latisha spent the day talking about and working through the attack. She showed her how to vent her anger and sadness through drawing and coloring. It was most productive.

When it was time to leave, he thanked her for coming to Bogalusa and walked her to the car ending with a quick, friendly hug. There was no passion, no overtones whatsoever, which made him even more fascinating.

PLAYING NICE

he radio played the whole way home, but her mind was somewhere else. Joshua was such a mystery. She knew he had been interested in her. Maybe he thought it was inappropriate, so he backed off, or maybe it was his emotions that were confused, and then again, was she reading too much into the whole thing? Besides, there was Nick. She knew where she stood with him; there was some measure of comfort. *To hell with it all*, she thought, *it'll work itself out*, but first, she had to get Nick and Seth hooked up with Joshua. She had a feeling together they'd uncover enough to start an air-tight case.

She wanted to talk to Nick but was hesitant. What would she say? What was there to tell him? She picked up the phone and put it back down, repeating the same steps a few times. "Dammit," she picked up the phone and punched in the numbers. "Mrs. Messina? This is Han—" and before she could finish, Nick's mother interrupted, saying she knew her voice and it was good to hear from her. She relayed that Nick was in the shower, but she would have him call as soon as he got out.

Only moments had passed, and the phone rang. "What's cookin', good lookin'?"

"Wow, that was fast. How are things goin'?"

They chatted a little about nothing of importance; she told him about her dad's interaction and conversations with Preacher Delery, suggesting it might lead to pertinent information for Nick to contact the preacher. After her brief overview, she gave him the phone number to the shelter, then ended her conversation before the tone in her voice divulged her adolescent fascination with the preacher. There would undoubtedly be a better time to tell him about her mean-nothing, schoolgirl crush on Joshua. They'd both laugh at the silliness. He couldn't get angry at her; after all, she didn't do anything but crush, or was it lust?

Finally home and fast in her bed, recollection of the past few days stirred up a hornet's nest of emotion. Getting to sleep seemed to be an impossible task. The country night beckoned her onto the balcony. The sky was dark, yet most clear, with an endless array of stars glittering in the heavens above. Her dad always thought of Southern Manor as a slice of heaven, and the majestic glittered sky amply proved the point. Somewhere off in the distance, she spied a small campfire. She couldn't help but have her curiosity piqued. She continued to watch the fire, each passing moment tempting her curiosity.

She slipped on a pair of cut-offs under her sleep tee and donned running shoes. She was going to investigate the source of the fire. She left the house, crossed the cut grass then navigated the woods. Although a little timid at first, she knew the woods in and out. She and her brothers had many adventures. Finally, she could make out three figures around the campfire when she was close enough to see. There was a large box topped with glowing candles and an assortment of what looked like fruits and vegetables arranged to perfection. Two of them passed a bottle back and forth. They handed it to the third one who took it then spit a mouthful into the fire, making it blaze even brighter. She couldn't believe her eyes.

The small figure had a shawl and was waving it around like a bird in flight, swooping low to the ground and then up over her head. She could hear muffled chanting. Hannah watched for half an hour; it was most weird. The person was obviously performing some sort of ritualistic dance, and then all three stopped and turned toward the woods and stood still for what seemed an eternity. Hannah felt like they were staring right at her, but she felt as though she had been well hidden. Finally, they stopped their gaze and returned to their dance, which was strange beyond anything she'd seen before. She decided it was time to go and quietly returned to the house.

Now there would be no way she could fall asleep; she laid down all the while her mind was spinning, trying to understand what she had seen. Finally, amidst the racing thoughts, she must've dropped off. The next thing she heard was the sound of her radio blaring the morning traffic report.

As she wiped the sleep from her eyes, the memory of the bizarre night came to the forefront of her thoughts. She readied herself for the city, grabbed a cup of coffee from the kitchen, and took off out the door.

She drove past Belle's quarters and the other quarters for the help; there was Lawrence's blue truck. Once again, her thoughts returned to the activities of the prior evening. It was hard to believe he would've been involved; voodoo rituals were something she'd heard talked about but never thought factual, merely old wives tales. Maybe the older crowd might participate, but certainly not the younger, more educated people like Lawrence. She couldn't imagine he'd be involved; he knew better. She was sure he too had heard the stories and maybe half believed, but she figured that would be where he drew the line.

Her mind flow jarred when her phone sounded.

"Hannah? It's Joshua; good morning. I wanted to let you know I heard from your friend, Nick Messina. Before I called him back, I thought I'd give you a jingle."

"I'm glad he called. I told him to; I think you can be of help in the investigation."

The conversation ended quickly, and he told her he would call her back after he spoke with Nick. She was okay with it, or so she said, and made her way into town.

The investigation started turning up numerous forgeries translating into illegal property sales. Both John Harris and Preston were up to their eyeballs in it. The findings also turned up some strange relationships which ended up plastered all over the paper and the nightly news.

As a result of these findings, John's wife threw him out. He was no longer under the employ of C&S, and it would be nearly impossible to find a reputable position after the massive scandal. That was if he didn't find himself in prison, given the dollar figures involved in the off-the-book deals. It would take a lot of time for the dust to settle on this one. It had received as much, if not more press than the development of certain properties on St. Charles Avenue. Millie, John's office piece, had offered to take him in, but it wasn't something he wanted on a full-time basis. He preferred life in the country club set.

Things were pretty rough between Grace and Preston, but it all came as no surprise to her. He had flaunted his improprieties about town for years. She had her own money; it didn't matter whether Preston was around or not; she would be fine. It sort of summed up their relationship anyway. It was all superficial and most puzzling as to why they stayed together. The closeness between Nate's wife and Grace had been waning even though they traveled in the same circles; their civility was merely that and nothing more. It became even more uncomfortable for their mutual friends. They found it more and more challenging for the two of them to stay out of the society pages given the recent scandalous situation.

Deidre and Sal were drowning in damage control. Hannah's department had much undoing for the C&S image.

Hannah, as usual, came in energized. "Good morning all, where are we on the ad? Did you see the paper this morning? Things are sounding a little better, and we're coming out of the sleaze."

Sal seemed to be bitchier than usual, and his facial expression was like he'd eaten something tart—lips pursed, nose scrunched, and chin held too high. "Hannah, darling, things have been a bit hectic around here this morning; we've just been able to get on the ad." He abruptly shuffled papers as though annoyed. "Lizzie called and said they had to rush Preston to the hospital during the night. They thought it was his appendix, but it wasn't. It seemed to go away as quickly as it came, but they kept him for observation. I told her it was probably stress-related due to all the B.S. here. She did her whatever voice and hung up. So, sweetie, this is where we are; I didn't want you to miss out on all the fun," he could be snarky extraordinaire.

Deidre made a hissing cat sound as she stood with her hand on her hip and turned to him. "Didn't we get up on the bitch side of the bed this morning, hmm?"

Sarcastically he retorted to Deidre. "Sorry, Little Miss Thing, don't get ya panties in a knot. Hannah's not bothered by me."

"No, but I am." She curled her lips with a look of disgust.

Hannah had heard enough. "Y'all are like children. Speaking of children, how's everyone been around here? Playing nicely?"

"As I told ya, hon, it's been a little crazy, which means everybody's thrown for a loop. It's better than it's been, but normal it ain't."

They settled in on the ad, and the day flew by as the clock rolled to five. Hannah had a way of putting away the crap and getting down to business without anyone feeling the pain; it came naturally. The three of them worked well together like a well-oiled machine. They pumped out more than many of the big P.R. firms.

Hannah remembered the trying time getting her dad to listen to her idea about starting a firm and handling all the P.R. for C&S. Her mind drifted back. When she returned home from her stint in New York, she planned to work for one of the oldest firms in New Orleans after spending a couple of months picking up her shattered emotional pieces.

Miles and Margot had been looking for a house on the Northshore. During one of Hannah and Margot's house-hunting excursions, the subject of opening a firm started to come to life. They saw several cottages for sale in the heart of Covington. It kicked off with them saying what fun it would be to have a shop in one of the cottages. The fantasy moved on, and it spun into Hannah opening a firm on the Northshore. The spark was enough to ignite endless thoughts over the next few days.

She approached her dad. He told her they'd been using the same firm for years and had never considered anyone else. Since C&S was such a loyal client, he felt sure they'd have a position available for her in their firm. She tried to explain to him it wasn't what she wanted. It went around and around over and over again.

In a last-ditch effort, she put an entire ad campaign together and a proposal showing the cost-effectiveness of her plan. She then made an appointment to do a presentation during one of the company's meetings. Margaret, her dad's secretary, had warned her it might blow up in her face. She reminded Hannah how her dad did not like surprises and tried to discourage her from making a presentation.

She'd never forget the look on her dad's face when he entered the board room. Their eyes quickly made contact, but Hannah turned and passed out the proposal along with the visuals. The response to the presentation was overwhelming, and everyone at the table seemed to like her ideas, everyone except her father. He just watched and listened as he would to any stranger. He thanked her for her time said they'd look over it and get back to her. She got her things together and left. As she walked down the hall, the last thing she heard her father say was it was time to get to the company's business.

The knot formed in her throat, and tears welled in her eyes. She made it to the car without a fallen tear, but as she pulled out in traffic, they streamed down her face. She drove straight to Mitch's bar and hoped he would be there.

When seen during daylight hours, the place was a dump, but it was the most happening place uptown at night. The college crowd was loyal, and it was packed every night of the week from about ten p.m. until two-thirty. It was only ten-thirty in the morning, but the doors were open, and they'd already sprayed down the sidewalk.

Crystal was the first to spot her, "Hey, girlfriend, don't you look like you stepped out of Vogue," she then yelled toward the back room, "Miiitch, where y'at? Hannah's here come up front." She turned back to Hannah, "take a load off. Can I get ya somethin'?"

Hannah still had her sunglasses on, but Crystal could see remnant make-up streaks on her cheeks.

"How about a Bloody Mary. You got the stuff handy for one of those?" Hannah asked.

"You betcha," she put it together, adding a spicy green bean, "honey, you okay? You look like somethin's wrong." Once again, she turned to the back and shouted for Mitch. She picked up a couple of napkins and handed them to Hannah. "That brother of yours has a new toy. Some guy sold him a couple of used foosball tables for a hundred bucks course, they're almost antiques, but he can touch them up and make a killing. Hell, he wouldn't need to do anything to them; those kids get so boxed they can't see anyway," she laughed.

Mitch ambled to the front; Crystal and Hannah were sitting on stools at the bar. "What in the hell are you doing here at this time in the morning? Rough night last night, and you didn't even stop in here?"

He plucked the sunglasses off her and saw the tears. He put his arms around her, "Aw, Han, who is he? Lemme handle it for you. Oh baby, don't cry," he stroked her hair.

She could feel him tensing, and she pulled away. "Before you get too much testosterone going, I'm pissed at Dad. Not pissed, hurt. Oh, I don't know, pissed, hurt, probably both?"

Mitch kissed the top of her head then stood with his arm around Crystal. "Hell, darlin' I can listen, but give advice, I don't think I'm the one to confer with about the old man. Every time I try to talk with him, it ends in a fight and me storming off. Reconciliation only happens on the phone. Man to man, shiiit, he blows me out of the water and pisses me off, but like I said, I'm good for an ear."

She told him the whole thing, her ideas, the meeting, and then the crushing blow she overheard. Both he and Crystal listened.

Crystal spoke first after looking through the packet Hannah had brought in. "You know I got a lot of respect for your dad. He's a helluva person, but the way I see it," she handed Hannah back the presentation packet, "This is good stuff, and Lord knows C&S needs to let its hair down and create a more modern image." Pointing to the material, she continued, "He has to have thought all this was good; maybe he wanted to read other people's reactions. Think about it; he treated you like any other P.R. firm; you gotta treat him like any other client. Business is business; take the personal out of it. Let him be the first one to bring it up, no matter how much it kills ya. It's business." She tapped the bartop, got up, and walked around the bar. "Mitch, you want some club soda?"

"What if he never brings it up again?" she wiped away the tears as they rolled down her cheek, "I don't know if I can do that. I gotta know, now." Her voice began to tremble, "What was I thinking? I know him well enough I should've never put him on the spot. I thought—"

Mitch took her hands in his and interrupted, "Wait, get a grip. Listen to yourself. How'd you ever play with the big boys in New York? Kid, let it go. He'll bring it up, maybe not right away. It'll bug the shit out of him when you don't confront him. He loves those confrontations; trust me, I know it'll drive the old man crazy."

They spent the rest of the morning together, and on into the afternoon, she felt much better. Mitch's place had a great hamburger, and after a few hours, the Mary had long worn off. She was going to give it the business-is-business approach. Hannah hoped her dad would be the first one to speak, and it was all she thought about the whole way home.

Hannah heard him when he came home and waited posed with an open book if he came to her door. She knew he wouldn't, and he didn't. Belle called up to announce dinner. She wondered who would be at dinner, would it only be the two of them? The lump in her throat was returning. She went the long way through the kitchen, Belle was walking toward the dining room with a fresh loaf of French bread. "Let me save you the trip; I'm on my way there." She took the bread and added some levity to her step like she hadn't a care in the world.

Her father was at the head of the table. He emanated power, "Good evening, Hannah. The aroma of the bread is such a tease. Break some with me?"

"Always," the one word that had been the steady in their years of battling. She would always be daddy's little girl, and he would always be there for her as she would for him. Life with her dad was always based on always.

Belle served dinner; table talk was limited and a little awkward. She knew he felt uncomfortable; she could tell. After dinner, he asked Belle to prepare some fresh coffee and bring it to them in his study.

"Join me?" he asked.

"Always."

Belle brought the coffee, and he asked her to close the door. *Here it comes*, she thought.

"Let's cut to the chase. I was surprised to see you at the meeting today. I wish you had clued me in on your plans. Nonetheless, I was impressed with your presentation; you certainly came prepared, and your numbers look impressive as well. I'd like to make this work, and I think it would be good for the company. I've already talked it over with Jeremiah, and both of us would rather keep business in the family; the concern, however, is Liz."

He intently stirred his coffee. "The others were most impressed, as well. Liz will bring up her son-in-law, who she thought would be a good addition to C&S since he's an architect. I couldn't make her understand that it wasn't prudent, not full-time, but that we could use him on a consultation basis. She thinks I'm out to get her or exclude her for some reason. She flares up over the least little thing; see the dilemma? Give me a little time to work out all the details."

He had been right; it had been a little sticky, but it all worked out, and Strategies had become an integral part of the C&S conglomerate as well as earning her a seat at the table during company meetings.

The knock on the think tank door zoomed her thoughts to the present; it was Margaret, "Hannah, Nick is here to see you. Send him back to your office?" Hannah nodded and excused herself from Deidre and Sal.

"Hey doll, what's kickin'?" he tickled her ribs.

She gave him a quick peck, and they sat down.

"Talked to your preacher friend. We're gonna meet tomorrow; he's comin' to town. You were right; he has a lot to say. Enough about my day; I'll use any excuse to see you. This weekend? Any plans?"

She played like she was thinking about his offer, "hmm, I'll have to check my social calendar, see if I can fit you in," she looked at him and smiled.

"Fit me in, you evil woman, playin' with my heart."

They planned for another weekend at Southern Manor, just the two of them, then duty called. There was another drive-by on Jackson Avenue that made three for the week.

"Sorry, doll, gotta go. They're at it again; the streets are getting wilder and wilder. See ya tomorrow night, after work," he leaned over and gave her a sweet soft kiss.

"Be careful," she rose and embraced him, "Nick Messina, you watch out for those bad guys, ya hear? That's an order. It seems like the whole world is going crazy."

"It's da heat."

She gave him a puzzled look.

"Da heat, hotter it gets, the crazier they get, later gator," he took one more kiss for the road, and she got back to work. It had been a full day, and they got a lot accomplished.

The traffic on the way home was light. She flew through the city to the sanctity of the bridge, her favorite part, lots of time for thought and reflection. Her mind drifted to the night before and the weirdness of the fire and weird ritualistic dancing.

The shrill of the phone startled her, making her jump and her heart felt like it was in her throat.

"Hannah? Joshua. I wanted to let you know I spoke with your detective and will be meeting them in town tomorrow. If you could break away, I'd like to go for a cup of coffee. I need to talk to you."

"Suppose I can. Talk about what? Everything okay, Latisha good?"

"Everything's fine, just want to talk with you; no big deal," he assured.

"Call me when you leave the police station. I'll make sure I'm available."

After the conversation was over, she wondered what he wanted to talk about—more fuel for the thought train. She was beginning to feel overloaded. The traffic on 190 had gotten bad; it was becoming an extension of the city.

Her cell rang again. "Miss Cain? Good afternoon; this is Detective Ford McLain with the Covington Police Department; your office gave me this number to reach you. They said you were on the way to the Northshore. Is it possible for you to stop by the station on your way home?"

"Yeah, I guess I can. I don't know where the station is, though."

He gave her directions and said he'd be waiting for her.

The Covington Police Station was what one would have expected, small but nice. As promised, Detective McLain was waiting for her and led her back to his office. They exchanged niceties and commented on the suffocating heat, a daily topic with everyone. The heat was brutal. His desk was piled high with a mass of papers. He dug through the organized mess and pulled out a file. He handed her a form to fill out. As she was filling in the blanks, he began to talk. I received a call from Detective Parsons from the NOPD regarding your father's death. He seems to be of the opinion that even though the crime happened in the city, he believes it originated here. Are you familiar with any of what I'm saying?"

She nodded in affirmation as she continued to fill in the form.

"He also indicated you were very close with your father and might have some information, maybe some insight into the dynamics of the family relations or business affairs. You did work with him, right?"

Again, she nodded.

"I'm ready anytime you are," and he turned on a small tape recorder on his desk.

He started with a recitation of the facts for the record, such as the date, time, and location. He went through the basics in a monotone drone. She looked at him blankly.

"Detective, I don't know how much help I can be to you. My father's death has been a big shock. It's all been overwhelming, and at this point, I'm not sure what's what. The things I know are only from other people, and I don't know if there are any facts to support their allegations." Her shoulders dropped, she drew in a deep breath and began her story.

She started with the funeral and Jeremiah's outburst and then went on about the argument between Mitch and Preston, although she admitted she had not actually witnessed it herself. Then discussed her visit with Jeremiah and the innuendos of Preston's improper business dealings and then tied it up with their visiting with Preacher Delery on several occasions. She told him everything she knew. He made notes fast and furiously, taking down names and stopping her for phone numbers or contact points. She gladly obliged.

"Miss Cain, you have been a tremendous help. Thank you for your time."

"Oh, you're welcome. Please feel free to call me if you have any other questions." Hannah gave him her card and scribbled her home number on the back. She was sure he had it since he had her cell number, but she wanted to make sure as an act of sincerity.

The sun was starting to set as she pulled into the drive casting a magnificent spray of golden light on the front of the main house. It looked like a scene taken from a painting. It was times like these that stole her breath. She slowly walked into the house, absorbing as much of the beauty as she could along the way.

"Hannah, that you?" Belle called from down the hall.

"Yes, ma'am."

"Darlin', this phone has been ringin' off the hook for you." She rounded the corner. She pulled a pad out of her pocket, lemme see, ya Auntie Elizabeth, Jerry, ooh he's kicks, Deidre and she said it was important to call her at her house and the preacher from Bogalusa, but he said he'd see you tomorrow. Then Nate's wife said to call as soon as you get in. She sounded terrible, like her nerves were all in knots. I never heard her in such a state. Chicken and salad for dinner."

"Thanks, you're right about tons of calls."

She returned all the calls. They were all about the same thing; Preston was wigging out. They said he was driving the nurses in the hospital crazy with lucid night terrors that left him screaming and symptoms with no explanation. The conversation with Danielle, Nate's wife, was odd. It was her laid-back demeanor everyone loved; usually, nothing bothered her, but when Hannah spoke with her, she found her anything but not bothered. She was a wreck.

"Hannah, there is something weird about this thing with Preston. As you know, Nate has been a basket case for a while, and don't get me wrong; I'm not complaining but listen to this. Nate is now completely out of his shell. He's back to normal like a switch went off in him, and whatever was going on inside of Nate stopped and at the same time entered Preston. Preston's never given two shits about anyone but himself, and suddenly he calls to see if Nate is okay. Get this, Gracie's even called acting like we're best friends, and then Lizzie called. I don't think she's called my house in ten years. I tell you, it's spooky," Hannah listened intently but said little.

The phone calls took an hour, at the very least, and when she hung up from the last call, she was exhausted. Her bites between words were less than filling. She went down in the kitchen for a sweet snack. The kitchen was spotless, and the house was still; it was eerie, almost chilling. It was the first time she had given much thought to being there all by herself. She felt small and insignificant; the house was mammoth, there could've been people across the house, and she would've never known. She looked forward to the weekend and, as a distraction, went out on the veranda to purvey the activity of the night. No sign of campfires, and all was quiet on the home front.

Joshua didn't like the bridge, in fact, one might speculate he had some kind of phobia about the whole thing, but he finally made it across. He didn't care for the city either, it was nasty and dirty, but then again, most people found Bogalusa almost terrifying and definitely nasty and dirty. The police station appeared in total chaos, the epitome of the hustle and bustle of city life. Like so many other big cities across the nation, he attributed it to the enormous plague of violence.

Seth and Nick were eager to meet with him. They led him into a dingy little office that barely had enough room for two of them, let alone three.

"Sorry, this is the only open space right now," Seth apologized.

They all sat, starting with casual conversation, and then Nick told the preacher he would be recording his statement.

"For the record, state your name," Seth began.

"Joshua Bennett Delery."

"Birthdate?"

"Ten, twenty-eight, eighty-two."

He continued with residence and other essential information. It ended with pertinent information relating to the case.

"Reverend Delery, it is our understanding you may have information regarding illegal transactions performed at Cain & Sons, and you had several in-depth conversations with the deceased, Tyler Cain. Could you elaborate?"

Joshua began, "I guess about a year and a half ago, Jeremiah Cain visited my church, a little church in Bogalusa, mostly African-American. After the first visit to our church, it is customary for the welcome committee to call on a newcomer's home. Our committee is small, to say the least; there's me and two others, both women. I've found men respond better to men.

I made my way to the home of Mr. Jeremiah Cain. We quickly developed a kinship. He would stop by the shelter sometimes, and I'd stop by his house. On one of those visits, I had the pleasure of meeting his brothers Tyler and Nate. We played cards until almost midnight. We decided to make it a weekly thing. Heck, some nights, we might only play a few hands but chaw the fat for hours. I was around when the ugly stuff started happening. I must say things at those games could sometimes get pretty heated. A lot was goin' on within the family." He had a pensive look on his face and adjusted himself in the chair, "from what I gather, it all started at some society ball. The whole family was there, and Nate overheard Preston's conversation with a business associate. Nate talked to Jeremiah and then to Tyler. At first, it had something to do with some building on Julia Street. After looking into it, Tyler found out Preston had sold some other properties and was in cahoots with some John fella. I think John Harris, his title evades me right now, but he had something to do with the land development aspect of the business," he ran his hand through his hair. "The fact is, they were forging Tyler's signature and dealing with some shady individuals, people Tyler would never have done business with, those kinds." He sat quietly, his mind lingering on something. He fought to bring the memories to the forefront of his mind. "John had introduced Preston to some fellas from one of the big hotel chains. They wanted to put a hotel on the property but would have to tear the building down; the city denied the request."

"Was it strictly John Harris and Preston involved in the hotel thing, or was everyone involved in the deal?" Nick asked.

"From what I gather, it's Mr. Page Foster's job to put buyers with sellers, and hotel people contacted him first. Mr. Foster recommended against it but brought it up to Tyler and Preston for final say-so. Tyler said if Foster recommended against it, then so be it. Preston was more reluctant but let it go. This was when things started to heat up. Preston worked the deal through Mr. Harris." The preacher pointed in the air as if drawing some invisible diagram. "Harris is the guru for real estate transactions and the goings-on of developments in the city. Page and Tyler thought the deal was over and done with, and they were onto other things. Now ya see, Jeremiah had some contacts in the city office. When these contacts called to apologize for not getting the approval pushed through, Jeremiah had no idea what they were talking about, so he called Tyler. See how it's developing?"

The preacher continued explaining about the conversations regarding the confrontation with Preston—stressing the meetings between the brothers were getting uglier and more heated. He went on to tell about a significant conflict at Southern Manor, "and, fellas, that's the way it all went down."

Nick mentioned to Joshua that Seth had contacted the Covington Police Department regarding the possible murder, and inevitably they would be in touch with him. The meeting lasted about three hours. Joshua had long been ready to leave, and on his way out, he called Hannah, arranging to pick her up.

Navigating the streets of New Orleans was a challenge in itself. It seemed every street was one way, the wrong way as far as he was concerned. He finally made it to her office.

Her appearance was like a breath of fresh air.

"Oh, my, Reverend, you look like they put you through the wringer. The boys at the P.D. grill you silly?" she got in the car.

"This is your town. Lunch or coffee?" He beamed a smile at her.

"You're right, this is my town, and it'll be lunch on me," she directed him to Emeril's. Her favorite table was available, and once they were seated, she asked, "how'd it go?"

He took a sip of his water, placed his hands on the table, and took a deep breath. "It's safe to say; I'm glad it's over. I don't look forward to the trial. It's exhausting, and things get all jumbled together."

Hannah sipped on a glass of wine, peering over the rim. "I know, I had the same type of thing with Covington P.D. It's hard to believe they think Preston could have something to do with the murder of my father. The man gets on my nerves, and he's a real pain in the ass, but murder or conspiracy of murder, I don't think he's capable. I know the detectives, hell everybody for that matter, think he's connected. I don't know; something inside me says he's not."

There was a pregnant pause as they both retreated to their private thoughts; she broke the silence. "What did you want to see me about?"

He looked her in the eyes. "I felt bad after the last conversation we had; I wanted to make sure I didn't offend you. I think you're special, and I didn't want to put a wedge between us or anything," he looked a bit sheepish but totally sincere.

With a smirk, she replied. "I'm a big girl, Joshua; I'll get over it. I have to admit; I have a hard time around you. Maybe it's the crisis thing you talked about, who knows, but if it's a friendship you want, I've got lots of that to give," she winked at him, "and it's okay, it's my crossed emotions, not your problem."

He laughed, "You are a pepper, Miss Hannah Cain," he took her hands in his, "I'm drawn to you, can't deny it, guilty as charged. Fact is, I don't wanna be; I'm not what you're looking for. It's not I don't wanna be, I'm just not."

Hannah cocked her head to the side, squinting her eyes, "What on earth are you talking about?" she was confused and had no trouble expressing it. "I'm not looking for anything, certainly not Mr. Right. Maybe he'll come around; maybe he won't. Either way makes no difference to me."

He felt her walls going up.

"What I'm saying is you have different expectations than I do, a different set of rules. That difference won't work." His sincerity was charming but wasn't working.

"Are you talking about sex?" she laughed.

He blushed, "well, yeah."

"How are the expectations different, do explain? What am I to you, some Jezebel? Thanks for all the credit. I've only been with a couple of men in my life. It's not like there's this long stream of lovers and one-night stands. I've sown a few wild oats, but certainly nothing to write home about. It seems I do a lot better without all the crap that comes from having a man in my life."

She paused, and her tone became much softer, "it was great to be close to you; oddly enough, I felt comfortable. After such an emotional evening, opening up some real bad hurt areas, it was great to feel secure." She took a sip of her wine, and then a devilish twinkle took to her eyes, "sorry, preach, you're a good looking guy and nice to boot, it's hard not to think of you the way I do, but it doesn't mean I'm going to try to jump your bones, give me a break."

Apologetically, "that's not what I mean, well it is, but it isn't. How do I put this?"

"Maybe you shouldn't."

He looked a little sheepish as he tried to explain. The more he spoke, the worse it got. He successfully put one foot in his mouth and was working on the other. *Good*, she thought. He kept on going, "things might be better if I keep the temptation at a distance, do you understand? I don't want to frustrate myself or you. It's like I want to be with you, but I can't, not that way, at least not now, understand?"

"You're sending mixed signals," she had him; she had somehow managed to turn the tables.

"I can't answer that; bear with me for a while."

She thought about what he was saying, "Joshua, I got an idea; let's say we leave everything alone. Whatever the underlying feeling is, I'm sure it will define itself one day. Until then, I need a friend. Someone that'll allow me to mourn and talk about my dad and how desperately I miss him. Who better than a spiritual counselor and my father's confidante?"

He had to get back across the lake, and she had a ton of work to return to; their lunch had to come to an end, but it had been good for both of them. There had been loose clarification.

Her message box was overflowing when she returned; she glanced through the seemingly endless sea of notes, the only one to strike an interest was one from Mitch. When she finally got him on the line, he asked if he and Crystal could spend the weekend in Covington; both of them needed to get away.

It was rare that Mitch or any of her brothers, for that matter, asked to come home for a weekend. She was thrilled. The four of them could visit. Of all her siblings, Mitch was the one Nick would get along with best. They'd already spoken regarding the crap with Preston the day of the funeral. She asked him if anything was wrong; he said no, they needed a break from the bar but didn't want to stray too far. It sounded good to her.

It had been telephone mania for the past few days, and the ride home would prove to be no different. She figured she better let Belle know about the additional company; proper preparations would need to be made, at least in Belle's mind. She didn't go for unannounced people in the house; she felt it was bad manners, even if it had been Mitch's home and she had raised him like she had all the others. It was Belle's way, and they all understood it and respected it.

By the time Hannah pulled into the drive, she knew Belle had the sheets changed, and she'd laid out fresh towels. Reginald, the master of errands and man of many hats, had probably returned with plenty of the day's catch from the market. It was Friday, the menu for the evening would be gumbo to start and some sort of fish.

Knowing it was Mitch, she'd probably fix his favorite of fried catfish and hush puppies. Belle loved them all like they were her own; she raised them for the most part. When they came home, she made a point to fix their favorites.

When Hannah had first moved home from New York, she had to tell Belle to slow it down on the gravy and sauces, the first five pounds came on fast, and if it didn't slow, it would parlay into ten.

Mitch's Corvette was loud to the point one could hear it about five minutes before he arrived at the house. Nick pulled up about the same time. He stopped to ooh and ahh over the Corvette.

Crystal walked ahead of the guys. "Hey there, girlfriend. When Mitch told me your man was coming, I couldn't help but think this was gonna be one helluva weekend. Party party," Crystal had enough energy for all four of them, "What's Belle cooked up for dinner? I told Mitch she'd probably fix catfish and hush puppies; I bet I'm right. She knows how much he looovves her fried catfish." She called back to Mitch, "Hon, what'd I tell ya? I was right; it's catfish." Crystal could talk anybody's ear off, but Hannah loved it.

"I hope y'all brought swimsuits; the weekend promises to be sunny and bright," she figured they had.

When Crystal donned her bathing suit, everyone, women included, couldn't help but stare. She figured Nick would enjoy the view. They settled in just as the first round of fish came out of the fryer. The feast began. After hours of talking and laughing, Nick and Hannah bid good night and headed upstairs.

Nick rubbed his full belly, "I think that's the best catfish I've ever had. Whatever the little woman does, it sure works. God, it was good."

His comment about the food made her think about the activities of the few nights before. She didn't think it would make the best pillow talk, but it was the stuff running through her head.

"Shower, oh thoughtful one," he grasped her attention.

"Sorry, got a lot on my mind."

"That's okay, but girl," and he waved his hand under his nose, "You still need a shower. Besides, I have the perfect thing to take your mind off your problems."

Playfully she slapped his arm, "You rude, rude man. Are you implying I am less than fragrant or that I just plain old stink?"

She began to take off her clothes, leaving a trail to the bathroom; he followed suit. By the time they reached the shower, neither one had a stitch of clothing on their bodies.

He scanned her naked body, "I love your body," he took her in his arms and raised her up gently, kissing her breasts as he lowered her to the floor. Small sweet kisses turned into longer lingering kisses filled with passion. Through the kisses, she mentioned if they didn't shower soon, they'd lose all the hot water. They maneuvered their way into the shower, hardly skipping a beat. The moment heightened with intensity, their bodies playing out the perfect symphony beneath the warmth of the shower. Her heart pounded in her chest as she tried to catch her breath. He watched her as he leaned back, panting against the shower wall, "Girl, you're gonna kill me yet."

It had been a long day for both of them, and they began to doze off quickly. The moonlight poured in through the French doors from the balcony bringing her out of the land of Nod. She hadn't closed the curtain, "Damn."

She padded across the floor and stopped for a peek out of the door. Rubbing her eyes, she wasn't sure if the campfire was blazing or not. Nick heard her open the door and followed her. "What're you doing out here? You're naked as a jaybird."

"I thought I saw something, but I guess not. Come on, let's go back to bed," Hannah took his hand, and they went back to bed.

He held her in his arms and kissed her forehead, "Hannah, I never want to be away from you. I want to be able to protect you always. Oh God, I love you," his voice seemed to quake. "Shh, you don't have to say anything, just sleep." She was glad he didn't want her to talk. What would she say? She liked him a lot, but love? She was perplexed; there were too many issues left unresolved, and she didn't have time for love, just like. They both fell back asleep.

At first, it was like quick flashes during a strobe light show. She caught brief specks, but she knew the pending nightmare was getting ready to overcome her at any second, and by far, it was her worst and the most recurring nightmare of all. Everything played in slow motion. The sound of the door buzzer echoed as she made her way to answer it. There he was, as always, at the door with the same sick smile. She tried to warn herself, but it didn't work, she invited him in again, anyway, as always. Maybe this time, she'd figure a way to get him out before it happened. Her anger, frustration, and fear mounted, and as a result, she began to toss and turn to the point where it woke up Nick.

"Hannah?" he nudged her and whispered. He put his arms around her to comfort her when she violently broke away, screaming, "Stop it, stop it," she woke herself.

Realizing she was fighting Nick, she apologized, her body still trembling.

"Hannah, are you okay?" he was past concerned.

Groggily she answered, "Yeah, just a bad dream."

"Wanna tell me about it? Musta been one helluva a nightmare—co'mere, you," he hugged her closely, "Lemme hug all those bad dreams away. You'll be safe now," he kissed her neck.

The morning arrived gently, and they lay for an hour enjoying the peace and quiet, "Nick, you want to go tubing today? I haven't done it in years. I bet Mitch and Crystal will go for it," they put on their swimsuits, and grabbed a change of clothes for the ride home.

She heard Mitch and Crystal stirring at the end of the hall, "Mitch? Crystal? Y'all want to go tubing on the Bogue Falaya today?"

Crystal stuck her head out. It was apparent she had very little on, "Give us a minute, let me talk to Mitch. I'm sure I can convince him to go, meet y'all downstairs."

They followed the aroma of breakfast down to the kitchen.

"Good mornin', y'all? I made some fresh biscuits and gravy, and the coffee came out extra good today if you're interested. Do you want some eggs or bacon, or is there anything you want me to fix for ya?

"Biscuits and coffee, that's the ticket for me. Thanks." Nick liked the old gal, "I slept like a rock last night; there's nothing like sleeping in the country, don't ya find?"

Belle looked up as Mitch and Crystal entered, "Lawd have mercy, child, it's a wonder ya can stand up with those bosoms."

It made everyone turn and look. Hannah thought Nick's eyes were going to pop out, which gave her a giggle. Crystal had on a pair of white shorts and her tiny bikini top. It looked like two patches on a pair of big creamy pillows.

Grabbing her plate, Hannah turned to Crystal and commented, "I hope you have some sunscreen; if not, we have some around here, probably the pool bathroom. Your twins might get a bit tender if scorched," pointing to the abundance of exposed skin.

They strapped the tubes to the top of Nick's car, loaded up the ice chest, and headed for the river. It was a spectacular day.

As dusk was just around the corner, the foursome returned home. It was right in time for dinner, which consisted of Pork Roast and all the fixings with sweet potato pie for dessert. The sun, water, and full stomachs guaranteed a good night's sleep.

Nick awoke early tiptoed downstairs as not to awaken Hannah. He grabbed a cup of coffee and decided to take a walk on the property. The grounds were beautiful. In the distance, he saw a couple of the hands loading up a truck. He waved, they waved back. He walked toward them and came upon an old fire pit he figured had been used for roasting pigs as he passed the clearing. There was a faint lingering of alcohol.

" Good morning, guys," he shouted.

The two men bid Nick a good morning. He recognized Reginald, but he had no idea who the younger man was. He extended his hand to them with a big smile, "Morning Reginald," and to the other, "Nick Messina, I'm a friend of Hannah's from the city."

They nodded, the older one spoke, "Good mornin', sir, this is Lawrence, Belle's grandson," Lawrence smiled.

"I can see why he's such a big boy if he's been eating Belle's cooking all his life. Shiiit, that little woman can cook. I saw the pig pit; which one of y'all do the pigs?"

"Lawrence's daddy; he does all the outdoor cooking," Reginald smiled.

"Don't think I've met him before." Nick shook his head from side to side as he furrowed his brows and bit his lower lip.

"Oh, he doesn't work here. He comes down now and then when Belle calls him. He doesn't like it much here, says it's too citified."

The two of the men laughed. Nick figured it must've been an inside joke.

He had kept them long enough from their work, so he started back to the house. He noticed a pile of burnt feathers, hay, and fruit as he headed back to the house. There was still the smell of booze like it was following him.

"Hey there, tall, dark and handsome," Hannah called down from the balcony. She looked like an angel.

Belle had prepared breakfast and was serving it on the veranda as Nick walked up.

"Where you been? You nearly gave me a heart attack, boy; take a seat," she pointed to the table.

He felt scolded, " I didn't mean to startle you, ma'am."

"Don't pay her no never mind, Nick," Mitch put his arms around Belle's waist, "this old girl gets a little too feisty sometimes, and when she does," he began to tickle her ribs.

"Mitch, you betta stop ya foolishness, or I'll put you over my knee," she loved his attention.

The girls arrived at the table, and the four of them enjoyed the time together; Belle sat with them and partook in the conversation. After breakfast, the four lounged by the pool, basking in the gentle morning sun.

Belle called out to Hannah, saying she had a phone call, then mouthed Lizzie was on the line.

"This is Hannah. Hi Aunt Lizzie, what can I do for you?" she listened and answered with a few sputtered uh-huh.

When she hung up the phone, she told Belle her Uncle Preston had taken a turn for the worse, and no one had any idea what was wrong with him; all they knew was that he was in pain and had a fever nothing would control.

"Hannah Lee, they say Gawd don't like ugly and Mr. Preston's done been ugly since the day he was born. I think he woulda knocked his own mama down for a Mardi Gras doubloon." Belle had a look of satisfaction on her face with a twinkle in her eyes and slightly upturned corners of her mouth.

"Belle!" Hannah was shocked, dropping her mouth agape.

"You gonna tell me it ain't the truth?" Hannah couldn't argue but was surprised by Belle's candor.

She went back to the table and told everyone about the phone call.

Mitch half-laughed, "Damn, Hannah, no one can find the cause, you know what that sounds like to me? Sounds like old Uncle Preston's got a curse on him," he shielded the sun from his eyes, "at least it seems like."

"A curse? Mitch, what? You sound as bad as the people from around here." She put her feet on Nick's knee.

Hence, a two-and-a-half-hour conversation on voodoo, hexes, curses, and the spiritual world commenced. The three of them, Mitch, Crystal, and Nick, had their tales to tell. Hannah argued for a while but gave up and listened to the conversation. She could hardly believe her ears, "Nick, you don't believe all the hokus-pokus, right?"

He leaned his chair back. "Hell, yeah, I do. I've seen too much weirdness to doubt it, and the more I hear about Preston, the more I'm inclined to believe it about him. Darlin', you never know who around you might be into all that stuff—you'd be surprised, gris-gris is some powerful stuff." He palmed her foot with slight pressure. She closed her eyes and smiled at his touch.

The night of the campfire popped into her head. After all, it was the same night Preston first started suffering from his unidentified maladies. She'd have to ask Belle. If anyone would know if there was truth to the old stories about voodoo magic, it'd be Belle. They enjoyed the rest of the day and bid farewell to Mitch and Crystal. Hannah had asked Nick to stay the night and ride into town together in the morning.

Laying in bed, Nick told Hannah he'd been talking to Ford McLain from Covington P.D. They had an opening in th eir investigative unit, and while they didn't hire for positions there, if he got hired on, he'd be their first pick for the job given his experience. Nick asked what her thoughts were about him applying for the position. He said he'd seen a small house in Covington for rent, and it would be large enough for him and his daughter, Michelle. Hannah listened quietly.

"Nick, if I were you, I'd wait and see. Look into Covington a little more. They don't get near the action you're used to; you might get bored." She was hoping she'd been subtle enough without offending.

Nick lay still but chuckled slightly, almost under his breath. Holding a slight grin, he asked, "Is there any reason you don't want me to move over here? I hope you don't feel like I'm rushing things. I've been thinking about a change for a couple of years. Michelle's getting older, and the city ain't what it used to be; I gotta look out for her."

Hm, she thought, was she being too assuming again? *Probably not.* "It seems drastic, and yeah, it scares me some. I'm still not ready for a serious relationship. I love being with you; it's great, but what if things don't work out between us? How would you feel being in Covington? Let's say things did work out. How will you feel about me working in the city?" She stared up at the ceiling with a slight feeling of trepidation—complete with a stomach full of knots and a flurry of anxious thoughts running rampant through her mind.

Cool as a cucumber, Nick rolled on his side, watching her sear the ceiling with her pensive stare. "To answer your questions, I don't know to all of the above. Let's wait and see how things shake out in the investigation; I have a feeling I'll be working over here a lot. We can have a trial run. Whaddaya say?"

She was thinking about it, and maybe it wouldn't be so bad. The dress rehearsal sounded like a good plan instead of jumping ahead of the game.

"What about Michelle? Where will she be in this trial run?" It was time for the quizzing to commence.

"With my mom." He responded with confidence. "I'll go get her for the weekends, or if we're still talking, some Fridays, you could pick her up on your way home. That is if we're still talking." He laughed.

"Smartass," she rolled over to face him.

RAISING CAIN AND MORE QUESTIONS

ays turned into weeks, and Halloween was bearing down on them. The investigative team and the District Attorney's office had worked closely, and a guilty verdict for property fraud was almost a sure bet. The NOPD and Covington Investigative Unit worked well together regarding Tyler's murder.

With the advancement of technology in the Crime Lab, they confirmed Tyler's identity, and there were strong indicators he had been dead before being dumped in the Julia Street building.

His body had been tossed on the floor, burying his left hand under his body which protected it enough from the fire to allow Forensics to gather information. They had completed the preliminaries, but they had to wait for the final report, and who knew when that would be finished. They had a few suspects in mind, and Preston was undoubtedly an easy and convenient possibility. Multiple accounts of Preston's tantrums and threats radiated from numerous circles. Several people gave detailed accountings about arguments between Preston and Tyler, very unlike the patriarch who kept things close to his vest. Preston had been enough to push even Tyler over the edge of gentility. Their most considerable disagreements had been over Julia Street.

The police could place Preston in Covington the night Tyler disappeared. Belle's statement regarding the massive blow-up between the two only a night before the fire was most damaging. The bad blood between the two men was fact, but hardly enough to get an indictment, yet it was plenty to whet their appetite and grab attention.

Essentially, Preston had been the last person to talk to Tyler from all accounts. When Belle returned to the study, Tyler and Preston had already left the room. She assumed Preston had stormed off, as was his personality, and Tyler had retired for the night. There wasn't any reason to think otherwise as all cars were in, and there were flickers of light coming from Travis' quarters suggesting he was watching T.V..

No one had seen Tyler since that night. His calendar showed an early morning meeting in Bogalusa, and it was naturally assumed he had spent time at Jeremiah's. His flight to London was scheduled to leave Sunday mid-morning; therefore, no one was alarmed when they hadn't heard from him over the weekend.

When questioned, Travis explained quite often on the weekend, Mr. Cain would take his personal vehicle for a spin to the coast or to see his brother. He liked his privacy and seemed to only use the big car and driver for going into town; it allowed him to clear his head and prepare for the day without traffic interference. On the days Tyler stayed on the Northshore, Travis would run household errands for Belle. Tyler was pretty much a man unto himself.

His private vehicle, a Lincoln Town car, had been in the garage on Friday night but was gone when Travis went into the garage on Saturday morning. He figured the old guy had gone for a drive.

They located his car at the airport, which coincided with his journey to London, although he usually would've gotten dropped off, but nonetheless, it was easy to explain.

The Crime Lab went over the car with a fine-toothed comb; someone had conveniently wiped the vehicle spotless. Under one of the seats, however, they found a matchbook from The Bourbon Pub. They were able to pull two good prints off the matchbook, which belonged to Eddie "the Flame" Germaine, a local punk affiliated with the Cardoza family. Those who knew him well said he was a piece of work. They said he was the kind to filet someone for a sideways glance.

The investigators were able to get a warrant for The Flame, and everyone was on the lookout. Seth and Nick felt confident he'd lead them to the money behind the deed if the DA offered a plea.

Tyler made enemies along the way, some with the same muscle he had and even a few with more. It was common knowledge that C&S was going into a hotel venture with the building on Julia Street and that renovations had begun. The only other issue at hand was the Canal Street property. Leonard Cardoza expressed interest in Canal Street, but Tyler refused to enter into any business dealings with the likes of the Cardoza family, which created stress and supposed threats. Thus given the mobster's notorious reputation, it was reasonable to put Cardoza as a prime suspect, but something inside of Nick kept pulling him toward someone closer. It would all shake out—it was just a matter of time.

As predicted, Nick had spent a good bit of time in Covington, and it looked like he might take the Covington position. The chief had immediately taken a shine to him, and with the Captain's okay and a little schmoozing with the guys on the hiring committee, it was almost a done deal.

Hannah had grown accustomed to having him around and was somewhat looking forward to the situation becoming a bit more permanent. Nick had been staying with her at Southern Manor but let her know that he'd be getting his own place when he made the move. She didn't argue.

Two days before Halloween, the decorating began for the annual "Raising Cain" Halloween to-do. The old place was a-buzz with party people. Lighting techs hung festive Halloween lights along the perimeter, the stage was in place, the dancefloor laid, and the decorator had worked his magic. They parked a hay wagon at the front gate decorated with scarecrows and boogeymen as the perfect touch. The invitations had gone out a month earlier, and from the acceptance calls, it looked like attendance, as usual, would hover around five hundred guests. Despite the run of family bad luck, Hannah thought it best for C&S and the family image to keep everything as normal as possible. She wondered if Preston and his cronies would show. She thought probably not.

Nick watched as she managed everything for the party while still reeling from her father's death and her uncle's criminal activities, which only added to the roller coaster ride of emotions.

The day had been hectic; she had tons running through her mind and found it impossible to fall asleep. The first cool front of the year had arrived; she hoped sitting on the balcony might help her relax and fall asleep. Nick was long asleep, and she could hear his faint snores from inside.

She had just gotten comfortable when the flickering of what looked like a fire caught her attention. It was coming from the area where they usually roasted the pig, but she knew that the roasting was happening at Jeremiah's. Rather than trying for a close-up view, she remembered her father had binoculars in his bedroom. She stole down the hall in search of them. After a short search, she lucked out and headed back to her room. Out on the balcony, she crouched down to get a good look. As before she could make out a few people. She sat there for about ten minutes and was completely startled when Nick came up behind her.

"What in na hell are ya doin'?"

She jumped a mile, "I'm looking."

"Yeah, I can see that, but whatcha lookin' at?"

He crouched down next to her and kissed her neck. She figured she better tell him about the first weird night. She whispered, "Look and tell me what you see."

She handed him the glasses. He casually took the binoculars, but his face became more and more intense as he watched.

"Damn, Hannah, ya say ya seen this before?"

"About six or eight weeks ago. I saw a blaze, the same kinda thing, but instead of getting binoculars, I decided to get a better look and walked to the second patch of trees over there. It was spooky. It looked like Belle, and two others were drinking and dancing by the fire. Oh, and there was this box all decorated with stuff."

"Any snakes?" he asked.

"What?" Her eyebrows arched in surprise by his question.

He took the binoculars away and pensively looked at her, "Snakes?"

"I don't think so."

"Did ya go back to see the next day?" His voice began to trail off. He remembered his walk on the property, the singed feathers, the pig pit, and it all started to point in the same direction. "C'mon, let's go down there. No point in sittin' here looking through these glasses. If it's who and what I think it is, they already know ya been lookin' at them. Put some jeans on; the mosquitos will eat ya alive, even with this little chill."

The whole time she dressed, she argued with him that perhaps she should mind her own business.

"Doll," he gave her a condescending look, "Whether you come or stay makes no matter to me, I'm going. I thought you might want to hear things first hand." He was dressed and ready to go.

By the time she finished dressing and got outside, the fire was out, but it didn't change Nick's mind about investigating the area. Hannah followed along. As they were approaching the site where the fire was slightly smoldering, Belle called out, "Mista Nick, good evening, what you children up to out here?"

"I was fixin' to ask you the same thing, Belle." They continued walking hand in hand toward the little lady.

"We were sitting by the fire tying up some loose ends." Sweat dripped off her face and glistened in the glowing smolder.

"Oh yeah," he asked, "What kind of loose ends?"

She shrugged, "A little bit of dis and a lotta dat." She laughed with her palms turned upward.

"Ya don't say?" He began walking around prodding at the smoldering fire, "Looks to me like y'all were laying some hex or curse. I can only hope I'm not on the receiving end of whatever it was." With his head still downward cast toward the orangey glow, Nick shifted his eyes to meet hers with a knowing kind of glance.

"Neva you mind that." She drew a pattern on the ground with a long stick, "The way I figure it, there's the law and the police, and y'all do the best ya can to punish evil, but there's some evil so dark you can't fight it the usual way, just like there's some sickness ya can't heal the regular way. So you call on those that's gone before you because darlin' they know. But then there's those people who think us country folk are plum crazy and put no neva mind to da spirits. Course I've seen for myself, yes sir, I seen babies come back from da crib death and their mamas so full of tears. It's a good thing, baby, ain't nothin' wrong with callin' on the spirits, it's like," she laughed, "Tendin' to family business."

Hannah was utterly overwhelmed by the whole thing, and her face reflected her befuddlement with exaggerated blinks.

"Hannah, baby," Belle asked, "Why you look surprised? Your friend here knows more about dis family than you do." Hannah started backing away, "You stop and sit here next to me, baby." She patted a stump next to her. Hannah looked at Nick for affirmation, "Hannah, come sit," Belle ordered.

He looked at Belle, "You gotta clear some of this up for ya girl; you ol' niggas done freaked her right out."

For the next couple of hours, Belle told Hannah about tales from the past and how the spirits had helped her family for years. She said Mr. Tyler, her daddy, had come to her, sometimes Porter, when they needed help from the great beyond. Belle also told her she'd gladly give her own life to save her or any of her brothers. She said she was sorry; she thought Hannah knew about the power of the spirits.

"What kind of spell or curse are you putting out there and on who?" Hannah was almost frantic.

"Bae, that's one thing I can't and won't tell you, just know it ain't on you," she chuckled.

The sun was beginning to come up, which reminded them the pre-party setup was about to start again and get crazier as the magic hour approached, "Nick, we better get a couple of hours sleep," they headed for bed.

Four hours passed as though only minutes. Hannah woke to Nick's prodding, "C'mon sleepy head, there's work to be done." He put his arm around her.

Hannah pulled the covers over her head, then popped right out, "Nick, can Belle get in trouble with the law? I wonder if she made Preston sick, the doctors couldn't find anything wrong with him, ya know? What do you think? How would you prove she had done it? I mean, is there a law or something about hexes or curses?" She had propped herself on her elbows and stared into his eyes.

"No, there's no law" He pushed her flat on her back and straddled her leaning close face to face. "I thought you thought it was all hokus-pokus, anyway," he laughed at her innocence; it was refreshing. The temptation of her lips was too much, and he honed in for a quick kiss.

"Do you really think Belle could've made Preston sick with voodoo?" Her eyes glistened like a child watching sparklers for the first time.

"Who knows, but don't worry about it, Hannah. I don't know a judge that would allow such a case to be in his court. They won't admit it, but many of them believe it or, let's put it this way, they wouldn't put it to the test." He leaned over again and kissed her goodbye; it was long past time he should've reported to work.

She managed to pull herself out of bed and get in gear. By the end of the day, the house was ready; all they needed to do the next day was set the linens. The band and the caterers would arrive and do their thing. She checked with Belle to make sure Mitch and Jerry's rooms were ready, and as expected, they were. Between Reginald and Belle, the house was stocked with everyone's favorites. Nick had met most of the family; however, he had never spent much time with Jerry. She thought it was going to be a most entertaining meeting.

The evening before "Raising Cain," the family gathered for their private party.

Jerry was the first to arrive, and to Hannah's amazement, he brought Jay. Each had a large suitcase, and it looked like more in the trunk of the car. She had a look of disbelief at the amount they packed. "You must have some kind of costume to have such massive suitcases."

"No, we thought we might spend a few extra days; that is if it's okay." He pushed his sunglasses on top of his head and gave her a broad smile.

"What do you mean, if it's okay, God Jer, this is your home, of course, it's okay. It's about dang time Jay spent some time with your crazy sibs." She looked at Jay with a smile, "I hope he warned you."

Walking toward the house, cases in hand, Jerry quickly commented, "By the way, I don't know if they RSVP'd or not, but I know Marguerite, Elise, and the whole gang are coming to the party. Everyone wanted to vacate the city, and I said, why the heck not? The more, the merrier, right? I did tell them costumes were a requirement for entrance. It should be a hoot."

Downstairs in the kitchen, things were more than wild. People were running here, there, and everywhere. Belle was calling out instructions like a war-time general.

"Belle, you have everything you need? Jerry told me we might have some extra overnight guests. I'm gonna run down and see if the guest house might need freshening up," Hannah was almost out the door.

"Already done, darlin', I figured there might be a few unannounced overnight guests," she was always one step ahead.

Jay entered the kitchen, "Hon, this place is great. When are you going to give me the 50 cent tour?"

Belle glanced in Jay's direction, "Besides the tour, you need anything else, bae, or are you fine for now?"

"Just fine, ma'am, thank you," he politely smiled.

"Where is my lazy brother? Wouldn't he give you the tour? Where is he anyway?" Hannah smirked.

Running his hand along the marble counter, he distractedly responded. "Oh, he's putting all our things away; I'm a bit impatient. I have heard oodles about this place since I met him, and I feel like I have to pinch myself to believe I'm actually here; I feel like Alice in Wonderland."

Belle gave Jay the up and down. He seemed a little too settled for Jerry, but maybe it was a good thing. The man was about as sissy as they came, but it was okay; she'd known Jerry's secret since forever. Regardless of his likes and dislikes, he was a good boy.

Hannah poured herself some ice tea, "Ya got ya fifty cents because the tour is about to begin. Starting, this is the kitchen, probably the most important room in the house. Belle's always got something on the stove or in the fridge and as they say, help yourself." She ushered him out of the kitchen.

Hannah brought Jay through the house, giving him the history as they went pointing out some of the more interesting paintings, sculptures, and furniture. They came to her father's study. She opened the door and dramatically welcomed him in. "And *this* is my father's infamous study," she sat behind the desk.

Jay stood in silence for a few minutes, "Jerry's told me many stories about your dad. I can almost feel his presence in the room." He held a stoic expression of awe and respect. One almost had to keep a revered silence.

"I know what you mean," she agreed and swallowed the lump from her throat. Her dad's death still felt like a bad nightmare, one she was eager to wake from.

"It looks just as I pictured it," Jay went on to tell her about some of the things Jerry had told him. Hannah listened as she tidied things on her father's desk. She hadn't been in the room much since his passing. When the investigators had come through his study, they had been careful to put everything back in place; maybe it was just a little off. A few loose notes wouldn't align, so she took them out and stacked them on top of the pile. Jerry made his entrance, arms stretched wide.

"There you are; Belle said you were doing the tour. Grand, isn't it, Jay?" Jerry sat in the vacant chair next to Jay. The two of them started talking. Hannah glanced around her dad's desk. It was strange to see his writing. She looked at the loose papers on his desk, then noticed his daybook underneath the pile. As she went for it, some of the notes fanned out. She was thumbing through his daybook when something on one of the notes caught her attention. She pulled the paper closer studying it.

"Girl, what are you looking at?" Jerry came behind her and looked at the scribbles. Her dad had sketched a triangle with arrows. There was C&S written in bold letters, which created the top of the triangle and pointed in either direction, pointing first to Pres, which had to be Preston, and then to the initials L.C. An arrow pointed in both directions between Pres and L.C. Her heart sank.

"Who's L.C.?" Jerry quizzed.

"I have no idea," she answered. In her heart of hearts, she knew it could only be one person, and that was Leonard Cardoza.

All kinds of thoughts ricocheted through her mind. It was more than evident from the diagram Preston linked somehow to Cardoza. She could fathom such a relationship, but not with C&S? Could her dad have been mixed up in all the mess? Her gut dropped in trepidation at the thought. She refused to believe it. She knew her dad was on the up and up; he'd always preached it and didn't tolerate other people's improprieties, for the most part. She had to strike those kinds of thoughts from her brain; they hurt too much. She folded the paper and put it in her pocket. As far as she was concerned, the secret would remain just that—a secret, and the police were on the right path with both Preston and Cardoza. It was better to leave her dad and C&S out of the little triangle.

As the three of them were leaving the study, the phone rang, "Y'all go ahead, I'll catch up." She answered.

"Hannah, that you?" it was Uncle Jeremiah.

"It is, and how is my favorite uncle today? Tell me are you bringing a date to the party?"

"There you go trying to make an old guy feel bad. There ain't a woman in a hundred-mile radius would want the likes of me. Hell, girlie, I'm near seventy-one, scraggly, and coarser than a goat." She sat listening to him as he went on and resumed thumbing through her dad's daybook.

Almost every day was chocked full of places to be and people to meet and then suddenly the pages were blank. She turned to June 11, the day they suspected the murder took place. There was no mention of his meeting on the Friday night with Preston, only a few brief notes, reminders she supposed of the London trip. It looked like he planned on going to Jeremiah's on Saturday, probably to drop off an itinerary and go over any last-minute business details needing a watchful eye. He used to tell her Uncle J. was like a good ol' hunting dog, "Give him a scent, and he'd be on it until he got called off." She continued to look back day after day, then there, clear as could be, the week before he had a luncheon date with L.C. at the Upperline.

"Shit," she said under her breath, angry and heartbroken at the same time.

"Hannah, you okay?"

"Yes, sir, Uncle J, thought of something I forgot, sorry."

"Almost forgot why I called," he chuckled, "I came across a letter your dad left here; he stuck it in my desk. I guess he figured I'd come across it one day. Says he left you and the boys a letter. You might want to look for them; if you get a chance, it's pretty interestin' stuff."

"I forgot all about them. Dad left the letters on his bureau in the bedroom, and I picked them up the day of the funeral." Talking to herself, "What did I do with them, crap?" She continued to one-handed tidy the desk.

"Calm down, missy, you'll find them," he laughed. "Darlin', I'll let you get to your frettin', and I'll see you tomorrow. Bye now," he hung up.

Talking to herself, "letters, letters, where did I put those letters?" She went into her room and went through her briefcase, suit jackets, and purses, finally finding them. Hannah sat down on her closet floor and carefully opened hers. She pulled the letter out, and a stack of hundred dollar bills fell in her lap; *how typical*, she thought. She remembered once getting in trouble at school for forging his name on a test paper. He put three humps in the "n" at the end of his name, and the teacher caught the difference. He was impressed by the teacher's thoroughness. She began to read the letter.

Dearest, dearest Hannah,

If you are reading this, then my time has come. There are a few things I would like you to know that may prove to be of value at some point in your life. I'm sure you are confused about how things look for C&S. Don't worry, it will all work out. Trust in Jeremiah; he won't steer you wrong. Nate is an ally as well. Lizzie is very protective over Preston and has her own agenda, which I haven't quite figured out. Preston is a piece of work. It will come out if it hasn't already that Preston had been less than honorable in his representation of C&S. He had been at the root of some underhanded schemes. Jeremiah has documents directly linking him to some shady dealings, and all have been reported. As Chief Financial Officer, he moved money around, creating such chaos with the paper trail that things eventually got lost in the shuffle. There have also been some other properties Preston has hidden money in, all to his benefit. I have confronted him about the situation, and he assures me he'll right his wrongs.

I've stuck Jeremiah on him; not much gets by the old guy. If there is anything funny or unexpected about my death, turn the matter over to your Uncle J. In regards to the company, Mitch is to take over where I left off. He is to shadow Jeremiah until he feels Mitch is ready. Jerry and Miles will have their share of my ownership, as will you. Each of you may sit on the board, but your vote will count as one. As a result of the untoward business practices, buy out Preston's family, they will readily go for the money and force him into retirement. This can be accomplished by selling the Lumber Yard. In the letter to Mitch, I have instructed that the purchaser must agree to keep Charlie Johnston on their payroll until he retires as part of the sale. Everything else is to stay in place.

Southern Manor, through my Will, has been left to the four of you; however, it is my wish that you live there. A separate trust has been established to provide for the property's staffing and day-to-day running—attorneys will handle this. If the property causes an unforeseen hardship, the court may decide on a sale. The proceeds will then be equally divided among you four.

On a personal note, I am very proud of you and feel blessed to have gotten as close as we did. I pray you find the love your mother and I shared, and you will pass on our memory to your children for future generations. Hannah, stay strong and re-establish your faith; that's how you'll get through all of this.

I love you and will forever, Dad

She sat on the floor sobbing. She missed him terribly but knew he would have been proud of how she was handling the debacle. He had raised her to be strong. She re-grouped put the other letters in her pocket for later.

"Hannnahh Lee, you up there, girl?" *Yep*, she thought, *Mitch is here.*

"Good God, Mitch, you could wake the dead," she trotted down the steps. "You crazy boy, leave your bags here; Reggie will bring them up. C'mon, I think Jay and Jerry are out by the pool. Belle's out there too, and I know she wants to see you, but before things get too wild, here's a letter I've been meaning to give you. It's from Dad." She hoped it wouldn't ruin his night. He folded it down, stuck it in his pants pocket, and continued to enjoy everyone's company. Miles and Margot showed up, and the pre-party was well on its way.

Nick finally showed up, "Sorry I'm late, doll."

"Better late than never, right?" she hugged him hard and led him in the direction of the family gathering.

"I gotta tell ya, today was great. I was able to help Covington apprehend a guy responsible for a string of robberies. I guess all those years with NOPD came in handy. I like the investigative unit. They're some easy-going guys. Looking over at the group, he watched Jerry work the crowd, "Lemme guess, Jerry's the buzz of the party?"

She looked over; everyone had crowded around Jerry as though he were some celeb; he made his way over to them.

"Jayzee," he dramatically motioned, "Come meet Hannah's beau." He put his hand out to Hannah's squeeze, "Nick, Hannah's told me a lot about you."

Things began to settle down; the rip-roaring conversations earlier in the evening began to wane as everyone was tired from the go-go day. It wasn't long before the crowd dispersed, and everyone went to their respective quarters for the evening. Hannah and Nick were the last ones to leave the patio. They helped get the mess cleaned up and then bid goodnight to Belle.

"How much older is Jay than Jerry?" Nick asked as they stripped down for bed.

"Quite a bit," she answered, "But he looked particularly weary tonight. Jerry can be a handful, especially with a few vodka tonics in his system." They lay in bed talking about what they thought everyone else was talking about in bed.

He felt comfortable next to her, "Your brothers are lots of fun. Musta been a challenge being the only girl with those three. Whatta brood. Had to be kicks growing up with them here, huh?"

"It was." Her heart warmed and picked up to a fluttery pace, thinking of the happy times with her brothers.

"Who knows, girl, you might be raising your own here." He held her hand, gently stroking her fingers. His eyes met hers, begging for a kiss and special closeness.

"Funny you should say that. I've been thinking a lot about babies lately. I've never wanted one before, but suddenly, I realize my time is ticking away. Hell, most the girls I graduated with are married with two or three kiddos."

He laughed, "Bet I could help there." Touching his nose to hers, he sarcastically commented, "Tell you what, doll, I'll buy you a dog." He gently kissed her, leaned over, and turned the lights out.

"A dog?" Her voice went up an octave.

"Yeah, ya know, a puppy—they're little and needy."

"I want a baby, not a dog. I just need to find the right guy to make one with."

"Hey now, maybe we need to practice first."

She held him close.

The morning came with a bang, the caterers arrived at the crack of dawn, and Belle had served up a continental breakfast, including Mimosas and Bloody Marys. The clan was grazing around the table. Hannah watched from the porch with Belle.

"That fella of yours, missy, is a fine man. He needs a little polishing, but you're good at that."

Hannah watched Nick as he moved through the family. He did fit in despite growing up in a totally different setting.

"Belle, ya think he's the one?" She linked her arm in Belle's.

"Oh, I dunno. Nick's the one for now, but foreva? Miss Hannah Lee, he would be if you could settle yourself. Don't think he'll put up with any nonsense, if you know what I mean. He's not the kind you go confessin ya soul to," she winked at Hannah

They stood in silence for a few minutes, "I been thinkin' about Preston" Hannah turned to face Belle. "Did you make him sick? I know you think he did my daddy wrong, but I can't see him having my dad killed. If it is voodoo stuff making him sick, why don't ya call it off and make him well." She looked sternly in Belle's beautiful, all-knowing golden eyes.

"I can't change the ways of the Lawd; sometimes He just lets me think I'm making a change. It's all in His hands. Maybe Preston got some changin' to do, and you know nothin' changes a man faster than lookin' death right in the face." She patted Hannah gently on the face.

For some unknown reason, Hannah came quickly to defend her uncle as she grabbed Belle's hand, "Preston's just Preston; he can't help the way he is. He was born as ass."

Changing the subject, Belle asked, "What do you think of Jerry's friend?"

"He's good for Jer." She turned to watch Jerry and Jay. " I hope he stays around, but I wouldn't blame him if he didn't. Jer can be a handful. He's high-spirited," Hannah smiled, "but he's a good person."

"Tell that to someone else, darlin'. I love that boy like he's my own, but it ain't Jerry's high spirit; he's just never satisfied. He's plum spoiled. Always 'fraid he's gonna miss out on something," she looked at Hannah, "just like you."

Hannah stood with her mouth agape and eyes wide open.

"Don't look so surprised; I know you two. Young Jeremiah was up to his foolin' round 'bout the time of your daddy's funeral. His little sideline friend called here; I told Jerry he's no good." She got close up to Hannah, who quietly took it all in. Belle amazed her. "Jerry backed off from the guy, best I can tell."

What could Hannah say? There was nothing to say. Belle was always right.

"Don't be mincing my words. I shore don't approve of they's ways, but Jerry's our boy and Mister Jay, he's a nice man, a true friend thick and thin. I guess they can't help the way they are. You children need to learn to be satisfied with what comes your way. The Lawd, He's been good to y'all. Go have yourself some breakfast; we got a long day ahead of us," and she swatted Hannah lightly on the butt.

The day proved to be splendid; everything fell right into place. The combination of the cool October breeze, the big moss-laden oaks, and the tiny sparkles of light throughout the property made for a magical setting. As with every other year, "Raising Cain" was a big hit, and the festivities went well on into the early morning. Everyone, including Belle, slept in until near ten, and then things crawled at a snail's pace.

A SLAM-DUNK?

eidre was her animated self, "Hannah, you outdone yourself this year, girlfriend. What a great party, it gets better n' better every year." Her hands punctuated her remarks.

"Thanks. I was pleased with the turnout." She went through the motions, but her mind was somewhere else; Deidre decided to let it go. Hannah had planned to find a recent photo of Cardoza, and her dad, then head over to the Upperline. Someone she thought might remember seeing them. Ever since she'd seen the scribbled papers in the study, she was plagued with the image of her dad and Cardoza. She had to find out for her sanity, but her thoughts were interrupted as she cast her eyes toward the direction of the television. "Quick, turn it up."

Plastered on the screen were Preston, Grace, and their attorney trying to block the cameras as they came out of the Courthouse. She couldn't help but notice how horrible Preston looked. The whole ordeal was aging him. Grace, on the other hand, didn't seem too bad off.

Their attorney had grilled them about staying out of the news and laying low.

The doctors could never come up with a good diagnosis for Preston's ailments; therefore, everyone speculated anxiety related to depression due to the stress caused by the legal mess he'd created.

Deidre broke the silence, "Girl, he looks awful."

"He does," Hannah agreed. She wondered how things were going in Preston's house. Certainly, it had to be strained.

The scene outside the Courthouse was utter mayhem at best. As the three came out, reporters inundated them, sticking mics in their faces shouting for comment. Their attorney ushered them away into an awaiting car.

"I don't know how much more of this I can take," Grace complained.

Their attorney opened his brief case and pulled out a file. He got on the phone with his secretary, "Baldwin here, any messages?" He listened and made notes as the person on the other end of the line rattled off numerous messages, "I need that number." He looked up at Preston and put his hand over the receiver, "D.A. office called."

In his usual snotty way, Preston quickly retorted, "Unless it's good, you need to let them know I'm not interested."

"For Chris'sake, Preston, don't be such an ass. If you hadn't been so—

Preston snapped, "Enough, Grace. Just shut up."

She clammed up and stared out the window. The car navigated the central business district streets, dropping his attorney at the Shell building. Preston instructed, "Call me when you know something and tell them not to bother—"

His attorney interrupted him, "I'll call you," promptly closing the door.

Preston looked at Grace, but before he could say anything to her, she turned her body away from him, signaling to leave her alone.

The car pulled up to their grand home on State Street. She didn't even wait for the driver to open her door. She quickly exited the car and bolted for her front door, heading straight up the stairs to their bedroom. Preston made his way to the living room and the bar. It had been a rough day. Even though he refused to confess to anything, he had a sickening feeling in his gut there was no way out. He'd always been able to bullshit his way out of other improprieties, but this was different.

He thought about how Harris had been spineless and rolled on him. Had it not been for John and his weakness, things would have never escalated the way they did. He felt sure he could've explained his way out of the land sales with Tyler, but John collapsing on the hotel deal at the same time pushed the envelope.

The phone rang; Preston stared as it rang, and then it stopped. The maid must've answered it, he thought. He hadn't completed his first sip of the drink he'd made when Grace flew into the room. "I'd appreciate it if you could tell your little whore not to call our home. She said to tell you she got the package you sent her."

"I have no idea what you're raving about, Grace," he took another large sip of his drink.

She picked up an ashtray off of the table and threw it at him. It was off target and crashed on the wall.

Preston barked, "Jesus, Grace, I've had enough of your spoiled bitch act."

She went for him, "I'm sick and tired of you and your women. I've had it up to here with you, Preston." She sliced the air with her hand across her chin. "You've really done it this time. You're flagrant cheating is disgusting, and it was bad enough you had to steal from your own brother, but—" she began to sob, "I won't protect you anymore."

He looked alarmed, "Protect me? He seemed almost amused, "Just how, Grace, do you protect me?"

Her eyes squinted to mere slits and hand on her hip; she spewed with venom. "All I have to do is tell the police you didn't come home the night of the fire. You'd be screwed."

He smirked, "You stupid cow. You know exactly where I was," he walked toward the bar and then slowly turned, "You think I killed Tyler. Don't you? My God, you stupid bitch."

She left the parlor and went back to her room. Exasperated and angry, she pulled a large suitcase out of the closet and opened it on the bed. In no time, she had it packed, turned it on its wheels, and carted it down the stairs. As she passed the parlor, Preston watched as she struggled with the bag.

Sarcastically he commented, "Where do you think you're going?"

"I've had all I can take."

"Grace, you're not going anywhere. We've got court tomorrow, and you're gonna be there."

"Don't you mean *you* have court tomorrow," she rolled the bag and headed for the door.

Preston jumped up and grabbed her arm as she got close to the door, "I said, you aren't going anywhere," and squeezed her arm hard.

She tried to move her arm from his grip. "Get off," she pulled away from him and opened the door.

"You bitch," he shoved her out the door, "Get out."

He went back to the bar and freshened his drink. On the way to his chair, he picked up the phone and punched in the numbers. "It's Preston. She's gone."

The person on the other side questioned as to who left, "Grace left, got time?" he smiled, "See you in a few."

He quickly called another number and waited as it rang, "Damn." He listened while the recorded message went down the list of selections. He pressed the appropriate extension only to find another prompt and another recorded message. He waited to leave a message. "Ray, Preston Cain here. I'm calling to find out about the D.A. and apprise you of a new development. Call when you get a chance; I won't be home; reach me on my cell," and he hung up. He picked up his keys and left.

The picture of Preston, Grace, and the attorney appeared on every station multiple times during the day. The phones at C&S rang off the hook with reporters and curious acquaintances. Hannah had her fill with the whole sordid affair. Preston's face glued all over translated into hours upon hours of P.R. clean up, leaving little or no time to sneak away to the Upperline. It'd have to wait.

Deidre looked at Hannah, who had her head propped and balanced in her hand. "Shit, where do we start?"

Hannah shook her head, "I don't know." She kept slowly shaking her head, thinking. "I'm gonna call Jeremiah and see how he wants us to posture ourselves." After a moment or two of reflection, she told Sal and Deidre to take ten and get a frozen cappuccino down the street. She handed them some money. She sat back in the chair.

Talking aloud to herself, she got up and started to pace. "What would happen if C&S filed a suit against Preston? Would that be better than?" she looked to the ceiling, "Dad, you gotta give me some help here."

She dialed, "Hey Porter, this is Hannah. May I speak with my uncle, please?"

"Shore thing, darlin'." He put the phone down, and she could hear him shuffle away.

Moments later, Jeremiah picked up. "Hannah," his voice boomed, "Have you seen the T.V.? Preston's slapped all over it."

She figured she better jump into the conversation before he got too long-winded, "Exactly what I was calling you about; I was wondering if maybe we should pull back a little. He did embezzle and, in general, screw us all over. Yet here we are doing nothing. Shit, we fired Harris. The only reason he didn't go to jail was he spoke up against Preston. Did you know Preston is still getting paid by the company?"

She could hear him chuckling on the other end of the phone, "good gracious, Hannah, calm down. I don't think we should change a thing right now. Preston has his hands full with the D.A." She tried to interject, but he kept going, "now, Hannah, they're gonna find him guilty; hell, it's just a formality. The man's as guilty as they come. Don't get in such an uproar; he's gonna pay, don't you worry. His punishment will be greater than any of us can even imagine."

She interrupted him a second time about Preston getting a paycheck.

"Hannah Lee, there's much worse things than not getting a paycheck or going to jail. Think about it. Until this whole mess, the family had always handled its own indiscretions. Sometimes family can be a lot harsher than the legal system."

Hannah started to interrupt, but he continued, "Family's the closest thing ya got, and well you lose them, ya got nothin'."

When Sal and Deidre returned with the cappuccino, she was still on the phone. They were trying to get out of the room quickly, but she motioned for them to stay.

"Uncle, the crew's just returned, so I'll have to go. I heard what you said, and I guess we'll sit tight for now. It's just hard."

She stayed quiet for a moment and then answered with a series of "uh-huh" and "right. Maybe next week. I'll talk to you later," she hung up.

"He says for us to keep on going like we are and for now no changes, not yet," the three of them got back to work.

Things in Bogalusa had become heated over the brutalities delivered by Tyrone to his youngest daughter Latisha. The story had been all over the nightly news, and the Bogalusa D.A. was moving fast on it. The reverend had tried to stay as removed as possible from the whole mess, but his picture appeared on T.V., pointing the finger of accusation toward Tyrone.

That evening, sitting in his office working on his Sunday sermon, Bettina called into him, "Rev'rn J. It's quittin' time."

"I'm almost done," he called back, "You go on, I'll see you in the mornin'."

She stood in the doorway to his office, "you gonna work yourself to death. Rev'rn J, what good will you be then? Put ya pen down and call it a day."

The more she fussed, the more he smiled, "Okay, okay, I get the point. Give me one more second, and I'll walk out with you."

He finished his work, turned off the light, and locked up the door. The two of them walked out together. What they didn't see was the figure of a man looming in the shadows.

Joshua stopped at Latisha's on his way home from the shelter. Like many of the houses in town, it was almost falling down. The weatherboards hadn't seen paint in decades, and the house had pulled away from the cement stoop. Latisha's aunt and some of the locals were sitting out front. As he got out of the car, they exchanged greetings.

"Rev'rn J. go on in, no need to knock."

He knocked on the screen door, pulled it open, and called as he was walking in, "Hello? Hellooo?" The house smelled of old grease, ground-in filth, and sweat. The pungent odor was overpowering, and turned his stomach. For the life of him, he couldn't understand how people could live in such squalor. It had nothing to do with lack of money; it was just plain laziness and dirty ways.

Latisha's mother came to the front. She had on a day dress, an old pair of house slippers, and wreaked of alcohol.

"Isso good to see ya, Rev'rn," her words slurred together. She had obviously been tying it on for a while. She sat in one of the torn chairs and pointed to one of the sofas covered with caked-on food and had the stench of years of waste. He didn't want to sit; he wanted to see Latisha.

She began a drunken whimper, "Isso awful. He's had his people come round, he's ev'l, Rev'rn, ev'l, ev'l, ev'l," she sputtered spit as she slurred her words out. "He's gonna kill me, he tol' 'em all," she sat there mumbling and shaking her head. Occasionally she would look up at him with glossed-over eyes. Her stare was empty.

He patted her on the shoulder and asked where he could find Latisha.

"She back there," she continued to stare into empty space.

He waded through the litter of dirty clothes and trash strewn from one end of the small house to the other—the deeper into the house, the fouler the odor.

He could hear the T.V. from the back of the house, "Latisha? It's Reverend J."

"I'm in here, " he could hear her footsteps on the old worn floor. She came out of the room and hugged him. She took his hand and led him into the back.

It was a communal bedroom. There was a bed in the middle and a couple of mattresses thrown to either side. It was apparent which mattress was hers. She had it pushed to the wall. It was the only spot in the room that was almost clear of refuse. She had crayon drawings taped up on the wall.

"I like your artwork. You do this?"

She beamed with a smile, "yeah."

He spoke softly, "They're real nice, Latisha. How you been?"

"Okay, I guess," she seemed pensive and reserved in her answer.

"Things okay around here?" he asked.

She shrugged her shoulders.

He spent the better part of an hour talking with her. She spoke to him freely about her drawings. She told him how when Hannah had been there, they had colored pictures together. She said she liked Hannah. "Wanna see something?" Her eyes glistened as she got up, went to the door, looked both ways. She came back and quickly raised the corner of her mattress, pulling out an old cigar box. There were an array of treasures in her box, from sparkling buttons to rubber bands. She pulled out a folded sheet of paper.

"Me an' Miss Hannah drawed this," once unfolded she handed it to him, "it's my daddy."

Joshua's mouth almost dropped, but he tried to hide his expression. It was a drawing of a man in a white tee-shirt and nothing else with an exaggeration of his erect male parts. The paper had a series of holes and had been crumpled many times over.

"You know what I do when I'm scared?" The little girl asked.

"No, Latisha, what do you do?" he wasn't really sure he wanted to know, but he asked anyway.

She rummaged through the box, pulled out a straight pin, and began poking the pin in the paper. "Miss Hannah said it might help me when I think about the scary things. I can even crunch him up and step on him," she demonstrated.

They heard the loud grinding screech of the screen door as it opened. Latisha hurried and folded the paper back, arranging it at the bottom of the box. He heard a man's voice and Latisha's mother's drunken retaliatory comments. It was not clear, but he could get the general gist.

Joshua thought it best he make his presence known. He walked into the hallway. The aunt, the mother, and a big black man were in the front room. When Latisha saw them, she tried to pull him back into the room.

"It's okay," he tried to reassure her.

She whispered back, "No, it ain't," she fled back into her room.

The black man looked up as Joshua emerged from the hallway.

"What the hell he doin' here?" the man directed his question to Latisha's mother.

Joshua thought he could calm the anger, "Good evenin', don't think we've ever met. I'm—"

"I know who you are," the man interrupted, "What I don't know is why you're here. Ain't you caused enough? I think you better be leaving," the man walked over and held open the screen door.

The aunt spoke up, "Terence, this ain't your house. Why don't you leave?"

"Shut up, bitch, before I beat your ass," the man pushed her.

Joshua grabbed his arm.

The man turned and looked at him with a cold dead stare, "You wanna piece?"

Although barely audible to others, Joshua looked right back in the man's eyes and, in a harrowing utterance, warned, "Better think again, big chief." He let the man go and walked out of the house. He could feel the eyes watch him as he walked to his car.

The more he thought about the run-in, the angrier he got. When he got home, the first thing he did was call the police station.

"Claude on tonight?" The answer must have been no, "Page him, please; this is—" the voice on the other end recognized his voice and identified himself; the preacher responded, "Good evening, Roy-Bob. I need to talk to Claude as soon as possible. Have a good night."

It was good to live in a place where everyone pretty much knew everyone else. It was time for him to cook dinner. Before his pop tarts had popped up, the phone rang. It was Claude. "You have time to come to my place tonight, Claude? Got some interesting things to tell you," he waited while he answered, "We can talk when you get here. See you soon."

It didn't take but a few minutes for Claude to arrive. Over a glass of ice tea, Joshua told him about the encounter at Latisha's, but more importantly, about the drawing. He wanted to make sure the charges against her dad stuck. They talked a long time about the beating and rape. Both men concurred if they had their way, they'd take the sorry S.O.B. into the woods with a bat. Claude told him they wanted to get the judge to rule against both the father and the mother. There had been previous calls about cuts, bruises, and burns on the little girl; up until that point, they hadn't been able to move her. He went on to say there had been very little help from child welfare. Joshua told him he knew of several good families to place the girl. They chawed on the subject of removing Latisha from her surroundings for another hour or so, and then both men called it a night.

Morning came fast, but the excitement of finding a home for Latisha gave him an extra bounce in his step. There was a wonderful nip in the air. It was one of those good to be alive kind of days. He was the first one to arrive at the shelter. There were no boys in the rec area, no sounds of life buzzing around; it was silent and peaceful. The door to his office was slightly ajar. He slowly opened the door. At first, he saw nothing out of the ordinary, and then his eyes were drawn to a big hunting knife stuck in the wall pinning a note, "SHUT UP OR DIE," he called the police. Within minutes they arrived.

He couldn't believe the whole thing. Up until this point, they had left him alone. It was known messing with the preacher was taboo. He wondered if the big guy they called Tee had been behind it. He hadn't recognized his face and was pretty sure he wasn't from the area. For the most part, Reverend Delery knew them all, at least their face, if not their name. This deed would have to have been done by an outsider; the locals would've never allowed the sacrilege. While the shelter was far from the Ritz, it was theirs.

By the time Bettina came into work, the place was buzzing with police, and the locals were gathering outside. Nothing had been stolen or damaged, except for the big gash made by the knife in the office wall. It was too coincidental this happened the same night as the encounter at Latisha's. Claude assured him they'd do their utmost to find the person responsible.

It had been a long day. Joshua finished up his hospital visits by six o'clock. He didn't particularly want to go home and didn't feel safe going back to the shelter, so he drove out to Jeremiah's for a visit.

Joshua arrived just in time for dinner. Porter had fried chicken made mashed potatoes, corn on the cob, and homemade biscuits, a welcome change from his usual dinner of pop tarts, cereal, or Spaghettios.

"Preacher, looks like you gotta whole lotta something on your mind. Porter told me he heard someone broke into the shelter."

"Yep," the preacher answered succinctly.

"Damn niggers," looked over at Porter, "no offense."

Porter was hardly shocked or offended. They had been close friends for a long time, and he knew Jeremiah didn't have a prejudice bone in his body. He was plain old honest and called the truth when he saw it. Often he himself had commented on the no-good, dope-dealing, welfare checking, food stamping, living off the rest kinda niggas.

"What'd they take?" Jeremiah knew how to cut to the chase.

"They didn't take anything." The preacher puckered his lips, narrowed his eyes, and nodded in complete disgust.

"Why in the hell did they break in, then, if they didn't take anything?"

"They broke in to leave me a note. It's a long story, and I'm too tired to tell it," Joshua waited a moment, " I don't mean to be rude. Here I am eating up your chicken and have the audacity to answer you like that, sorry. It's been a long day."

Jeremiah chuckled, "You don't have to be apologizin'; you're welcome to come and relax; you'll tell me when you want to, I know that."

The phone rang, Porter answered it. He handed it to Jeremiah, "It's Miss Hannah."

He took the phone and began a series of okays, and sure, "you'll never guess who dropped in for dinner tonight." He waited a minute as she continued to talk, "you're right, he's right here, hold on," he handed the phone to Joshua.

He got up from the table with the phone glued to his ear and went into the hallway. They could barely hear what he was saying. The conversation was short-lived, and when the preacher came back into the kitchen, he seemed a little brighter.

"Things okay in Covington?" Jeremiah said with a twinkle in his eye.

"Yes sir, you know Hannah, she's got a lot to say one can hardly get a word in edgewise," he thought he sounded evasive, "this'll be one day I'll be happy to put behind me. For the next hour or so, Joshua told Jeremiah and Porter about the knife, the note, and the prior evening activities. "That's the big news rattling around the streets of Bogalusa," the preacher concluded.

The evening ended; Joshua bid farewell and headed for home. His mind flashed to Hannah; he couldn't help but notice the burst of energy he got when they spoke. It had been a while since he'd spoken to her. The whole Latisha thing had taken his time; it'd been crude and nasty. When he thought back on it, the note should've come as no surprise. Latisha's father had cursed at him the night the police arrested him. He'd also told him he'd better watch his back. Joshua thought those were just the idle threats of a disturbed man. He surmised he had been wrong; the threats were anything but idle.

After the preacher left, Jeremiah and Porter sat on the porch for their nightly sip while the dogs had their last prowl of the property for the evening. Jeremiah couldn't remember how long their nightly routine had been in place.

"Porter, what you think about the preacher and Hannah? I think he's keen on her; he sure seemed different after talking with her. It's amazing what a woman can do for your spirits."

Porter scratched his fleecy hair and gave one of his big-toothed smiles, "I see what you're saying, but I think she might be a little more of a handful than the preacher can manage. You know she's hard-headed and got her own opinions about everything. But, like you, I gotta say, he seems fond of her. He just doesn't know what he might be getting into," they both had a good chuckle. Porter bid a good night and started for home.

As he trudged toward his house, he heard Jeremiah calling for Spook and Shine. He could hear the crunching of pine needles and fallen leaves on the dry hard ground. Something caught his attention. There was a heap on the ground, but it was too dark to make out what it was; he'd have to get a closer look. As he got closer, he couldn't believe his eyes.

"Oh my Gawd," his voice quaked, "What ya done now, Spook?" The pup laid there on the ground, silent and still. He picked him up and bellowed to Jeremiah. "Cain, Cain, c'mere."

Jeremiah hit the flood lights in the trees. It illuminated the entire area. He saw Porter coming to him with something in his arms. In a millisecond, he knew what that something was. Porter laid the lifeless body on the porch. The front of his shirt was soaked in blood. He wiped his drenched hands on his pants. Blood was everywhere.

There were tears in both men's eyes. Jeremiah stood on the front porch, and at the top of his lungs, he called out to Shine. He wiped his nose and eyes and, like the protective father, went out to Shine as he bounded in. He knelt and gave him a little tussle. "C'mon, boy," Shine ran up on the porch. He nuzzled his dead pal as if to wake him to play.

"Cain, who would do such a thing?" he put one hand on Spook and pet Shine with the other, "there's some sick people in this world."

Jeremiah agreed and asked him to call his family to see if anyone saw anything. "With all the folks we have on this property, someone has to have seen something out of the ordinary."

Porter called home, and before he could say anything, his son-in-law told him there was a stranger on the property, and he'd tried to ring the main house, but there was no answer. He said he thought he heard something and when he looked out of the window, someone had pulled up into the woods, gotten out of the vehicle heading to the main house on foot. His son-in-law said he went on the porch but decided to go back in and get his shotgun. He said just as he came back out on the porch; he could hear one of the dogs surprise the unwelcomed guest. He said he called out, and the person bolted back to his car and took off. He tried to chase it, but it was to no avail—the black SUV maneuvered the grounds too fast. The only thing he could tell was he thought it had been a white man; at least, he moved like a white man.

"Maybe we should call the police," Porter sensibly suggested.

"Nah, we'll take care of this ourselves. Tell your son-in-law I said shoot next time; we'll ask questions later."

Porter shook his head, "He done right, Cain. You cain't just shoot; you know that."

Jeremiah grumbled, "I'll get the grave dug; you go on home. Tell your son-in-law he done good. Good night, my friend."

Porter patted Jeremiah on the shoulder and ambled toward his house. As he got closer to home, he started peeling the blood-soaked clothes off his body. Porter put them in a plastic bag and then the garbage. Both his daughter and son-in-law were waiting as he walked inside. At first, they were alarmed when they saw him. He still had a good bit of blood on his body. He told them about Spook and then got in the shower.

After his shower and before bed, he went out on the porch. As expected, the house lights were still burning brightly. He could see Jeremiah sitting on the front porch and suspected he'd be there another couple of hours. He was going to wait in hopes the uninvited guest would return.

Morning came, neither of the men had much sleep. It was going to be a slow, sad day. He knew whoever the intruder was; he hadn't come to kill his dog; they'd come for him. In his mind, he was ready for them. He was ready to pay them back for Tyler's death and now Spook's. He looked forward to the encounter.

The morning was spent over a lazy breakfast. While Porter did the cleaning up, he went out on the property. About an hour later, he returned.

"C'mon Porter, go get ya shotgun. I got us set up." Porter came out onto the porch. Jeremiah had set up target practice. "Thought we might be a little rusty, no time like the present to fine-tune our shot."

There was no point in arguing. It took a few moments, but Porter returned shotgun in hand. Neither were very rusty and picked the targets off with ease. Jeremiah was satisfied.

Long about suppertime, Claude from the police department stopped by. Jeremiah went out to personally invite him in, "You came right in time for dinner—vegetable soup from homegrown vegetables. Nothing better than having your own out the garden.

He accepted the invitation. Porter's daughter-in-law had called Claude earlier to tell him about the incident the night before. She pointedly asked the sheriff not to tell Mr. Cain she'd called, but she was worried. The sheriff told her he'd known Jeremiah a long time and knew how to handle the situation. He knew the old man could be difficult at the best of times.

Shine stuck to Jeremiah's side. Claude thought this would be the perfect intro, "He's turned into a handsome pup; where's Spook?"

"I may be getting' older, but I ain't stupid. You ain't been here in a month, and then you show up tonight. I don't know who called you, nor do I care. Let's cut through the shit; just don't mess up my dinner." Jeremiah walked into the kitchen.

"You shoulda called last night, ya know that? I don't wanna be fightin' with you. You know you shoulda called and made a report." Claude followed right behind him.

"To tell ya what, someone killed my dog? What would they do? Put out an APB or maybe a highway block. Shiiit, that guy was long gone. Now want a beer or some ice tea?"

"Beer sounds good," getting back on the subject, "We coulda been on the lookout for a dark-colored SUV; I think your daughter-in-law said it was a Land Rover and advised state, as well. Who knows, slim chance, but we mighta caught the guy." They argued all through dinner, neither giving in nor giving up, "You gonna call me next time?"

"Next time, I'm gonna shoot the bastard, and then I'll call you. I doubt he'll be back, but maybe I'll get lucky. Boy, I'd like to get a piece of him, sick son-of-a-bitch." The thing about it was Claude knew Jeremiah meant every word of it. They spent the rest of the night speculating and then grabbing much-needed sleep.

THE HEAT IS ON

Things in the Big Easy were heating up, and the offices were busier than ever; Hannah was determined to find time to make it to the Upperline. If she couldn't get answers to her satisfaction, she decided she'd turn it over to Nick. She was sure she could convince him to handle it with sensitivity.

The trial was going terrible for Preston, and the only plea they were offering was five to eight years in prison. He wasn't about to take it. Although his marriage had been a farce, Preston was having a hard time with the prospect of going through the remainder of the trial alone. He had to put pride aside and beg her to come home. His attorney said it was the first smart move he'd made in years. He also recommended that Preston make every effort to be congenial. Both he and his attorney were glad Grace reconsidered the separation.

Nick and Seth had made headway on the murder; the indicators pointed to Cardoza. They could easily link Eddie "The Flame" to Cardoza, but Nick still had the feeling Preston was involved in some kind of way. Seth tried to get him to drop it and work with the evidence they had in hand; it was enough. They knew Eddie Germaine had done the deed. It was just proving Cardoza ordered the hit.

Leonard Cardoza was a well-known name in New Orleans. He had been linked to several heinous crimes but had no convictions. This episode of Eddie's, which he hadn't been involved in, was something he didn't need and sure as hell didn't want. Following several annoying visits and a plethora of harassing phone calls, he had put the word on the street he wanted to talk to Eddie, but The Flame laid low.

Eddie had high-tailed it to the Gulf Coast. A friend of his had loaned him the keys to her condo in Gulf Shores. Their relationship had been a secret, and he'd be safe there. For all practical purposes, Eddie was a good-looking man. He had a mass of dark hair and a chiseled masculine face, perfect for wooing older rich women and their money. It was a little different with this one; he truly liked her more than he had all the others. He figured it had something to do with her talking down to him and treating him like the trash he was.

The condo was first class all the way. For days he lounged in the sun, sipping colorful fruity drinks and watching young babes as they pranced up and down the beach. He liked to look, but that was it. He'd found out long ago that while beautiful and tight, young girls liked to talk, and that was something way too dangerous for a person in his line of work.

He was just rolling out of the bed when the phone rang; it was his friend, "How's things goin'? He asked.

He listened while she talked.

"When you comin' ova here?"

He listened again.

"I'm good. It's kinda lonely here, and I thought—"

She cut him off.

"Okay, then. Yeah. Bye."

It was a short-lived conversation and mostly one-sided on her part. The condo association provided the morning newspaper and delivered it early every morning. Eddie opened the door to get the paper and noticed a middle-aged woman doing the same thing next door. They smiled at each other. *Not bad,* he thought. He went back into the condo. The T.V. had been on all night; one of the daily morning shows was on; he sat reading the paper listening to the yack yack in the background, occasionally looking up at the television. There was a knock on the door.

He got up, "I'm comin'. Who's there?"

"Sorry to bother you," the female voice responded.

He opened the door to find the neighbor from the picking up the paper encounter.

"It's no botha; how can I help you?" he tried to put forth his charming side.

The woman explained she had locked the bathroom door with the bath water running and couldn't get anyone to answer the phone in the office and thought maybe he could help. He couldn't help but think getting into locked doors was one of his specialties; he was sure he'd have no problem.

She watched him as he tinkered with the lock, and in seconds he had the door open. She smiled, "Thank you," and trailed, waiting for a name.

"Eddie, Eddie Germaine, and ya welcome," he played the same waiting game.

"My gosh, I'm so sorry, how rude of me," she put her hand out, "Grace Cain."

He almost choked but managed to keep it together, "Call if ya need more doors unlocked," smiled and went back to the condo.

Just as he left, the phone rang; she answered it, "What is it now, Preston?" She listened as he humbled himself.

"I don't know; I don't even know if I want to come back to you. Maybe it's just better if we end the whole thing. Our marriage has been nothing but a joke. I have to think about this some more."

He pleaded with her, but she remained determined, "I'll let you know my decision in a couple of days. My bath water is about to overflow; let me go." He continued to argue, "No, Preston, you're the one that fools around, not me. I've more than had my opportunity, but I took our marriage a little more seriously than you and refrained." The badgering went on, "When? Don't be so stupid. You ask when, um, right before you called that's when," she paused, "Who, really? I suppose he's a new condo owner, and I must say he's extremely handsome."

"That's pathetic, Grace. Nice try, give me a break. Let's say for argument it's true, what was the man's name, hmm?" he was on the edge of returning to his cruel, sarcastic ways.

She had trouble recalling his name, but then it clicked, "Edward Germaine, do you really care, Preston? Are you that concerned?"

"Enough of the game, Grace, come home," he waited for an answer, "this is the last time I'm going to ask you."

"I'll be home in a couple of days; I think we need time apart right now. Maybe you might learn to appreciate me."

The conversation ended cordially for a nice change. In her heart, she knew it wouldn't be much longer until he went to prison; even if it ended up being more like a country club, it would be hard for him. She didn't put much past him, but she found it hard to picture him as a killer; it didn't fit. She had to admit to herself he had been acting cagey, and it might have been possible he knew something about the murder, but in her heart, she felt it couldn't have been more than by proxy.

She knew where he had been the night of the fire. He had been at Brandy's, his most recent conquest. She even knew where the girl lived and had seen the two of them together. He knew very little about discretion or plain didn't care.

After they hung up the phone, Preston laid back on his bed. He contemplated his future, was scared and didn't want to go to prison. For the first time, he admitted to himself the terrible acts he had committed. He had seen Tyler's power and wanted it. He was tired of begging Tyler to expand the business, to get more in touch with the current trends, but Tyler continually said he liked things the way they'd been. The process had been tried and true; why change? If it wasn't broken, why try to fix it? Preston could see the possibilities they were missing out on, and Tyler would have no time for his suggestions. Preston knew if he could take a couple of deals and make them big money, then Tyler would have to take notice and maybe listen. The ring of the phone dashed his thoughts, making him almost jump out of his skin.

"Are you up yet?" it was Lizzie.

"Good morning to you, too, Elizabeth. I was just thinking about you. What are you doing for lunch?"

"I didn't call to chat, Preston. I wanted to let you know I was going to Gulf Shores for the weekend. Do feed the cat, if you will." She was quick on the phone and ready to hang up. He thought he better act fast, or this might be the last chance he had for someone to talk him out of a confession.

"I'm gonna take the D.A.'s offer." There was dead silence for what seemed an eternity.

"Let's talk. Can you come over here? I'm trying to get my things together to leave and still have a few errands. We can pick up a sandwich on the run." The two of them were cut from the same cloth. She could identify with him as they were both out for themselves and had little regard for anyone else. He had whined to her on many occasions about Tyler's disinterest in him. Personally, she found Tyler a bore and lacking sophistication for a man in his position. At heart, he was still a country boy, just with a bit of spit-shine.

In no time flat he had made it to Lizzie's; it was only a few blocks to Octavia Street. He went in through the kitchen and called up to her. She told him to come up while she packed.

As he entered her room, he saw her luggage, "I thought you said you were going for a weekend, not a month."

"What are you talking about? I know you're just as bad. It's part of the gene pool, I think; both my girls inherited it as well." She continued grabbing a few items out of her closet.

He sat in the bedside chair. "Lizzie, I've been thinking this whole thing over. I don't think I'll have a chance with a jury; maybe Baldwin can negotiate a little more if I agree. He's advised me to take the offer, each time I've said no, and he's come back with a better one, but I think it's now or never." He could hardly keep still, constantly repositioning himself.

"I don't know what to tell you, Preston. Five years is a long time. See what the terms are; after all, in essence, all you did was take what was already yours. It *is* our company, too. I think the D.A. has forgotten that one," she went in the bathroom with her toiletry bag but continued to talk to him. "What's Grace say?"

He hadn't told her about their fight and that she had left him, "I didn't ask her," he responded.

She came out with the bag. "Why the hell not? It affects her life, too, not just yours."

Skirting the issue, he answered, "I know, I know. I will, maybe in a couple of days."

"Why wait? What is wrong with you?" he sat there tongue-tied. Again she asked, "Well?"

"Because she won't be home until then, that's why. I'm not going to drop this on her over the phone." He cocked his head to the side, raising his eyebrows.

Lizzie stood with her hand on her hip. "What a ridiculous time for her to go out of town. The woman must be insane. Since she's not around, I guess she'll have to live with our decision, right?"

They spent the rest of the morning together and part of the afternoon and decided Preston would go with the advice of his attorney. He eventually owned up to Grace leaving him. Lizzie wasn't too surprised but advised he better keep his pecker in his pants, at least until things settled down.

Meanwhile, things at the office were busy as ever. Page had his hands full with Julia Street. Due to the fire and damage, all that was left was demolition. The phones were ringing off the hook; everyone wanted the land. The stakes were getting pretty high and still rising.

Hannah, Sal, and Deidre had managed to keep a tight rein on P.R. while constantly dodging the badgering press regarding the company's views on the embezzlement, the rumored action on the sale or development of Julia Street, and, of course, the looming investigation of the murder.

The weekend had finally arrived, and Hannah was more than ready for it. She had picked up Michelle on the way home. She knew Nick had been looking forward to seeing his daughter and enjoying a weekend of peace and quiet.

The days had grown shorter, so it was nearly dark when Nick arrived at Southern Manor. After settling in, he popped a beer and waited on the front porch for his girls to arrive. He called her.

The ring of the phone was startling. Michelle answered, "Hannah Cain's phone, may I ask who's calling?" she giggled because she knew it was her dad.

He made his voice real deep and serious, "this is Detective Messina. May I speak with Miss Cain, and who may I ask is speaking?" she giggled again.

"You certainly may; this is Miss Michelle Messina, daughter of the one and only Super Cop." Hannah looked over at her; she was precious and adored her daddy. Michelle handed her the phone, "It's my dad."

"Really?" Hannah smiled. "Hello, is this Super Cop?"

"Where are you? I've been sitting on the porch waiting for hours."

She quickly retorted, "Hours my foot, but if you really want to know I just turned into the driveway, you should be able to see my lights any second."

"Right now," and he walked down to the driveway still on the phone, "I've missed you all day today."

"I've missed you, too," she whispered.

"I love you," he sounded so seductive. Hannah lowered her window and stuck her head out with lips puckered, ready for a kiss. He gladly obliged.

Miles and Margot stopped by for a visit when they dropped off Lauren. The four of them sat in the parlor. Belle had prepared enough for an army, so they joined Hannah and Nick for dinner. During dinner, Miles asked Nick if he had heard about all the excitement in Bogalusa.

The question perked up Hannah's ears, Nick nodded.

"What excitement?" she had to know.

Miles was the first to answer. "Some bad egg broke into the community center. I heard that a note was pinned to the wall with a big hunting knife. Supposedly, it was a death threat to the preacher up there."

Hannah looked at Nick, "Is Reverend Delery okay?"

Nick seemed matter-of-fact about the whole thing. He didn't share in the enthusiasm, "he's fine. Maybe a little shaken, but he'll be alright."

She seemed upset and questioned, "Who did it?"

"They don't know. The thought is that it's linked to the rape of a little girl."

"What rape? What little girl?" Margot hadn't heard anything about the episode with Latisha.

Hannah told the story that she had been at the shelter when the girl was beaten and raped. Nick cut the story off; he seemed to be somewhat angry.

"They have a couple of suspects, but nothing concrete yet," Nick's comment seemed to punctuate the ending of the conversation. Things at the table became uncomfortable. It wasn't long before Miles and Margot left.

Hannah had been quiet for the remainder of the night. Nick didn't notice, or if he had, he didn't say anything. Michelle and Lauren wanted to swim. Hannah gave the okay and sat on the porch swing while the girls frolicked in the pool.

Nick came out, "did I do somethin' wrong? You seem distant since dinner."

She was still upset, " I didn't like the way you acted when I was talking to Margot. You might as well have told me to shut up. At least that's how it felt."

"Sorry," he started to get pissy again. "I see enough ugly all week long. I sure as hell don't need it at the dinner table," realizing his tone, he apologized again. "Maybe I better go to bed. I'm sorry, I don't mean to hurt you," he leaned over to kiss her and stopped, "Don't move."

She wanted to jump and run, but she sat perfectly still. "What is it? Is it a snake?"

"No, I just need to see somethin'." He walked behind her and started talking to himself. "If I came behind, like this," he put his hands close to the back of her neck. "That's it." He went into the yard. From where he stood, he could see the garage. He went into the house and then came out with his flashlight. He slowly walked the path to the garage. Stopping along the way, but it was no use; he'd have to wait until morning, "ya pops ever come out here?"

"You mean in the yard?" she asked.

He qualified, "No, on the porch, specifically the swing?"

"Yes, all the time, especially after dinner. Dad said it was the perfect ending to the day. Why?" he had her curiosity.

"Call it a hunch for now."

Hannah called the girls out of the pool and headed inside with Nick, "a hunch? What was that all about?"

"I've been bugged recently. Seth thinks we got all we need on your pop's case," he stopped, "Hannah, I feel uncomfortable talking to you about this," he went silent. She put her hand on his.

"It's okay; I can handle whatever it is about my father's death. I don't think there's much I haven't already heard. Besides, there's something I think; maybe I should have already told you about a note I found."

His mind was on one track, and her comment passed him by, "it's not that I think you can't handle it exactly. We got one shot, that's it, one. Anytime we're getting down to the wire, and it looks like we've got the perp dead to right, I get anxious. It's all them little facts that get ya if ya not careful. Somethin' just don't feel right on this, and I don't wanna blow our chance. Anything I say to you could jeopardize the case. Nothin' personal," he looked to her for understanding.

"Okay tough guy," she whispered in his ear, "Remember I'm not the one that pissed in your Cheerios, though."

He laughed, "Gross," she had broken his mood, "where did you hear that? That's gross, Hannah."

They went arm in arm up the stairs, "you don't wanna know where I heard it."

"Okay, then don't tell me," he figured from the comment it must have been Michelle. Most definitely, he needed to get her out of New Orleans.

Later as they lay in bed, Nick asked, "What is it you wanted to tell me?"

"Show you," she corrected.

He took it completely wrong, "Oh baby, show me."

"Not that kind of show you." She hesitated but finally got up and brought the note back to him, "before you look at this, you have to promise me you'll talk to me before doing anything. Promise me."

"How can I promise without knowin' what I'm promisin' about?" He had no idea where she was leading him.

It took a while, but she finally told him about straightening the papers on the desk and finding her dad's daybook, and while browsing through it, she noticed a loose piece of paper with a triangle of arrows. She continued seeing lunch plans in the book and then launched her own investigation into the matter. She showed him the note and then the daybook.

"Damn, Hannah, yeah, you right, you shoulda shown me."

She knelt in the bed and put her hands on his shoulders, "calm down, tough guy. I'm dead serious about this. If any of this implicates my dad in any wrongdoing, I want the whole damn thing dropped." He felt the gravity of what she said and understood; regardless, it didn't change what he had to do.

"It don't work like that, dammit," he shook his head, "Why in the hell would you hold back and not tell me?"

Tears welled in her eyes, "Cause I don't want L.C. to be Leonard Cardoza and—"

He interrupted, "It probably is, but it still doesn't mean your old man did anything wrong. It gives us more leverage against Cardoza. See?" He turned his body so that she would spoon next to him. As she cuddled next to him, he held her tight. It had been an eventful night, and he welcomed sleep.

Even though it was Saturday and any chances of CIU being in were slim, he passed by Covington P.D. anyway. He lucked out; McLain had gone in to catch up on paperwork.

"Ya gonna love me for this," Nick was pumped. "You need to go by Cain's place today. I think I know where they got the old man. He musta gone out on the porch swing after his meetin' with Preston to think or somethin'. There's scuff marks on the porch under the swing."

Ford looked up, "that's brilliant, Nick." Then sarcastically, "Of course there are scuff marks under the swing, it's a swing for Chri'sake, you drag your feet." He looked back down and continued, "Why am I gonna love you when you don't send me flowers anymore?"

"Seriously, if you stand behind the swing and look down, it's obvious;

you can see it clear as day. Put ya pen down and at least take a ride with me; I'll even buy the coffee."

Ford rode over with him, and just as Nick had said, the marks did, in fact, appear to have been caused by some kind of scuffle. There had been enough force to gouge the floorboards. They enacted how they thought it could have gone down. Nick's phone went off.

"Damn, it's Seth," Nick walked away as he answered the call. He watched as Ford walked the way to the garage, stopping every so often to take a closer look.

Nick called from the porch, "Ya find anything?"

Ford walked back toward the house, "Maybe, I'm gonna call LT, see what he says. You might've stumbled on to something."

"I gotta get, something's up. Call me if y'all find anything," Nick went back into the house and ran up the stairs. Hannah was still sleeping.

As he tip-toed out of the room, she rolled over, "Just where are you sneaking off to?"

"Seth called, something's come up in town," he sat on the bed next to her. He ran his hand over her form. Through the sheets and covers, he could feel the contours of her body.

She exaggerated a pout. They went to kiss when the phone rang.

Hannah answered, "Good morning, Millie. What can I do for you?" Hannah listened intently, "You're kidding me, okay, thanks for calling." She grabbed the T.V. remote and scrolled to the right channel.

"Hannah, what's up?" he looked toward the set. A newscaster theorized about an emergency meeting between the D.A. office and Ray Baldwin, Preston's attorney. She summarized the rumor was Preston was taking a plea.

Down at the courthouse, Preston waited pensively outside of the office. The door was closed. He could hear loud voices but couldn't make any of them out. His heart pounded hard and fast; it felt like it was coming out of his throat. He could barely swallow. His hands were cold and clammy. He closed his eyes, hoping this was all a nightmare and it would be gone when he opened his eyes, but it wasn't; it was very real. The door opened.

Ray came out. He turned back to look in the room, "This changes everything; I'll have to consult with my client."

He took Preston by the arm, and they walked out of the waiting area. "What's going on," Preston was a nervous wreck.

"They've changed the offer," he was on edge.

"What is it now?" They hurriedly walked down another hall and then into a private room.

"They believe you had prior knowledge of the murder, that makes you just as guilty as the guy who committed the murder. I don't know how much of a case they have, but New Orleans D.A. has filed to postpone your case in light of the new information from Covington P.D. What they're looking for from you is information. The more you are willing to give them, the more they are willing to negotiate."

Preston began to whimper. "Ray, you've got to be kidding. I don't know anything about my brother's murder. Jesus, Tyler, and I didn't see eye to eye on many things, but to know about my brother's murder and not do anything? Oh, my God." His body began to tremble. He grabbed the trash can and heaved his guts falling apart right before Ray's eyes.

"Preston, get control," he barked.

Slowly Preston began to pull himself together. He couldn't believe what he was hearing. A million thoughts started running through his head. What could he possibly tell them to amount to any negotiation?

"What happens now?" He sounded pathetic.

" You'll be arrested as a fugitive from justice by the NOPD. Then Covington police will pick you up and charge you for the murder of your brother. Given your family's influence in the area, there's a chance we'll be able to post bail. The keyword here is chance."

He pleaded, "But I didn't do anything."

They sat in the little room waiting. Eventually, two police officers from Covington arrived.

The reality of the situation began to unfold as they handcuffed him and led him to the awaiting police car. They read him his rights, and that was about it. Baldwin stood and watched as they pulled away. Once again, the sickening feeling was returning. He felt like he was going to die. His chest tightened to the point each breath drawn posed an arduous task. He wanted to scream but knew it would be to no avail. The lump in his throat was getting bigger, and he could barely swallow. His mouth was so dry his lips stuck to his teeth when he tried to speak, and each word had an almost crackling sound. There was no point in saying anything; they didn't care.

He started thinking. They'd have to allow him one phone call. Who would he call? Who could he count on? Lizzie was out of town, as was Grace, and he couldn't rely on them anyway. Nate was too stupid to be of any help. He had to think. There was Jeremiah, but he was too crazy, no telling what he'd do. The only one he could think of was Hannah. He wondered if she knew they thought he had something to do with her father's death. She couldn't have heard the new theory yet; she'd have to be the one he called. She would listen.

The girls and Hannah played in the pool and then played beauty parlor. She dried and styled their hair. Plans were to go to a matinee, but the phone rang.

"Hannah, God, I'm glad I got you. I'm at the Covington Police Department. I need you to come here quickly. I need your help," she knew it was Preston, but for some reason, it didn't sound like him.

"Preston?" she asked.

"Yes, yes, Hannah. I don't have time for questions, just get here," he sounded a little more like himself.

"Okay, I'm coming," she hung up. She called Nick.

"Hey doll, whassup?"

"You'll never guess who's called me and from where," she sounded almost giddy.

"I give."

"Preston from Covington P.D. He wants me to come there; he said he needs me. What do you think? I told him I'd come. Part of me wanted to hang up on him, but part of me felt sorry for him." She couldn't believe her own words, but it was true. She did feel sorry for him.

Nick told her to stay put; he turned around, then immediately dialed Seth with a brief update. Surprisingly the return trip went by fast as he recounted the whole daybook episode—the triangle between Cardoza and Preston and the speculation Tyler might have gotten too close, knew too much. This certainly added another dimension to an already perplexing case.

After speaking with Seth, Nick called Ford McLain, the Covington investigator asking to be in on the Preston interview. He was able to get him just in time. Ford most graciously agreed to hold off until Nick arrived.

Finally, after the calls to Seth and Ford, he called Hannah back and told her he'd meet her at the P.D.

Nick had only talked with Preston a few times during the preliminary investigation of Cain & Sons following the anonymous letter. During that time, all he found against the obnoxious little man was way too much pomp and arrogance. It took weeks of going over contract agreements and an array of real estate files that required a specialist from Baton Rouge to assist and examine the numbers game. Overall, it was pretty cut and dry. Preston's name appeared all over the place. The forgery of Tyler's signature could have been the only sticking point, but Harris had testified he had been with Preston during the transactions. It should have been a slam dunk. Keyword being *should*. Nick found it disturbing that the D.A.'s office was having such trouble, but he also had experience with the city government to know that it was hardly surprising. It seemed logical to him; why couldn't the attorney keep a simple thing, simple?

Hannah pulled up to the station. She didn't find any of it very intimidating but she wasn't the one in the hot seat. There were a couple of police officers hanging around the door.

They smiled as she approached, "Good afternoon, ma'am."

The older one held the door open for her. She could feel their eyes as she walked past them to the open window.

A pleasant-looking man sat on the other side of the window. He had his head down and was busy at work, humming as he went along.

"Excuse me, sir."

The man looked up, "How can I help you, little lady?"

"I'm here for Preston Cain," she politely smiled.

"You're gonna have to take a seat out there for right now," he smiled back.

"Thank you," she sat on the vinyl bench. One of the officers from outside came in and made small talk with the guy behind the window. She figured the conversation was in her honor. With these kinds of men, it always was.

She glanced at her watch; it was two forty, she wished she was at the matinee with the girls, but Travis had the pleasure. Another twenty minutes and the gentleman from behind the window called to her.

"Miss, I need you to fill this out." He had a clipboard with a form for her to fill in her name and who she was visiting. He opened the door and told her to follow him.

Preston was waiting there. His face visibly brightened when he saw her, "Oh my God, Hannah, I can't tell you how grateful I am you came."

She nodded but remained silent.

"Honey, there's been an awful misunderstanding, and I want you to hear it from me," he whispered, "They think I had something to do with your daddy's death."

She whispered back at him, "Well, didn't you?"

He looked shocked, "N-no, I didn't. I may have gotten caught with my hand in the cookie jar, but that's a far cry from," and he whispered again, "Murder. I can't believe you would even think I'd be capable." He honestly looked hurt, "you have to believe me," he hung his head.

"Whether you did, or you didn't, either way, won't bring my father back. Somehow, Preston, I believe you. Make no mistake; I'm the only one that does." She dropped her voice to a whisper, "What you've put the company and me through; I should let you sit and rot." She turned her head away from him.

"What can I say, Hannah? I don't know, but you can sure as hell bet I'm sorry for whatever mess and wrongdoing I've done, but I didn't"

She cut him off, "I bet you are."

They looked at each other for a minute or so.

She broke the silence, " I have a friend that might be able to help, maybe get you out of here so we can talk like human beings. I'm not sure, though. Where's Baldwin?"

He shrugged, "Hell, if I know. He hasn't done much for me yet. Find out what you can, darlin'."

"Okay, call me if you need to; I'll get on this right away."

An officer escorted her to the front of the station. As she passed the little man who'd let her in, she saw Nick. He was joking around with the guy and the officers who had been outside.

He jumped up when he saw her, "Hey, Doll. You got here faster than I thought you would. Pete tells me you had to wait." He shook his head.

"I didn't know she was a friend of yours, Nick. Look, Miss," he began.

She cut in, "Don't let him give you a hard time. You were doing your job. Anyway, you guys have a great rest of your day." She grabbed Nick's hand and led him into the parking lot.

She turned and faced him. "Before you say one word, I don't think Preston was directly involved with my father's murder. Don't look at me like that. Nick, I've worked with the guy for a couple of years, and Lord knows I've known him forever. I've seen him lie, and he's not lying now."

He smiled, "I thought you said you didn't know him very well. Hannah, think about it. Don't look at him as your uncle; look at him like the man that ordered the hit on your dad. You'll see him differently."

"You're wrong. When I first came here, I believed he was somehow involved in it. I really don't think he is. Do me a favor; when you interview him, go with an open mind."

"I always do," he almost seemed insulted.

"And," she said in a sweeter than normal voice.

"And?"

"See if you can get him out of there. He can stay at Southern Manor. He won't be out of anyone's sight."

He was obviously annoyed. "Hannah, what is wrong with you? This isn't some game. Until I have some reason to believe he is innocent, as all the evidence points differently, I am not doing anything to help him get out. I hate to think what the bail would be." He shook his head. "You don't get it, do you? Let's say he didn't have anything to do with—" he was angry and began mincing his words. "Dammit, he fucking forged your father's name and stole over half a million dollars from C&S. What would make you want to help him?" He had his hands firmly on his hips with a rigid posture.

Hannah shook her head looked down at the ground, biting her lip. "Never mind, Nick. I guess you're right, like always." Now she was angry, piping angry. He had hurt her feelings and insulted her. What gave him the right to think his opinion was the only thing that mattered, and she was wrong? He had talked to her like she was stupid. The score could've always been made up regarding Preston's indiscretion. Jeremiah could opt to do a distribution to Nate, Lizzie, himself, and her father's estate. She was now beginning to see what Jeremiah was talking about when he said the family took care of its own matters. Nick didn't understand how it could work out. He'd have to learn if they were going to take their relationship to the next level.

STEPPIN' OUT

hey both arrived at Southern Manor about the same time. Travis had not yet returned with the girls. The more she thought about their conversation, the more she seethed. She didn't acknowledge him; she walked into the house and straight up to her suite. He followed, taking two steps at a time. He was annoyed with her, but he didn't want to fight with her more than anything. They could talk the whole thing through. There had to be a happy medium.

"Hannah, stop."

She turned at her door, "What?" The venom dripped from her mouth.

"What? Don't be like that. C'mon, I don't wanna fight. I'm trying to be rational. It's hard to be objective when it's your own family. You forget it's what I—"

"Don't even go there," she interrupted. "Believe me; I never forget what you do for a living. The thing is, Nick, you don't give me any credit."

He got mad all over again. "You're right, Hannah. It's all my fault, always is." He walked down the hall toward the guest room; he turned in. She could hear slamming. She walked into her room and slammed the door closed.

After a few minutes, he came to the door. He called in, "I'll get Michelle in the morning if that's okay?"

She opened the door, "That's fine." The tears were streaming down her face.

It broke his heart. He couldn't bear to see her cry, especially since it was his fault. His eyes teared. "Aw, Han. I'm sorry, I'm so sorry." He stepped in and held her in his arms.

"I'm sorry, too, Nick. I don't want to fight. This whole thing is hard."

He stroked her hair, "Look; I gotta go back to the jail. I wasn't supposed to leave; I was waiting on Ford when I saw ya. I gotta go." He kissed her tears, "I promise to stay objective, okay?" He crossed his heart. "Promise I'll come straight back here when we finish. I love you."

Hannah took his bag from him and put it on the floor inside the door. "I love you too."

His heart pounded; she'd never said she loved him before. He felt like a teenage boy as his stomach did flip-flops.

She fell on her bed feeling totally and completely in love. It was the weirdest emotional roller coaster. Pissed to the boiling point one second and then dreamy in love the next.

Nick made it to the jail in record time. He figured he had probably violated every traffic law in existence. Ford was outside waiting.

He could tell the Covington detective wasn't too pleased. "Sorry, something came up; thanks for waiting."

"Two more minutes, and I was going in." Ford made his point.

The two went in together. Preston recognized Nick immediately. "Hello, Detective Messina."

Nick nodded.

Ford gave Preston some papers to sign saying he had been informed of his rights and began the interview. He turned on the tape. "For the record, state your name."

He went through the routine of establishing identity, date, and surroundings. Preston was fully aware of why they arrested him. "For the life of me, I can't figure where y'all got your information. I didn't have anything to do with my brother's death."

"Tell me about the last time you saw your brother, Tyler Cain." Ford continued.

"It was at his house, on the Friday before his death. We had words at the office. I wanted to make amends and went to his house later that night. He told me I could visit."

"What was the nature of your disagreement?"

"It was in reference to a business transaction he wasn't happy about."

"What exactly was the business transaction?"

"Gentlemen, we all know about the transaction. Do we really need to re-hash this?"

"Answer the question." Ford had little time for Preston's irritating tone.

Preston sat there for a minute. He knew they knew about the fraudulent contracts, but he didn't want to admit it to a tape recorder in case they used against him later. "I don't know if I want to answer anything without—"

Nick interrupted before he could say without his attorney present. He had signed the papers. Everything he would say would be admissible. "Preston, you're right, we know. We know all about the transaction. We need to make clear for the record the transaction only included venture and had nothing to do with arson."Nick leaned forward, drumming his fingers on the table.

"No, no, it had nothing to do with the fire. It was for the demolition of the property. I made sure all permits were filed. As you know, the city turned it down; thus, nothing ever came from the transaction." It wasn't until he finished speaking that he realized Nick had gotten him to admit the crime for the record. Because he was afraid, he was unable to think straight.

Ford started up again. "Okay, you've gone with cap in hand to make amends, proceed."

"Yes, I did." Preston firmly nodded.

"What if I were to tell you we know for a fact, you and Tyler quarreled, and he told you to leave? It was far from making amends. At least no kind of amends I've ever made."

"Yes, quarreled, but no more than we ever did." His face flushing to bright pink.

Ford shook his head, "Preston, stop jerking me around. You and

I both know you and your brother had a real go of it. What I want to know is how *bad* did he piss you off?"

Preston sat; he wasn't budging. Exasperated, Ford left the room. Nick put his hand on Preston's shoulder, "I know you were only trying to keep C&S up with the times. The old guy didn't get it. They never got it, did they"

Preston sat silent.

"I know how it is; in the police department, we have those old guys stuck in their ways when there's a whole new world out there. Boy, things could be way easier if they could get with the program. They don't mind the donut eating, behind the station beating reputation, where, hey, a guy like me, I work hard to improve the image. While it's not the same, there are some similarities." Nick hesitated, "You wanted to keep them up with the times; I don't blame you; it's frustrating." He paused again. "Hell, no one would've bought into y'all doin' anything on the sly if it wasn't for Harris; he was the weak link."

"Damn right he was. You're right; I was pissed. What the old guys didn't accept was we, Nate, Liz, and I, have as much claim on the company as they do. That night I pointed it out to him. He didn't want to hear it. He didn't ask me to leave; I was on my way out. I was disgusted."

"Yeah, I don't blame you," Nick agreed with him, "What ya do next?"

Preston lied, "I went home."

"No, you didn't. Don't start lying to me now. Man, I'm the only one who understands where you're comin' from, capiche?" He whispered low but right in the direction of the recorder. Preston didn't notice. He was looking at him eye to eye, "Where'd ya go?"

Preston whispered back, continuing to look Nick in the eyes, "Brandy's."

"Ya went straight there?" Nick asked.

"Yeah," he actually looked ashamed.

"You have any idea of the time?"

"Ten, ten something. The news was still on channel four." He gave all appearances of telling the truth.

"Any problem with me talking to Brandy? Think she'll corroborate your story?"

Preston had to think about it for a moment. "Hell, my wife knows. She even knows I was there on the night in question. Why not? Talk to Brandy."

Ford came back into the room. Preston watched him as he walked around. He stood squarely behind him; it was most uncomfortable having the detective standing over him.

"Where's she work?"

"She's a nail tech at," he hesitated, "Does he have to stand behind me. He's breathing down my neck."

Ford came around and sat on the table next to Preston, who rattled off his girlfriend's phone number.

"She'd probably be more cooperative if you called her at home." He went on to tell Nick he paid for an apartment for her in Mid-City.

"The old love nest," Nick winked at him.

Preston started to whine, "Detectives, I'm getting tired. Haven't you asked me enough questions? When can I leave?"

Nick looked straight at him, "I'm gonna tell you straight. I don't think you're gonna be able to leave anytime soon. It's up to the judge and the D.A. I'm pullin' for ya. I even told the D.A. he should at least let you go to your nieces. I said I didn't think you'd be a flight risk, but people with your kinda money, Mr. Cain, can disappear at a moment's notice. It's a risk. Ya gotta give me somethin' to give them." Nick leaned back in his chair.

"But, I don't have anything to give you," he whined. "I already told you everything. I stayed the night at Brandy's, then went home Saturday morning to Grace's bitchin. Then the next thing I know, the phone's ringing, and it's the alarm company. They told me the building was on fire."

Nick looked through his pad, "Ya know anyone by the name of Eddie Germaine?"

At first, he answered an abrupt no but then stopped to think. "Wait, the name sounds familiar. Why? I don't know where I heard it, but I've heard it before. Who is he?"

Nick pulled out a picture of Eddie, "Does this man look familiar?"

He looked the picture over, "No, should he?"

"Not necessarily," Nick answered. "I'm going for a Root Beer. Ford, you want one? Preston?"

Ford took the hint and walked out with Nick, "Whaddya think?" Nick asked him.

"I watched him close when the two of you were in there alone. I don't think he's lying, but he might be of better use locked up. The real slime might surface if he thinks we think we have our man." Ford shrugged a shoulder.

"I don't know. I couldn't make any lies, but he might be that good. You know, some of those people think they're above it all. Besides, no one's gonna do nothin' to get him out before Monday. He needs to reflect on his sins, man." He put in a couple more quarters, and another came tumbling down.

He handed the drink to Ford. "Thanks," Ford popped the top, took a couple of swigs, and turned to Nick. "I know what you're saying about Preston possibly manipulating the situation. He's too much of a puss to be that practiced. He doesn't know anything; I'd bet lunch on it."

Nick went back in and handed Preston a soft drink, "Where were we?"

"You asked me if I knew the man in the picture, and I told you I didn't. Detective, how much longer is this going to go on? I'm exhausted."

"Preston, I got good news and bad. Your choice as to which one comes first."

The fear had turned to exhaustion which turned into aggravation, "I don't care."

Nick went on, "I'll give you the good first. The interview is over for the night; the bad news is you're here until Monday morning. Since you'll have time, you can think over anything you might have seen or heard. Something I might be interested in. See you Monday morning."

"Shit, I want to call my lawyer." It was the straw that broke his back. Preston didn't humble well.

"See ya Monday." Nick left.

Hannah was waiting for him to get home, heard the car pull up, and the engine cut off. Naked, she positioned herself in the bed with the sheets draped seductively, revealing the right amount of skin to be arousing. She heard him as he plodded up the stairs.

Nick's mind was on the interview. Over and over, Preston's answers played like a loop of audio while an association between the verbal and non-verbal language filled in details. Perhaps Hannah had been right. The more Nick got to know Preston, the more he was convinced the little man didn't have the spine. Trying to weasel a way out would've been closer to Preston's style. According to most who knew him, it would've been closer to his practice. Regardless, Nick still felt neither the fire nor the murder had anything to do with Leonard Cardoza. It would've been too easy; instead, someone wanted the police to assume it was Cardoza. Nick knew he'd have a helluva time trying to get Seth to look anywhere else. He was like a pit bull; once he was convinced that he knew the facts, anything else was moot, and it was exactly how he felt about Cardoza.

Quietly he opened the door. It hadn't been that late, but the house looked battened down for the night. The room had a soft glow of candles. She was a vision of beauty, almost angelic. The light of the candles illuminated the sheen of her hair. Her irresistible pouty lips were a kiss just waiting to happen. She had a lusty twinkle in her eyes, which let him know that there was no escape in no uncertain terms; the adventure was just beginning.

He stood at the foot of the bed and stared into her eyes, then studied the lines of her body beneath the sheets as his clothes dropped piece by piece on the bedroom floor. He felt his heart race creating a hot flush feeling that passed through his body like a wave. She was deliciously intoxicating.

As he pulled her to him, she wrapped her legs around his waist. The plans she had made as she prepared for his return home had been perfectly orchestrated, and the night proved to be filled with hours of passionate touches, kisses, and love. As she drifted into slumber, she whispered, "I love you," He pulled her even closer.

"I love you, too."

Sunday morning came fast. Hannah awoke to knocks on her door. "Hannah," the voice called out. Knock, knock, knock again. This time even louder, "Hannah!" It was Michelle's voice. Hannah quickly looked over at Nick, who was sound asleep.

"I'm coming, hold on," She grabbed a tee and quickly put it on. She could hear Michelle breathing outside the door. She unlocked the door and barely cracked it. "Is something wrong? Are you okay?"

"It's my dad." She was panicked. "He left. His bag is gone, and he didn't sleep in his bed. Where'd he go?"

At first, Hannah went blank, not knowing what to say, but the door pulled from behind just as she started to answer. "I'm right here, darlin'."

She hugged him and looked up at him. "Don't do that again. You scared me."

"I'm sorry I didn't mean to scare you." He gave her an exaggerated wink.

"That's okay. I'm just glad you're okay." She squeezed him tighter.

Hannah was waiting for some kind of question regarding her dad sleeping in his girlfriend's room, but it didn't come up.

The three of them climbed into Hannah's bed and turned on the T.V.. There was an Evangelical program on which Hannah immediately changed.

Michelle looked over at Hannah. "How come you don't go to Mass?"

Nick scolded, "Michelle, that's rude and none of ya business ta boot.

"That's okay. It's a good question." She pondered the thought. "I don't know; I just don't. Why do you want to go?"

"Yeah."

Her dad thumped her on the head. "Yeah? What's this, yeah? How bout yes, ma'am, huh? Besides Michelle, I promised your memaw I'd be back for dinna and Mass. It means so much to her. You wouldn't wanna go an' disappoint her, huh, squirt?"

Hannah was feeling guilty. She hadn't thought about the church thing before. "I tell ya what, Michelle. I promise next time you're here on a Sunday; I'll take you to Mass. Deal?"

Michelle smiled, "Deal."

Nick hurried Michelle along, and they bid farewell. They had an hour to get across the lake, pick up his mother and make it to Mass. It was going to be a tall order. Hannah brought Lauren home. Michelle's comment played on her. She started wondering why she never went to church. It was an interesting question; she didn't have an answer other than "just cuz." She would change that today. She had a brilliant idea.

She turned her car around and headed for Bogalusa. She wondered how good Joshua was at preaching. She had only passed by the church once before and wasn't exactly sure how to get there, but she'd manage.

Hannah slowly passed the church, looking for a place to park. Fortunately, her car was so small she found a spot where an ordinary-sized vehicle would've had to pass up. She could hear the sound of joyful singing and eased into the church, hoping to blend in since she was late. *Fat chance of that*, she thought. Hers was the only white face in the congregation. Everyone noticed when she entered, even the preacher.

One of the ushers handed her a service bulletin and found her a seat right in front. All eyes watched as she made her way to the front pew.

Joshua went through the weekly announcements, births, deaths, injuries, sickness, and the like. At the end of the list, he addressed the congregation. "Can we give Sister Hannah a warm Holy Grace welcome?"

The entire church shouted, "Welcome, Sister Hannah." She could feel the heat rise to her cheeks, knowing full well they'd be red as cherries. Now she knew why she didn't come to church. It took a few minutes, but she gained composure and vowed she would get even with him if it were the last thing she ever did.

Apart from the barrage of "amen brother" and "Praise Jesus," his sermon was excellent. He had a way of bringing Scripture into everyday life. The sermon was about, "Everyone's special, We're all His Children." A large lump developed in her throat; she held back the tears. He moved her. It made her look at her life. For the first time in a long while, she felt a sense of belonging, even if she was the only white person in the congregation.

At the end of the service, she filed out with the rest of the crowd. When she got to the reverend, he hugged her, "Hannah, it's so good to see you. What a wonderful surprise. Can you stay awhile?"

"Sure." She hung around.

"Well, Miss Hannah," a friendly voice followed a warm hand on her shoulder.

She turned; it was Bettina. "Hi. How are you?"

"Girl, what you doin' in Bogalusa?" She, too, hugged Hannah.

They chatted for a few minutes. Bettina introduced her to her husband and two children. The church had cleared out, and the good reverend was at her side.

He was genuinely glad to see her; it showed all over his face. "How have you been?"

"Fine," she answered. "But the real question is, how are you?"

"Ah, I see you heard. I'm okay. What do they say shaken, not stirred?" She followed him to the back of the church, where he removed his preacher garb that he had over his clothes. She averted her eyes when he started to remove the robe. He laughed. "What? You didn't think I had pants on under my robe?"

Her face turned beet red; nonetheless, she put her hand on her hip and, with a sassy smirk, said, "I didn't come all this way to Bogalusa to have you pick on me. Here I am, trying to get a little religion, visiting a friend, and what do I get?" She smiled through her pretense.

"It is so good to see you." He'd been smiling from the moment he saw her come out of the church. "You want to go get something to eat?"

"Actually, I was thinking of going to my uncle's. You're welcome to come along." Seeing the look of disappointment on his face, she changed her mind. "Heck, I can see him anytime. Please, I'd love to go to lunch with you." Her words sparked a glisten in his smile.

He took her to the local Western Sizzlin' where she could splurge to heart's content on the food bars. Her palette was not accustomed to family-style food bars. It was an adventure, but she enjoyed his company. They talked about his church, the people, and then the sermon. She told him what had led up to her coming to church, and as she unraveled the story, something inside burst like a dam with a breach. From nowhere, tears started flowing down her cheeks. Her deep inner pain was bubbling up from within; she had to get out of there before she made a scene.

He paid the bill and joined her outside. They sat in her car, and he held her while she poured out her soul. "I-I feel so alone." She could hardly catch her breath. "You said I'm never," she gasped, "a-lone." She looked down, grabbing a tissue from her purse. She looked at him with question and hope. "Is it true, the part about calling me by name and knowing the number of hairs on my head, or is it just a quaint thought?" She had difficulty speaking through the sobs, but he sat there listening. "If He loves me so much, why has He let me h-hurt so bad?" She swallowed hard as she felt her insides were about to pour out.

He patted her hand and leaned in closer to her. "God has a plan. We maybe don't understand it, and sometimes it seems awfully unfair, but Hannah, He's right there with you. *That* you've got to believe, in those darkest times, it's our faith in our Heavenly Father that pulls us through. I don't pretend to have the answers; I just believe. All I have is my faith which I'm offering to share with you."

He offered to drive her car, but she followed him. She sat on the sofa. Her eyes were red, and her nose stuffed up. "I'm sorry. I don't know what came over me." She continued to wipe her eyes and nose. "Can I use your bathroom?"

While she was washing her face and looking to see the damage caused by her sudden fit of hysteria, he put a pot of coffee on and found a box of Kleenex. He had a feeling there was more to come.

Coming back in somewhat composed, she said, "Joshua, I'm so sorry." She sat, and they visited for a while longer over coffee and Oreos.

Relaxed on the sofa, Joshua told her all about what had been going on with Latisha's father and the threats he had made when he had him arrested. He also told her about the incident at Latisha's house the night before the note at the shelter. "Since then, I've had a lot of hang-up calls. I don't think it's anything worth worrying about. Besides, I've kept Claude, our sheriff, informed."

Hannah turned sideways to face him. "How's Latisha doing? I haven't seen her lately." As though making a mental note, she said, "I need to."

"She's doing pretty good. You made a big impact on her. She showed me the picture she made. Pretty good suggestion. It's helped her feel more in control; how 'bout you?" He held her hand.

"How about me, what?" She started to get defensive.

He didn't back off. "Have you drawn any pictures lately? Maybe practice what you preach."

"Doesn't work on adults, " she said matter-of-factly.

Her body started tensing, and the barrier was going up fast. Joshua moved on to other subjects. Eventually, they got around to the murder. She caught him up to speed on the progress, Preston's arrest, and the phone call. He had seen the coverage when the news team speculated about the plea bargain.

"By the way," she asked, "Did my dad ever talk to you about a guy named Leonard Cardoza?" She held her breath for the answer as he thought.

"Nope, not familiar. Why? Was that the guy Preston and John Harris tried to work out some deal? Maybe not."

She told him about the note and then about his planner and the Upperline lunch with L.C.

Joshua shook his head. "Ya got me there, don't know."

They talked well into the afternoon. Hannah found it to be peaceful. It was hard to imagine that only a mile away, if that, people were living in squalor and filth. They talked about Latisha's world; it was common ground for both of them. He carefully went over what he had witnessed the night he had stopped in. Hannah confirmed his findings were not a one-time incident. She described a similar situation the day she had visited Latisha. The only difference was that her mother was passed out in the bedroom. They turned the television on to watch the news.

"As soon as this is over, I gotta bolt. I didn't realize how late it was." She seemed preoccupied.

They watched in silence. Preston's picture flashed to the corner of the screen while the newscaster told the story.

She slid down into the sofa and, out of the blue, began to recite her story. "We had decided to move in together." She looked straight ahead blankly. "We were planning on getting married in the spring. Davis had already left for work."

The tears were building up in her eyes, and the bile pushed up into her throat. She put the Kleenex to her eyes. "The doorbell rang. It was Peter, Davis' older brother and one of the senior partners of the agency. He had a file with him. It was a big account. I mean really big, a career-maker all by itself. He handed the file to me. 'It's yours.' He said. I was on top of the world. I sat on the sofa. I thought, wow, I've made it. As I was looking it over, he sat and moved close to me, putting his hand on my knee."

Hannah's body began to tremble. "I stopped reading and pleasantly asked what he was doing. After all, he was one of the partners, and he had just dropped a huge account in my lap; otherwise, I wouldn't have been as nonchalant about the whole thing. 'You want the account?' He asked. I said, of course. Then he told me there was a price to pay for it. I was shocked. I handed the file back to him and told him I didn't want it that bad; he could give it to someone else. He told me not to be so childish and that my decision to decline posed a whole new set of problems. By this time, I was piping mad and insulted." She could feel herself getting more fidgety and becoming increasingly nervous.

"I told him I couldn't believe he was acting like that, and if he didn't have respect for me, he should at least have respect for his brother. I told him to leave, but he refused. I had never had someone defy me so emphatically, and I got outraged. Again, I told him to get out. He said, 'You just couldn't play by the rules, could you?' His voice was mean, condescending, and threatening. I got scared. 'No, you think you're better than the rest of them.' By this time, I had moved well across the room. He got up and walked toward me. He had a menacing look in his eyes. I wanted to scream but couldn't. I guess the fright of it all rendered me paralyzed. It took everything I had to charge toward the door. He grabbed my arm, slapped me across the face, and then threw me to the ground. I couldn't believe it was happening. He was on top of me and ripped my blouse. I fought harder. He slapped me again and told me to shut up. He forced himself on top of me, grabbing my body. He squeezed my breasts; he knew he was hurting me. His teeth were clenched together, and when he spoke, it was guttural and disgusting. With each painful thrust, he growled even more demeaning utterances. I felt like I was being ripped apart. When he finished, he got up and left, taking the file on his way out."

She sat there. As she spoke, he saw the pain in her eyes. She turned her head away, "The weird of it is, I feel guilty. Logically I know I did nothing wrong, but still, I felt guilty. What if I hadn't been so eager to accept the file? I still wonder if there was some way I sent the wrong signals."

He turned her head back toward him, "Hannah."

She looked down; she felt ashamed.

He touched her chin, tipping her head back, and looked her in the eyes. He could see the betrayal she held inside. He held her tightly. "I'm sorry you went through that."

Her body was still tense, but he could feel her slowly letting go.

"Have you told anyone besides me? What about the New York police?"

"No. No one."

He pulled back from her and looked deep into her eyes. "That's a horrible weight for your heart to bear."

She started to put her head down. He lifted her chin. He tilted his head and slowly came toward her, delicately pressing his lips to hers, and she welcomed the affection pulling away enough to unbutton the front of her dress. "Am I being too forward?" He didn't say a word, but his eyes said it all. Maybe it was the emotional impact or a deep desire he'd had since meeting her, whatever; he welcomed her invitation, and they moved into his bedroom.

Gradually they began to reveal the hidden more secret parts of their bodies. The intensity of the moment steered them into each other's arms and the warmth known only to lovers. It was beautiful. Afterward, they lay quietly, refusing to let words destroy the moment.

It was still light outside. Hannah figured she better leave before nightfall as the road back to Covington could be dangerous, especially in the dark. He walked her out to the car. "Been thinkin' 'bout that L.C. thing you asked me. The only thing I can come up with, darlin', is an appointment your dad had with your Aunt Lizzie. They went to lunch, but I don't know where. Ya think the L.C. could be Lizzie Cain and not Leonard Cardoza?"

She touched his nose with her finger and sweetly retorted, "I wish. But it's Lizzie Delahoussaye, and that would be L.D., not L.C., but thanks for the try." With a flirty wave, she drove off.

The whole way home, Hannah re-lived the passion and beauty they shared. Oddly enough, she felt no guilt. Somewhere inside, she knew it would never happen again, and that was okay. It didn't redefine her relationship with Nick; Hannah felt confident he was the one, and eventually, they would marry and start a family of their own. No, the intimacy shared with Joshua was a one-time thing, but very, very precious. Their time together crossed any boundary she had ever experienced. It transcended the physical plane connecting on a more spiritual level, like the coupling of souls.

As Joshua lay still in his bed with his eyes closed, he could feel her presence. Her scent was still in the air; the fragrance of her perfume filled the air with a touch of gardenia. Her kiss was still on his lips; he could almost feel the faint tickle. The back door creaked open; he wondered what she had forgotten, or did she come back for an encore. He could hear her soft footsteps gently make their way back to his room. He sunk deeper into his bed, waiting to hear her voice call to him. Silence. He waited another moment but gave in to temptation.

His curiosity was peaked. He opened his eyes and sat up. Before him, at the foot of his bed, stood a stranger. He had a cold empty stare. Joshua had never seen the man before.

"What do you want?"

The stranger stood there silent.

Joshua pointed to the watch on his dresser.

The man stared straight into the preacher's eyes. He brought his right hand up from his side. Joshua never even heard the gun go off. Everything was still, silent in an unnatural way, peaceful. His body fell back in the bed. His chest burned with intensity, but the pain vanished as quickly as it came. Memories of the afternoon ran through his mind. He could see her smile and the sparkle in her eyes. He turned his thoughts to the journey that beckoned him. He could feel his spirit ascend to a radiant tunnel of light. It was time to go home. He closed his eyes for the last time.

A BEACH FROLIC

reston had whined so much that the officer at the jail figured he better get in touch with Nick, or no one would have any peace.

The shrill of his phone made him jump. "Shit!" He grabbed his side.

"Nicholas!" His mother had a different name for him with each of her moods, and this mood was disapproval. Anytime he might have a slip of the tongue, she would lash out with a stern, "Nicholas!" She rarely just called him Nick; it was usually Nicky if not bae, sugar, or dawlin'.

"Alright, Ma." He looked at her apologetically.

"Messina here," he answered the phone. The officer apologized for the call, but Preston had ranted and raved, saying he had vital information and wanted to speak with him right away, hence the call. Nick said he was on his way.

Usually, he would've put off seeing a suspect until the following day, but this gave him the excuse he wanted to be with Hannah. As soon as Mass and Sunday dinner with his mom were over, he headed for the Northshore.

It was a picturesque evening, not a cloud in the sky. Tiny twinkles littered the sky like diamonds. Nick felt like a school kid; his stomach tied in knots in anticipation of being with her. He couldn't help the broad smile that came over his face. It was good to be in love, he thought.

Everything looked relatively quiet at the St. Tammany Parish jail. He thought, what a contrast, compared to Central Lock-Up in New

Orleans, which was a zoo, morning, noon, and night with a constant backdrop of yelling, cursing, screaming, and crying. The Big Easy had its share of card-carrying crazies, not to mention all the folks that caught up in the chaos while on vacation. He stopped for a minute to shoot the breeze with the officer managing the front desk. Again, the officer apologized for the inconvenience.

"Like I said, no problem. It comes with the territory, don't sweat it." He patted the officer on the back and headed down the hallway.

"Where the hell have you been, Detective?" Preston couldn't even wait for Nick to sit. "You know you asked me about that person Edward Germaine? I've been thinking and thinking. I finally figured out why the name sounded familiar."

Nick waited. "Well?"

"I have to get out of here. Do something. I can't stand it. The smell is disgusting." Preston looked pathetic.

"For tonight, as I told ya, my hands are tied. I'm gonna get on it first thing in the mornin', now tell me about Eddie."

Preston could be obstinate. "First, get me out of here."

Nick was getting aggravated. " It don't work that way. Personally, I don't care if ya tell me tonight or tomorrow. One way or the other," with a smirk, "ya gonna tell me."

It looked like Preston was sulking; he wouldn't talk.

Nick got up and was halfway down the hall when Preston shouted for him to come back, which he did.

The two men sat face to face. Reluctantly he began whining, "My wife left me."

Nick shook his head, "What's that got to do with anything. Jesus, Preston, are you tryin' to piss me off, or is it you're just plain stupid?" He started to get up again.

"No. Wait. The point was if you let me finish, my wife went to Gulf Shores. We have a condo there. While I was on the phone with her, she mentioned we had a new neighbor, Edward Germaine. This Germaine character may be the same guy you're looking for."

"When was this?" He had Nick's attention.

"Friday. Friday morning." Preston answered.

"I assume you have the address of your condo or the name of it?"

Preston shrugged, "It's probably in my wallet, the address, that is, but it's real easy to find. It's two doors down from the Holiday Inn. It's a corner unit, number 201. If you want, I can take you there."

"Not from here; you can't." He got up to leave, but Preston grabbed his arm, and, for once, he felt kinda sorry for the poor bastard. "I'll do whatever I can to getcha out in the mornin'."

From one of the offices, he called Seth. He told him what Preston had said, and they decided Seth would get in touch with the Gulf Shores police department while Nick would meet them at the condo."

He called Hannah. After a warm greeting, he jumped right into the crux of the matter. "By any chance, do you know where Preston's condo is in Gulf Shores?"

She sounded surprised, "Yeah, why?"

"Long story."

"Are you planning a get-away? If so, you don't need to use Preston's; we have one, same place."

Figures, he thought. "You want to give me directions?"

"Nick, what's this all about?"

"I don't have time right now, doll; it'll have to be later." He was rushing her off the phone.

"Okay, but then you'll tell me?"

"Promise." She quickly rattled off the same directions Preston had given him. "Thanks. Love ya." He hung up the phone.

In a flash, he was out of the jail and on his way to Gulf Shores. There was a burst of adrenalin running through his veins like he was on the runner's block waiting for the pop of the starting gun. Perhaps Preston was right. Maybe this was the same guy, and if so, they could get him to testify against Cardoza or whoever the guy was that ordered the hit.

Just as described, the building was two doors down from the Holiday Inn and easy to spot. The Gulf Shores police were parked on the side of the highway, obviously waiting for him. They had already contacted the property management office to ascertain the names of the condo owners on the second floor. There were six: Preston, Tyler, Lizzie, Nate, and two non-family members owned the other two. From the parking lot, they could see lights on in only two condos; one was Preston's and the one next door.

The Gulf Shores police had already obtained the warrant for the arrest of Edward Germaine. All that was left was finding him. They knocked on the door of 203. They could hear someone coming to the door, then after a series of clicks, the door opened.

An attractive middle-aged woman answered. Her voice was raspy. "Can I help you?"

Nick stood there perplexed, embarrassed, and pissed. "Uh, We're looking for Edward Germaine. Is he in?"

"I'm sorry, officers, you have the wrong condo. There's no one here but me. Try checking 205 or 206."

He couldn't believe Preston had led them on this wild goose chase, but, more so, he couldn't believe he'd fallen for it. "Sorry to have bothered you, ma'am."

He checked on the two rentals, and as far as the management offices knew, both were vacant. On the way down in the elevator, he apologized to the other two officers. "Man, I thought I had good info." He had been totally humiliated.

The door to the elevator opened, and before him stood a tall, dark-haired man waiting. Their eyes met. The dark-haired man suddenly realized who he was looking at and started to run. Nick drew his gun, ordering the man to stop.

As they secured the cuffs, Nick began to read him his rights. "Edward Germaine, you are being arrested for the murder of Mr. Tyler Cain. You have the right to remain silent —" It felt good, so good, to finally make headway. He made a mental note to get Preston out as soon as possible. The little snake had been right.

It had been a long night. The drive back to Covington seemed like an eternity. He didn't like to transfer suspects. For some reason, it made him unsettled. He was glad when they arrived at the jail.

Nick could hardly keep his eyes open by this time but knew he'd better get the paperwork done. There would be time for sleep later. After a little over an hour, he had finished the report, and up until then, the only thing Eddie had to say was, "Lawyer." So until the lawyer had crossed the lake, all they could do was sit and wait. He went out to his car to catch a few z's.

Just after daybreak, there was a light tap on the window. He nearly jumped out of his skin. Seth stood there with a big smile, a big cup of coffee, and a bag of biscuits. "Time to get up, little Mary Sunshine."

His back ached from sleeping in the car. As he turned his head, his neck cracked like the sound of a string of firecrackers, pop, pop, pop. He was stiff. "I feel like I've been run over by a Mack truck."

"Padna, you look like it too. Ya want this coffee?" Seth leaned on the hood of the car.

Nick got out of the car, and between sips of coffee and bites of biscuits, he ran down the night's activities, bringing Seth up to speed.

"Perp say anything yet," Seth asked.

"Yeah, Lawyer." He took another long sip of his coffee.

A few minutes later, Ford from the Covington police department pulled up. Nick had left word on his voice mail when he was en route to Gulf Shores. He had forgotten to call him when he returned.

"Got your message, Messina." Ford nodded to Seth, and the three of them waited together.

Despite the circumstances, it was peaceful. The morning had broken, and the sun was a brilliant orange contrasting with a sky painted in deep lavender and multiple shades of blue. As soon as eight o'clock hit, Nick excused himself and made his way to the D.A.'s office. He'd promised Preston, and he was going to make every effort to keep his word.

He explained the series of events to the assistant D.A., and the wheels of freedom began to turn for Preston. Nick was pretty sure the white-collar charges would stick. He returned to the jail. When Nick arrived, he noticed the green MG. He picked up his pace.

Hannah was charming her way into seeing Preston just he walked through the door. "Hey, doll." He kissed her tenderly. "You look beautiful; you're glowing. Something's different. You do something new?" The corners of her mouth turned up.

"No. I was just asking this nice officer if he could bend the rules, just a little, and let me see my uncle."

Nick asked the officer if it would be a problem. A click and buzz signaled the okay. As they walked down the hall to see Preston, she quizzed him on the night and commented on how tired he looked. He said things had gone exceptionally well, and he had good news for Preston.

There was a spark in Preston's eyes when he saw the two of them. Through tears, he said, "Hannah, it's so good to see you. I was beginning to think everyone had forgotten about me."

Nick cut him off, "I got good news for ya. It looks like you're getting out in the next coupla hours. Don't know what the New Orleans D.A. is gonna do, but more than likely, they'll be after you again. I hope you've learned from all of this to cooperate."

Nick left Hannah and Preston to visit while checking on Eddie's progress.

Eddie's attorney had finally shown up so the questioning could begin.

The attorney began, "From what my client tells me, y'all don't have much. You're spitting in the wind." His wrists rested on the papers.

"Don't think so," Ford said. "We've got two clean prints from your client in the vic's car and a DNA match from under the vic's fingernails. Seems like we have a lot to me. I think a jury will think so, too, especially since your client has a rap sheet as long as my arm. The D.A. might work out a deal if your client hands over Cardoza."

Eddie flew off the handle with animated arm gestures. "Cardoza? Whatcha lookin' at Cardoza for? I don't know nothin' about him."

"Gimme a break, Eddie." Nick tossed his pen across the room. "Everyone knows you work for Cardoza. Ya gonna let the big man get off with nothing while you fry? If it were me padna, I'd be singin'."

Eddie threw his hands in the air, exasperated. "There ain't nothin' to sing; I don't know whatcha talkin' bout."

Nick leaned back in his chair. "Lemme paint you da pic-cha. C&S won't crawl into bed with Cardoza on accounta Tyler Cain—Mr. Cain thinks your boss is too sleazy. Cardoza figures if he gets rid of Mr. Cain, he can muscle his way past the others. So, he tells you to whack Cain, put his body in the Julia Street buildin' an' torch it. Sound like a familiar bedtime story to you?" Nick's patience was wearing out.

"Man, you been smokin' ya socks, Detective." He leaned forward, slapping his hand on the table. "I'm telling ya Cardoza had nothin', nothin', ya hear me, to do with Cain getting' whacked." He leaned back in his chair.

"Alright, wise guy," Nick pointed at him with a grimace.

Ford got right up in Eddie's face. "We really don't care who ordered it; we got your signature all over the place." Eddie shrugged his shoulders.

Nick got up and started to walk out of the room. He turned at the door. "Ya know, Eddie, you're one stupid piece of shit. If it were me, I sure as hell wouldn't fry for no one, but hey, my mama didn't raise no fool." He turned his back to leave.

They rotated in and out of the little room, hoping that a one-on-one might gain Eddie's confidence. So far, it hadn't worked. They returned him to holding. They decided to let it rest for a while and try again later. After hearing about the DNA and fingerprints, his attorney watched the show without a peep.

They sat down to re-hash the evidence during the break for what seemed to be the hundredth time. They had him dead to right. They knew it had to be a hit, Eddie, himself, had nothing to gain to knock off Tyler. The challenge was getting him to admit who hired him. Cardoza had motive, the muscle, and the money to make it happen. Nick still had an uneasy feeling that it was closer to home. He had been told more than once that he was the only one who thought that, and there wasn't a reasonable explanation, so to drop it and work with what they had.

Ford suggested, "Maybe y'all can get someone to i.d. Cordoza from the restaurant he and Mr. Cain went to."

Rubbing his stomach, Seth grinned, "I can handle that m'boy."

Seth asked where Eddie was going when they nabbed him at the elevator. Nick said Eddie was staying at a friend's condo, and the other units appeared empty. They figured Eddie was staying in 206. There were a couple of shirts and pants hanging in the closet along with other items one would expect someone to take when going to the beach.

"You sure that's where he was staying?" Seth asked.

"Yeah, it had all his stuff," Nick answered.

"Did y'all check with the owner? He could've been the one to put out the hit."

Nick told him they'd called the owner, but the owner said the management office handled everything and to check with them. The guy at the management office said he had no record of it, but it could've been one of the other managers. To say the least, it was messy, and none of it set well. The right hand didn't know what the left hand was doing. Nick told Seth he'd had both owners' names run, and they were squeaky clean, not so much as a parking ticket. He figured Eddie must have picked the lock or stolen keys when someone wasn't looking.

They sat quietly, each in their own thoughts. Nick decided to take a break and look for Hannah. According to the officer, they released Preston, and Hannah had taken him with her. He said it hadn't been more than thirty minutes before. Nick tried her phone, no luck. When he called the house, Belle said they had been there but had taken a ride to The Pearl, but Hannah had instructed her to tell him no matter what time it was to come over that there'd be a key in the plant on the right side of the door.

As they hung up, it hit him. He went and requested the envelope with Eddie's personal effects. He went through them. There were only three keys, two to the car and one that had the appearance of a door key.

Seth and Ford were still in the break area. Nick tossed the key on the table. "If this is what I think it is, then the owner or the managers are liars, or someone else gave him the key. I'm gonna check it out."

"Nick, while you're at the beach, I'm going back to NOLA and get a photo of Cardoza and one of Mr. Cain and head to the Upperline. Maybe they'll throw me a few crumbs while I'm there. But, before I leave, I need a moment of your time."

Seth suspected Nick was making a change but wanted to hear it from him. They'd been partners for a long time, and the thought of training another partner didn't thrill him.

As they were walking out, Seth shook his head at Nick.

"What?"

"What, nothing. That's what." Seth answered.

"Well, if it ain't nothin', then stop lookin' at me." Nick retorted.

"Man, of all people, I thought you were my friend. Then I hear from a nobody at the station that you're making a move. Piss me off, Nicky, piss me off. The least you coulda done was tell me. Man, I know you're hot on the skirt; I don't blame you. But I figured you woulda told me first."

"I did tell ya. I told ya I was thinkin' about comin' over here."

Seth stopped and looked at him with a downcast expression, not his usual jovial self. "To live, not that you were leaving the department."

"I ain't signed nothing yet, so there's nothin' to tell." They continued to their cars.

"You let me know before it happens? I don't wanna come in one day, and boom, I have a new partner. Ya know?" By this time, they were at Seth's car.

"Seth, you go get the i.d.; my gut says we're gonna hit paydirt with the key."

Seth pulled off, and Nick started on his way to Gulf Shores. Before he knew it, he had arrived at the complex and pulled into the parking lot. He immediately went to 206 but couldn't get the key in the door. When he finally did, it wouldn't turn. He tried again lifting while he turned the key. Nothing. After several attempts, each with a different twist, he dejectedly admitted it wasn't the key to the door after all.

He leaned against the door and looked down the hall, searching for answers. He walked to 205 tried the key. No good. Then 204, again, no good. He wasn't going to give up that easily. Then he tried 201. Bingo, it worked. He stood at the door, pushed it open, and called in. The room in front of him was dark. The curtains had been drawn, and it didn't look as though anybody was there.

"Jesus, this doesn't make no sense." He ran his hand through his hair. "Why would Eddie have a key to Elizabeth Delahoussaye's condo? Don't make no sense, but it's interesting." It was like a light bulb went off in his head. "Shit, I shoulda seen this all the time. Why the fuck would he have even come to these condos. Coincidence? I don't think so. I'm an idiot. Why didn't I see this?" Thoughts binged through his head like some pinball machine. One idea to the next, and it all started lining up.

He rode back to Covington. About ten minutes outside of Covington, the fatigue hit him, and he couldn't wait to get back to Southern Manor and her arms.

It was just after ten. Nick could tell from the dim light she had her side lamp on, so she was waiting for him or had fallen asleep reading. The days had run together, and it felt like an eternity since he'd been at the house.

She was sitting up in the bed when he walked into the room. Her face had a bright redness from hours of crying. Tears flowed from her eyes.

"What's wrong, doll?" He hated to see her so upset and held her as she sobbed, figuring she'd tell him what was wrong when she was ready. Gently he stroked her hair. He could feel her nuzzle closer. He wanted so desperately to take away her pain.

Through muffled words and sobs, she said, "Joshua's dead."

He had to get his thoughts together and think who Joshua was for a moment. He didn't want to seem uncaring, and she spoke like he knew this person. All Nick could say was, "I'm sorry," and held her tight. He had hoped he could fill in the blanks as she explained the whys and the wherefores of this person's demise.

"Wanna tell me about it?" He had to get the ball rolling.

"After Preston was released, we rode up to Jeremiah's. I could tell something was wrong when I got there. Uncle J. was really upset." Her voice began to tremble. "When Bettina got to the shelter –"

It suddenly dawned on in him, and he interrupted her, "Reverend Delery? When? How?"

"That's what I told you, Nick. Someone shot him last night while he was in bed. When Bettina got to the shelter this morning and found Joshua hadn't gotten there yet, she worried and called the police. They went over and found the door open. I-I can't believe it." He lay down next to her on the bed. Her muffled sobs slowly came to an end.

The next morning came faster than usual. Nick had so much on his mind. He wanted to first run down Mrs. Elizabeth Delahoussaye. He was most interested in what she had to say about why her condo key had been in Eddie's pocket. At the same time, Ford would approach Eddie about Mrs. Delahoussaye and see if there was any waiver on his part. He still couldn't put the whole thing together just yet. A few more whittles, and it would begin to take form.

Liz lived on Octavia Street in the heart of the Garden District in uptown New Orleans. Her home was impressive, even by Garden District standards. Due to her ex-husband's indiscretions, Liz was able to end up with just about everything plus substantial alimony. She reveled in her elite style of life and had very little time for those outside her station, a trait that would grind on every nerve in Nick's body.

He pulled in front of the massive home, knowing full well his vehicle would be more than conspicuous and would leave her neighbors with enough gossip for a month. As he pushed the doorbell, he could hear the deep, resonant chime. Through the beveled glass door, he could see a figure moving toward the front.

"Yes, may I help you?" The gentleman's voice had a sophisticated British accent.

"Detective Messina with NOPD. Is Mrs. Delahoussaye here?"

"Yes, sir, I believe she is." He opened the door and ushered him in. "Please wait here; I will let her know you are here."

He waited in the foyer. While elegant, he couldn't help but notice the house's cold, inhospitable feel. It was equally as impressive as Southern Manor but lacked the warmth and welcoming charm. He could vaguely hear voices, then the sound of footsteps, gradually drawing nearer.

"Detective, how good to see you again." Her tone was drippingly sweet and way-too rehearsed for his taste, "What can I do for you? Please come in."

They took a seat in the parlor.

"Mrs. Delahoussaye, do you know a man by the name of Eddie Germaine?"

"Isn't that the man your partner already asked me about?"

"Yes, ma'am. I find it strange that you don't know him because he had a key to your condo in Gulf Shores when we arrested him. We got him exiting the elevator at the complex." He watched; she didn't flinch.

"Well, how on earth did he get a key to my condominium? I, too, find that very strange, Detective." She acted like she was thinking. "He must've stolen it from the Management office. I will have to tell my brother about all of this. It could be a dangerous situation. You see, many of our family members own condos in the same complex. We could all be in danger. I was at the condo all weekend, alone. A woman alone, it could've been horrific; I would've been an easy target."

Nick pulled out a picture of Eddie and showed it to her. "Have you seen this man?"

"No, can't say I have. Is that the man you arrested? What was his name, Eddie? How did y'all catch him?"

She didn't bother to ask why they arrested him, only how. Nick found it curious. He believed she knew way more than she was letting on.

"Now, when did you say you went to Gulf Shores?" Nick had decided to ask a few more questions and then be on his way. He needed to get a better read on the situation but didn't want to come on too strong. It needed to be amiable so she'd let her guard down and maybe slip. He wanted her too comfortable.

"Friday afternoon. I spent the morning with Preston, running errands here and there, and then took off to the beach. It was perfect timing for happy hour." She gave him a flirty smile. He had a feeling she was the kind of woman who acted prissy and soft, but without the pretense, was naturally 100% bitch.

"Ya know, you're right. A woman like you all alone on the beach—" He slowly shook his head, "Prime target. I know you said you went alone, but were any of your friends at the beach? Like did you run into any of them at happy hour?" clicking his ballpoint pen rapidly, making her a bit uneasy.

"Um, I saw a few people I knew, but I wouldn't call any of them friends, Detective."

He could tell she was getting tired of the question-and-answer game. Too bad, he thought he'd ask a few more, but not enough to really piss her off. "Any strange guys buy you a drink? Anyone scoping you out that you could tell? I mean, being you were alone and all, hey, you couldn't blame a guy, could ya? See anyone like that?"

"No, not really." He could see her thinking. The wheel of deceit was spinning fast and furiously; he had seen it many times over and could identify it right off the bat.

Playfully he asked, "Not really? Hm, is that like kinda sorta?"

She didn't understand, cocking her head to one side.

"Ya know, people are all the time sayin', 'kinda sorta, but not really?'"

"Oh." She nodded like she understood. "There was one man. Let me see that picture again."

Nick handed her the photo.

"It could possibly be him. The light was dim. I'm not sure. He said he was staying in a condo at the end of the same floor as my place. That's scary. He didn't buy me a drink or anything. I remember thinking it best I leave before he did so we didn't have to ride the elevator together." She rolled her eyes. "Nouveau. You can tell."

"Yeah, I can see where that might be awkward being y'all were on the same floor." He stood up to leave. "Thanks for your help, Mrs. Delahoussaye. Oh, and be sure to have those locks changed. Who knows who Eddie could've given a copy of the key to?"

"Goodbye, Detective."

He couldn't wait to get to Covington and find out what had gone on with Eddie. Ford was in his office buried behind a stack of papers.

"Hey, padna." Nick sat in the empty chair in front of Ford's desk. "Anything shake out with Eddie?"

"Hell no. You?" He answered as he continued to work on a report. Nick waited for him to finish his thought.

Ford looked up. "Okay, what happened?"

"My guess is, before you say anything, hear me out." He punctuated the thought with a raised hand. "I think she's shackin' with Eddie. She neva asked once why we arrested the man, just how we caught him. Ya know why she didn't ask because she already knew why. I don't know if she asked him to do it or if he just did it on his own; whatever, I tell ya, she knows he did it. I wanna have her accounts checked. See if she's taken out large sums of money. It's hard to believe Eddie would do it for a piece of ass without money involved."

Ford started to say something, but Nick interrupted, "Wai, wai, wait. I almost forgot. She also made a point of tellin' me about some guy lookin' at her durin' happy hour. She says she's not interested, rolls her eyes, an' says it's on accounta he's nouveau. But here's the part, the bitch is lyin' cause there was no one in any of the condos except hers and Preston's."

"Are ya done?" Nick nodded his head to the affirmative. "You think you could get Eddie to roll on her?"

Nick shrugged his shoulders, biting his bottom lip with a contemplative look in his eyes. "Don't know until I try, right? I also want to talk to Preston to see what he knows. From all I can tell, he and Liz seem to be pretty tight. Course, I don't think either one has a loyal bone in their body."

Ford followed him into the jail. Nick waited for Eddie in one of the interrogation rooms. He was debating how to handle him – like best buds or flies on shit. It would depend on Eddie's tone, he thought.

The first thing Eddie did when he entered the room was go for a cigarette. Nick could've played it either way. Like everywhere else, there was a no-smoking policy, but sometimes the officers let it slide. Nick reached in his pocket and pulled out a book of matches, and handed it to him.

"Thanks." Eddie took a long drag off of the cigarette.

"Lizzie wanted to know how you were getting along? I told her pretty fine, but she really ought to come see you since she gotcha into the whole mess."

Eddie's eyes flashed in his direction. *Bingo*, Nick thought, *got him now*.

"Who?" Eddie tried to remain calm.

"Liz, Lizzie." Nick locked his hands behind his head and closed his eyes. "Your squeeze."

"Don't know any Lizzie."

Nick leaned forward in a whisper, "Aw, c'mon. I know all about it; you don't have to lie to me, padna. I know how it is with them rich bitches. Believe me, I know firsthand."

"Yeah, I heard some of the guys' talkin'. They say you hosin' the daughter, right?" Eddie gave him a sly smile. Nick wanted to rip his head off but played the game instead. If anything else didn't come from the conversation, at least he knew what the water cooler gossip was.

Eddie continued. "Man, I dunno what you're talkin about. I got an ol' lady, an' one bitch is enough. Sometimes I can't even deal with her." Eddie popped his jaw, making smoke rings, then blew them away and crushed his cigarette under his heel.

"Hey numbnuts, I know you're lyin'. Ya know how I know, ya had her key in ya pocket. That's where you were goin' when we nabbed ya ass. Now for the last freakin' time – what about Liz, she pay you or did ya give her a freebie to get some of the sweet stuff?"

Eddie sat with his jaw clenched like some kind of vice grip.

Nick could tell he was getting to him. "Look, man, she's playin' ya. You been around long enough, pal, to know when a bitch is playing you. She gotcha to do her dirty work, an' now she walks away free and easy. But you, you lookin' at da needle. You think a woman with that much money can't buy love? I'm sorry, padna, but she ain't gonna pine away for you. All ya gotta do, ma man, is tell me she gotcha to do it. That's it, an' the needle goes away."

Eddie's stern hard look took on a different look, almost pathetic. Nick saw before him a middle-aged man with nothing to his name but the clothes on his back. Up close, he could see the gray roots edging their way out with the rest of the harshly dyed black hair. For years, Eddie had gotten by on his good looks, but that too was passing like all things.

"For grins, Detective, let's say I tell ya whatcha wanna hear. What happens afta that? Eddie played with a piece of thread, balling it up, then straightening it out. He looked up, "Well, *padna?*" He said sarcastically.

"I can't say fa sure, but my best guess is you'd get twenty to life, and she'd get the needle, but it ain't up to me. Who knows, the D.A. might go lighter than that, but you are in St. Slammany, as it's lovingly called. They don't take no shit here, not like N'Awlins. I guess it all depends on what ya can give them. What I do know is if ya go to trial, you won't get no leniency."

Nick sat back in his chair. Eddie would have to make the next move.

"Get da D.A." He stood up and requested to go back to his cell until the D.A. arrived.

Nick put a call into Seth, caught him up on the morning's activities, and made sure he'd be available to pick up Liz following Eddie's confession. While they were on the phone, Seth read Nick his messages. There was one from the Bogalusa police department. As soon as they hung up, he put a call into Bogalusa.

The call had been from the detective investigating the Delery case. He said he found something that might be of interest to him. They had been able to pick up a few identifiable prints. There were several in the kitchen and the bedroom. He went on to tell him it was pretty evident that the reverend had company earlier in the evening before getting shot, as there was evidence in the bed suggesting he had danced the horizontal mambo. The door had several different prints, but one, which was only a partial, was from Eddie Germaine. He said he had gotten word that they had Eddie at St. Tammany jail, which Nick confirmed. The Bogalusa detective said he would be coming down to Covington sometime later in the day.

Nick took a moment to buzz Hannah. It seemed like forever since he'd had quality time with her. He missed her desperately; his heart longed for her and ached in his chest. "Hey, doll."

Playfully Hannah responded, "Wait, give me a second, I recognize the voice, is it –"

Nick interrupted. "I know it seems like foreva. I miss you, too. It's been crazy. You gonna be late tonight?"

"Not if I have a better offer!" She chuckled.

"How 'bout you an' me, dinner and then, um dessert. An' I know exactly what I want for dessert." He paused. "Oh, doll, between you an' me an' na lamp post – ya know the L.C. you've been worried about? Try Lizzie Cain on for size."

"I've heard that somewhere before, but as I said, it's Lizzie Delahoussaye, L.D."

"I dunno; from what I understand, ya pops always referred to her as Cain. Check fa ya self; it's in all the legal documents related to the company. How ya like dem apples? We're not 100% but damn close. Everything is pointin' in that direction."

"Like what?" she quizzed.

"Ain't got time, gotta fly, doll."

"See ya tonight. Be careful, Nick."

"Will do. Love ya."

"I love you, too."

They hung up, and his stomach was doing flips. He still hadn't gotten used to Hannah telling him she loved him, and he hoped he never would.

The Assistant D.A. showed up to negotiate with Eddie. Before heading to the back, Nick filled him in on the situation, including the call from Bogalusa. The A.D.A. said he had seen the newscast and thought they already had their suspect in custody, someone linked to a man that had beaten and raped some little girl.

Nick said the new evidence was linking it to the Tyler Cain murder. The reverend had been one of the key witnesses. He had vital information, and it was predicted his testimony would have been most damaging to the defense.

Eddie was waiting for them. They went through the formalities filling in the forms, informing him of his rights, making sure he knew what he was doing and the ramifications.

"Yeah, yeah, I understand." Eddie impatiently commented. "Now, ya wanna hear or not?"

"Go ahead." The A.D.A. seemed nervous. Nick wondered if he had ever been this close to a murderer before.

"Lemme see, 'bout six months ago, I meet this woman, Liz Delahoussaye. Anyway, we hit it off pretty good. She wanted a roll in na hay, and I wanted someone to support me in the lifestyle I deserved. It was a nice arrangement. She got the wood; I got the dough. We was getting' it on by the pool when her brother walks in. He got all bothered an' went in the house. We cleaned up and went inside. I stayed in the kitchen, but I could hear him.

"He was whinin' 'bout some guy threatenin' to oust him an' how he should have just as much power. He went on and on. He musta messed up real bad cuz he was worried about da law rainin' on his parade. Now, she told him she'd fix it, but he was gonna owe her big. Then they had a few words, an' he left outta there. She's a tough girl; she don't let no one push her around. Don't let the sweet face confuse ya. She's one cold-hearted bitch. So, she says, 'Eddie, what kinda work you do?' An' I tell her—anything she wanted. She lays it on me, ya know. There's this guy causin' all kinda trouble for her an' she needs him outta da way. She asks if I know someone that handles such annoyances, that's what she said. Cold-hearted, right? I said, yeah, I knew someone, how much was she willin' to pay? She said fifty grand, half up front, half afta. I said, for that kinda money, sure I knew someone, and I'd handle the arrangements. Now I don't know if she knew I was gonna do the deed. Women don't wanna think they messin' around with some murderer. But, if ya askin' me if she ordered it, yeah, she most definitely ordered it and paid. Now whatcha give me?" He leaned back in the chair with a cocky grin.

"Not yet. About the crime?" The A.D.A. seemed a lot cooler than before.

"Ya want me to tell ya how I done it?" He seemed aggravated.

"How else would we know you're the one who committed the crime? Maybe you know about it, but maybe you're not the one who did it, and for some reason, you're confessing." The A.D.A. had a face of stone.

He looked at Nick to explain the comment of the A.D.A. "Now, why would I do that? You people, I tell ya."

"Mr. Germaine, continue." The A.D.A. leaned back in his chair and folded his hands on his chest.

"Whateva," he looked totally put out. "I tell Liz I need some info about the guy, like where he works, lives, any habit he might have that would make sense for him to be outta his regular routine, ya know? Somethin' to buy some time between his disappearance an' findin' the body. I tell her my contact don't wanna know the name, makes it too personal. She gives me all the information in a plain brown envelope, includin', get this, a copy of his calendar.

"I see he's got two trips planned, back to back. One to Mississippi an then ta Europe, how convenient. I tell her the guy'll do it Friday night; then he'll bring the body in his car to the airport. She says the airport would be good for the car, but the body needed to be dropped at a construction site on Julia Street. It was a vacant building, and I'd have to get the guy to torch it. I tell her she'd need to pony up more money. She said, fine, how 'bout anotha ten?" He turned his palms up with expression. "I said I thought my friend would go for that, but it would have to be with the upfront payment. So thirty-five before. She thought about it, got up, and handed me a big black athletic bag. She said she added an extra five for me as a management fee an' then told me to leave. She also told me ta meet her at the Gulf Shores condo the followin' Friday an' gave me a key. It went down perfect. I had a friend drop me off at the guy's house. When I got there, I could tell he had company, so I waited in da bushes that run by da porch. Man, I didn't even have to go into the house. Afta his guest leaves, he goes on da back porch. It was easy. I got him from behin' with a wire. I drug him to his car, an' we got the hell outta dodge. I dropped his body at the vacant buildin' an' torched it, then dropped the car at the airport and cabbed it inta town. I tell ya, whadda blaze. Ya could hear it poppin' blocks over. So? I get the deal; I've given you all the information there is to give. Everything ya wanted."

"Yeah, you get the deal." The A.D.A. packed his papers away and left. Nick stayed.

"Okay, Mista Detective, you can call 'em to bring me back." He folded his hands across his chest.

"Nah, not yet. There's one more person who wants to see ya." Nick called the Bogalusa detective into the room. The detective said he had him dead to right, and Bogalusa didn't make deals; his sleazy ass was gonna fry. Nick saw no point in hanging around, so he headed out. When he got to the door, Eddie made a parting comment.

"Hey, Detective, ya know, I could tell da preacher man wasn't used to getting' any cuz, he forgot to close da winda. The breeze would come along, an' the blind would sway just enough to get a peek. Boy, he had himself one sweet piece of ass. She was tight. She, sure enough, rocked his afternoon. Didn't get a look at the face, but I'd know that li'l green MG anywhere!" His eyes darted toward Nick with a cunning evil look, then said, "Hey, padna, I gave you dat one fa free."

Nick left. So many thoughts were going through his head. Was Eddie yanking his chain, or had Hannah really been in the sack with the preacher? He remembered the Bogalusa detective had said there was evidence Rev. Delery had been entertaining, and there were a lot of identifiable fingerprints. Nick didn't know if he really wanted to know.

He found himself rationalizing the whole thing. Before he knew it, he was pulling into Southern Manor. Hannah's car was parked in its usual spot. It had been a hell of a day already. He decided to let sleeping dogs be at least for a while.

A SOUL OF BLACK

I t was good to see her. Nick hugged her tight. "You love me?"

Her smile warmed his heart. Hannah looked deep into his eyes. "Of course I love you. Are you okay? How about something to eat?" He decided right at that moment he didn't want to know if Eddie had been on the level or not. What was important was she loved him. He could see it in her eyes and feel it in her touch.

They spent the rest of the afternoon lazing in a hammock by the pool. Nick told her about going to the condo, finding nothing at first, and then running into Eddie as they got out of the elevator. He told her how they had been in a deadlock. It was all topsy turvy and nothing made sense. And then, miracles of miracles, when he called Southern Manor hoping to reach her, Belle relayed the message about a stashed house key by the door for him, and the light bulb went off. He went back to the P.D. and looked through Eddie's personal effects, and low and behold; there was a key.

"See, doll, cuz of your message about the key; it jogged my mind to see if Eddie had a key to the condo, and we were able to put it all together. If it wasn't for you, who knows?"

His phone went off, startling both of them. It was Seth.

"Nicky, she split."

"Whaddaya mean she split? Shit. Somebody musta called her."

"Nah, I don't think so. Her butler, or whatever he is, says she went to the beach. I called the guys in Gulf Shores, and they'll be waiting for her in the parking lot." Seth sounded exhausted but pumped that maybe they'd be able to put the Cain murder to bed.

"I'd love to be there when it goes down. Keep me posted—"

Hannah interrupted. "What's going on?" She was full of questions. "Who split? This is—"

"Simmer down, girl. Gimme a chance. What happened was Seth went to pick up your aunt, but she was gone by the time he got there. The English butler guy said she'd gone to the beach. Seth called the Gulf Shores P.D., and they're gonna be waiting for her. Whadda surprise. It would be great to see the expression on her face."

"Why don't you call them and tell them to wait until you get there? As long as she doesn't try to take off, just let her go about her regular stuff, then you can be there when it all goes down." She could see he was thinking about it.

As he picked up the phone, she calmly went inside. She hurried to get her purse, jumped in her car, and took off for the beach. She figured by the time he realized what had happened; she'd have a good fifteen to twenty-minute head start. The more she thought about everything Nick had told her about how Lizzie had planned the whole thing so calculated and coldly, the more enraged she became. Lizzie was out for herself, one hundred percent. Hannah had always known that, but this, this was inconceivable. She actually orchestrated the murder of one brother, arranged an attack of sorts on another brother, and then planned to pin it all on her supposedly closest brother, Preston. A sequence of faces flashed through her brain – all those who had been affected by the whole sordid thing – her father, Jeremiah, Joshua, Preston, not forgetting her and her brothers – so many lives altered forever.

Hannah made it to the beach in record time. The Gulf Shores police were discreetly parked across the street, waiting for Nick. She saw Lizzie's car and pulled alongside. In seconds she was in the building and on the elevator. It was the first time she really gave any thought to what she might say or do. She couldn't back down now.

With determination, she knocked on the door.

Lizzie was a little shocked to see Hannah but had always been pretty quick on her feet and recovered in an instant.

"Hannah, darlin', I didn't know you were at the beach. Do come in, Suga." Lizzie turned and walked to the bar, her lavender silk ensemble flowing as she glided. "Can I get you something to drink?"

Hannah was beside herself. "Something to drink? Something to drink?" Her voice jumped an octave.

"What on earth is wrong, dear? Are you alright?" Lizzie raised an arched eyebrow.

"No, Lizzie, I'm not alright. I'm far from alright." Venom dripped from each word. "How can you even ask me that?" Her hands clasped tightly together.

"Child, what are you ranting about? You must not be feeling well."

"What? What about my dad, for one? How could you do that? I know all about it, Lizzie. Everything—" Hannah's voice hitched, and she could feel the tears welling in her eyes.

"Oh, you do?" and she sharply turned. The words graveled out of her with a hideous sound, one that penetrated the very essence of Hannah's soul, causing her to shudder. "You couldn't possibly know what it was like little daddy's girl. Do you really think anyone at C&S ever took you seriously? Grow up, Hannah. Like me, you too are stuck in the Gentleman's Dance at C&S. Face it; a woman has no place at C&S. Never once in all these years was my opinion sought on anything. Not even the color of the office paint. Look at it." She laughed with sickening sarcasm. "They put Nate in some high faluting position. They might as well have hired a monkey. Why I think a trained monkey might have a longer attention span."

"You make me sick!" She backhanded Lizzie across the face.

Lizzie fell to the side but caught herself on the bar and swiftly righted. "I'm sorry you feel that way, dear," she said in a smug tone.

Hannah's mouth dropped as she realized Lizzie had a gun. She wondered if she'd had it all the time hidden in a pocket; whatever the case, it was there now and pointed straight at her. "We really could have had such fun. It's such a shame. I thought you had a lot of potential."

Just then, the door flew open. Nick and two Gulf Shores officers had their weapons drawn as they burst into the room. For a brief second, Nick and Hannah's eyes locked, then as though in slow motion, he caught Lizzie's slightest movement. Reflex took over, and before he realized it, he had pumped three shots into her. She staggered back and fell to the floor.

Hannah collapsed, drawing her knees into her chest, her body uncontrollably trembling. She was numb, all emotion drained, leaving her with an empty pit in her gut. He put his arms around her, stroking her hair. "You're okay, Hannah. You're okay." His heart was racing with the thought of what could have been.

For just a moment, everything seemed to stand still. The screech of sirens pierced the otherwise peacefulness of the beach. Before long, officers and medical personnel traipsed through the room. Nick couldn't get Hannah to move, not even budge an inch. A paramedic responded quickly to her and managed to get her onto a gurney and into the ambulance. Nick tagged along, never letting go of her hand. It took everything he had to fight back the tears. From what he could gather from listening to the paramedics talk to each other, Hannah was in shock and needed help quickly.

Hannah remained unresponsive for days. The doctors explained she could very easily snap out of it or stay in her state of mind indefinitely.

A week had passed, and there hadn't been any sign of change. Nick knew this morning would be no different than any other during the past week, but he continued his daily routine of going to Mass and then picking up a bouquet of fresh flowers, just in case.

He slowly cracked the door and peeked in. His heart sank; it appeared nothing had changed. Hannah lay asleep, curled in a fetal position. He walked to the sink to add water to the flowers.

From under the covers, he heard, "Are those more flowers? What'd you do buy a flower shop or something? Boy –"

He couldn't hold them back; the tears streamed down his cheeks. "How ya feelin', doll?"

"Alright, I guess. How about Lizzie?"

Nick shook his head. "By the time they got her to the hospital, she was already D.O.A."

The tears slowly ran down her cheeks. The series of events that had transpired over the past year was unfathomable. Who would've ever thought that bitterness could run so deep? It was hard for Hannah to comprehend the hatred and anger. Life had taken on a whole new meaning, and she knew that the sharpness of the pain would dull in time.

With a few weeks of therapy, Hannah was making progress. There would be some undeniable emotional scars that would hopefully fade with time and a lot of hard work but would never completely go away; in Hannah's mind, that might not be such a bad thing. She had grown so much. Therapy enabled her to acknowledge her vulnerability and the pain of the rape. Through family and partner counseling, she unveiled her New York secret and learned to accept the support of her family and Nick. Healing occurred on many levels drawing the family closer together creating bonds for a lifetime.

The stay in the hospital had opened many doors, and through a series of tests performed during the acute stage of her trauma, a most unexpected and interesting discovery emerged. Hannah was expecting. Nick could not have been more excited. The family worried if the trauma would cause problems with the pregnancy or baby, but Belle assured the happy couple there was nothing to worry about, and as far as Hannah and Nick were concerned, that was as good as it could ever get.

The calendar flipped quickly, and before they knew it, the Fourth of July was upon them. She sat on the back porch swing and watched Nick play with Michelle and Margot's kids. It was good to be surrounded by family, she thought. She remembered all those fun Fourths she had spent running wild with her brothers and their friends while the grownups visited with each other. Now they were grownups, how crazy.

She watched as Belle shooed the children from the sweets table. She had stood guard over the desserts for as long as Hannah could remember.

It had been a very odd year. Hannah missed her father, and the reality of his death was finally sinking in. Looking at Nick, she thought he would have approved, but then she smiled, knowing full well regarding her dad, no one ever stacked up for her. Nick would've worked his way into her dad's heart, and he would've respected him. He would've passed the loyalty test, the most important thing.

Things at C&S had finally simmered down and were somewhat back to normal. Mitch had been an excellent addition to the company, and he seemed to take to it like a duck to water. Misguided Preston was sentenced to eighteen months at the country club for cons, but okay. She managed to visit him a couple of times, assuring him there would be a place for him at C&S when he returned. Eddie Germaine was on death row waiting to pay for the murder of Joshua Delery. Somehow it just didn't seem like enough. Jeremiah was as feisty as ever, and she'd grown close to both him and Nate.

A loud thud plunged her into the present. Nick ran up on the porch laughing. "Oops, doll. You okay? Sorry, we'll keep the ball in the grass next time." He retrieved the ball, leaned down, and put his mouth close to her very pregnant belly. He tossed the ball back and sat next to her on the swing with a huge smile. He gently rubbed her belly. Life was good.

Many Thanks To...

My dad, Big Bill, for teaching me about making it in a man's world and to the love of my life, Doug, for exemplifying all that a husband and partner should be. Thanks for having faith in me.

Our tribe of children, their spouses, and grandchildren—I've ordered pom-poms for all your cheerleading and support.

The network of co-workers and friends that have listened to me ramble about thoughts for more books.

To G.Lee and K.N. Faulk for skillful yet loving editing, and Paige Brannon Gunter, my forever editor, and creator of clever anecdotes and words of wisdom.

To Cyrus Wraith Walker, who once again masterfully designed my cover, beautifully formatted the interior, and kept me on track.

To the many readers of my books...spreading the word, your thoughtful reviews have made all the difference.

OTHER BOOKS BY THE AUTHOR

CENSORED TIME TRILOGY
A Quarter Past Love (Book I)
Half Past Hate (Book II)
A Strike Past Time (Book III)

Friends Always

BE ON THE LOOK OUT FOR...
Price To Pay (2nd Edition) If you already read the 1st edition, no need
to get the 2nd
Untouchable Love
Leave No Doubt
Fit the Crime Series (working title, so far. Coming in 2023)

Visit my website corinnearrowood.com
Reviews are appreciated

ABOUT THE AUTHOR

Born and raised in the enchanting city of New Orleans, the author lends a flavor of authenticity to her story and the characters that come to life in the drama of love, lust, and murder. Her vivid style of storytelling transports the reader to the very streets of New Orleans with its unique sights, smells, and intoxicating culture. Once a masterful event planner, now retired, she has unleashed her creative wiles in this suspense-filledstory...*A Seat at the Table*.

Lightning Source UK Ltd.
Milton Keynes UK
UKHW011955020522
402399UK00004B/93